a love to behold

Praise for A Love to Behold:

This is a book that may cause you to think deeply …
and to wonder … both of which are good to do! It
raises some important questions about enduring love
in a way that allows readers to ponder possibilities
and experiences that they may have previously not
considered or addressed. *A Love to Behold* will introduce
you to a new kind of love story; be open and attentive to
your personal response!

—Ann Osborne, PhD, ThD, BSc,
Life Energy Balance

Wendy, in writing so sensitively about love through
the ages, offers some profound insights to her readers.
Touching as she does on physical, emotional, mental,
and spiritual issues, she opens her readers up to new
ideas … or to very old ideas through new approaches …
to matters that touch both sides of the veil. I much
admire her bravery and lack of self-concern in addressing
such issues, which many are drawn to examine and
embrace even as we are cautioned against it!

—Evelyn MacKay, author of the
newly released *Without Halos,
Without Wings Connecting with
Angels in the Thin Places*

a love
to behold

Wendy Stross

Table of Contents

Act III: Writing the Love

For Ernie

Everything That Was Broken

Everything that was broken has
forgotten its brokenness. I live
now in a sky-house, through every
window the sun. Also your presence.
Our touching, our stories. Earthy
and holy both. How can this be, but
it is. Every day has something in
it whose name is Forever.

—Mary Oliver

ACT I:
ARCHIE RETURNS

Prologue—Summer 2017

Coming Home, Anne, and realizing you weren't here upset me deeply. When I learned the truth of us, my first thought was that I had to see you. But that was not to be. My spirit guides explained that I didn't have the first inkling of what needed to be said.

At the first opportunity, I came to your house—you were alone in your bed. It was early morning. You had not yet woken, and so I was free to sit and gaze at you. Over forty years since we last held each other. Such a long time! My life was hard without you in it.

Lying on your side, you had one arm flung over your head. You were still beautiful, older but the same. Your dark hair was streaked with grey—it suited you. I took hold of your hand, the one above your head. You stirred ever so slightly, but your eyes remained shut.

When they opened, I could see you observing your hand with concentrated focus. Once or twice, you glanced at me and I wondered if you knew I was there. I guess I should have left then, but I loved the feel of you. How long we remained like that, holding hands, I have no idea. It was ever thus with us—space and time just faded away.

Eventually, I slipped my hand down your arm and away. Only then did you move — your hand reaching for mine.

CHAPTER 1

Anne—December 2017

Had Anne known this day would come? If so, she had long forgotten, or perhaps she'd simply ceased to care—given up. It was Saturday morning, two weeks before Christmas, and Anne had friends coming for dinner.

She had no idea why she fussed so. After all, she had known Kat and Charlie for more than forty years. She looked at her to-do list: groceries, wine, clean house, make dinner. She had hoped to have the Christmas tree up and decorated, but there had been no time.

Her husband, Jack, didn't much care for Christmas, so most of the preparation was left to her. Ordinarily, this had never been a problem. Anne loved Christmas, and through the years she had taken great pleasure in all the planning and festivities that marked the joyous season when family and friends gathered together. This year, however, she had been feeling empty, despairing even. She had a sense that something was missing. Maybe it was her. Somehow, she'd gone MIA.

Anne was struggling but she didn't know why. Jack always said how everyone wanted to be her—that she had a great life. And she did. She knew that. She had a phenomenal husband who loved and supported her in all her endeavours, even those he questioned the wisdom of, like getting a doctorate in history instead of going into law. Their two children, Alex and Lizzie, were now grown, successful, and happily married with kids of their own. And Anne loved being Nana to her three wee granddaughters. So, what was going on?

As Anne moved through the grocery store, she went into auto-mode, getting only the items on her list. It was party season and the store was crowded, so much so that Anne berated herself for having left her shopping to the last minute.

After she was finally able to exit the store and stow the groceries in the trunk, she sat in her car, knowing she should get going. *I have things to do.* Still, Anne sat.

Her father had died earlier this year, and it would be Anne's first Christmas without her dad. Her mom was still alive, but Anne had always been a Daddy's girl. The bearer of big hugs and appreciation, he had made her feel loved, special, calling her "the rock of the family."

She had not cried when he died. He had been so very ill with cancer and she had felt—dare she say it?—relief that his suffering had ended. *Maybe this is grief I'm feeling now. I'm missing Dad.* And with that, the tears came. Anne realized, not for the first time, that she was emotionally spent and physically exhausted.

When someone pulled their car in next to hers, Anne blew her nose and took a deep breath. As she turned the key in the ignition, Anne decided to stop at "the Gathering"—an annual event sponsored by a local store that specialized in spirituality. She'd received an email about it and, if she was being honest, it was one of the reasons she'd rushed through her shopping.

Anne had always been spiritual, and this past year, perhaps because of her father's death, she had become more so. In particular, as a historian, she found ideas of reincarnation, past lives, and the eternal nature of one's soul endlessly fascinating. And even more intriguing to Anne was the possibility that one could communicate with spirits of the dead, deceased loved ones who had crossed the veil. Sometimes, when writing about a historical figure, she had felt their presence, as if she had called them forth to aid her in the project she was working on. Curious, Anne had once asked her mentor, Fiona, if this had been her experience, specifically as it pertained to her research on an eighteenth-century woman of infamy. "Yes," Fiona had answered, but didn't elaborate further.

At just 10:30, the church auditorium was already humming with activity. Tables of various vendors, healers, and mediums were scattered throughout the room.

Anne's friend Jennifer called to her, "Hey kid, what are you doing here?"

"Procrastinating! I've never been to this event and was curious." Jennifer was an energy practitioner who did reiki and reflexology. "Do you have a table here?"

"No, this kind of event isn't conducive to my kind of work— too busy and noisy. Actually, I'm just leaving. My daughter has dance in an hour. See you at Friday yoga?"

Anne nodded, waved bye, and started to wander. Everything from aromatherapy, crystals, jewelry, Christmas decorations, and baked goods, as well as various healers offering their services, could be found in this one room. Still, nothing really grabbed her attention.

I should go, she thought.

But then, out of the corner of her eye, she spotted a woman seated at a table; her sign read SUSAN BARKER, PSYCHIC MEDIUM— READINGS $60 FOR 30 MINUTES.

Anne had had readings from mediums before—some good, some not so good. She was not familiar with Susan Barker.

Anne circled the room once more, but found herself drawn back to Ms. Barker, who looked to be around fifty, was heavy-set, and reminded Anne of a beloved great-aunt. She was available at the moment, so Anne pulled out three twenties and sat down for a reading.

At the outset, the medium asked if Anne had any particular questions, to which she replied no. While she hoped to hear from her father, it was her practice never to lead the medium—an effort on her part to remain open to whatever messages came through.

For the first fifteen minutes or so, the medium was pretty on track. Anne's grandmother had come through, saying Anne had come by her love of books from her.

Anne nodded and smiled. One of her favourite memories was of the day her grandmother had taken her as a small child to the adult floor of the local library. Looking up at the towering shelves lined with books, Anne had been filled with a sense of wonder and awe—a feeling that this was hallowed ground upon which she stood. And so began her lifelong love affair with books, as well as the spaces in which they were housed. To this day, Anne felt most happy alone reading a book, or lost in a library reading or doing research about people, places, and times that transported her beyond everyday life.

"Was there something at the end whereby she couldn't talk?"

Impressed, Anne said, "Yes, she had a stroke that affected her throat. She could neither swallow nor speak."

Ms. Barker said that her grandmother regretted that she had been unable to say some of the things she'd wanted to say. That she was very proud of Anne and of all she'd accomplished as a wife and mother.

Moments later, Sue looked above Anne's head, her eyes widening in surprise.

"Your soul mate's here, standing behind you!"

Startled, Anne leaned forward to ensure she'd heard correctly. "I'm sorry, what?" And then, shaking her head, she said, "You must be mistaken. I've been married over forty years, and my husband is very much alive."

"He says you dated before your husband. He had his own business and drove a truck for work."

Anne was drawing a complete blank. *Who could she possibly be talking about?* Anne had never really dated much before her husband. If this person were her soul mate, surely she would remember him?!

She shook her head again.

"Sorry, I have no idea who you're talking about."

The medium then looked up at her "soul mate" and said, "You need to step aside."

And for whatever reason, this agitated Anne. *Clearly, my soul mate is here for a reason. But he's been asked to step aside.* Anne sighed. *Finish already.*

But Ms. Barker had more to say. She addressed the issue of the history book Anne was writing: the never-ending project based on her doctorate, a cultural history of obituaries in eighteenth-century London. "You need to finish it," the medium told her. And with that, the session was over.

Shaken, Anne booted it to the car. Sadly, her dad had not come through. Instead, a mysterious soul mate had come forth, and for the life of her, she had no memory of him.

But then, as Anne drove home, a face came to her, a name. *No, that would have to mean he was dead.* She felt a storm brewing deep within, but pushed it back down.

In typical Anne fashion, she went home, cleaned the house, made dinner, and she and Jack spent the evening enjoying the company of their two dearest friends.

She thought she had hidden her turmoil well. After dinner, however, as they were sitting in the living room and chatting about an upcoming trip to Italy the two couples were planning, Charlie, who was seated beside Anne on the couch, leaned over and whispered, "Is everything okay, Anne? You seem a bit down tonight."

Anne assured him that she was fine. "Just a little tired. Too much Christmas, I guess."

Charlie nodded and turned his attention back to the others. Anne loved Kat and Charlie, but they had never met anyone whom she'd dated, other than Jack—someone they'd known and loved since high school. So she saw no real reason to talk about a past boyfriend now, let alone a supposed soul mate that until today she herself had forgotten.

After Kat and Charlie left, Jack went to bed while Anne stayed up to clean the kitchen. It was something she did, her way of winding down after a party. Only when the dishes were in the dishwasher and the kitchen was neat and clean could she retire.

But tonight, as she washed the pots and pans, her mind was preoccupied, as it had been all night. She was thinking about someone she had once dated, once cared for—Archie. Actually, his name was Archer McAllister, but everyone had called him Archie. She hadn't thought of him in years.

But now, as she stood at the sink, she couldn't stop thinking about him. His presence seemed palpable. When they had dated, she'd been very aware of their strong, almost mystical connection. And now, as in the past, Anne felt him near and sighed.

It was past midnight when Anne finally crawled into bed. Due to her husband's snoring, she'd recently moved to her son's old room, and she quite liked the arrangement. She slept better. Exhausted, she quickly fell asleep.

Around seven the next morning, she got up to use the bathroom, then returned to bed. Still troubled by the events of the day before, Anne fell into a deep sleep. The dream that ensued was remarkably vivid.

It was a bright, sunny day, and I was lying on a lounger outside a cottage situated on a hilltop, overlooking a lake. The sun's rays were strong and, closing my eyes, I felt myself drifting off to sleep. And then out of the silence, I heard shouts.

"Anne! Anne! Wake up! Wake up!"

Rising to my feet, I looked down at the lake and was amazed to see a number of people paddling canoes, heading to shore, toward me. In stillness, I watched them.

The man in the first canoe was waving to get my attention. "Anne!" He looked very much like a good friend I had known at university. By this time, some of the canoes had landed and people were starting to come ashore.

As I descended the hill, I was startled. To my left, a man on a horse was galloping toward me, and for an instant I feared for my safety. This, however, was not a knight in shining armour horse— more like a Howdy-Doody horse.

The next instant, I felt the horse behind me, standing on his haunches with his front legs wrapped around my neck. He was softly nibbling the top of my head, and I was quite relishing the horse's affectionate overture when reason prevailed. There is no way a horse could sustain this stance!

I looked down and saw arms. A man was gently embracing me from behind, kissing the top of my head. It felt heavenly.

Eventually, he released me, and as I turned around, I saw a fairly tall man with light brown wavy hair walking away.

He then turned and smiled somewhat sadly at me, before again turning and walking away.

Upon waking, Anne knew the man in her dream had been Archie. In life, he would often come behind her to embrace her, to hold her.

The dream had felt so real, she felt compelled to record it. For the last twenty years or so, Anne had kept a journal, faithfully recording dreams, events, poems, or ideas that she thought might lend some insight into her life, her spiritual being and journey. In the various readings and spiritual workshops she'd attended, she had learned that dreams were one means by which spirit—higher self, spirit guides, God, angels—communicated messages to a person. *Perhaps Archie came to tell me he loves me.*

The next few days passed in a flurry of activities and Anne had no time to find out if, indeed, Archie had died. Sunday, Jack and Anne set up the Christmas tree, not without the usual angst and fight over the tree lights.

To appease Anne, Jack took her to dinner and a movie, *The Man Who Invented Christmas*—about Charles Dickens' inspiration and the writing of his classic tale, *A Christmas Carol*. The movie was disappointing to say the least, a Hollywood production and not reflective of the historical Dickens in the slightest. However, in all fairness, Anne was feeling a bit disgruntled, so maybe this had coloured her review.

Monday, Anne had an appointment with her naturopath, who was helping her to get her health back on track. After her father's death, Anne had developed a harsh bronchial cough. Her doctor had thought it might be pneumonia and prescribed antibiotics. Still, the cough persisted.

This past March when she and her husband had been on holiday in Germany, Anne had been on two respiratory puffers, cold medication, and cough syrup, just so she could make it through the trip. By late August, Anne found herself continuing to struggle physically and at her wit's end. It was then that she'd sought out a naturopath and, so far, Anne was impressed with her approach; the cough seemed to be slowly dissipating.

It was Wednesday before Anne found the time to go online and search the obituaries for Archie's death. Though the last few days *had* been busy, she knew part of the delay had been procrastination. A part of her didn't want to know Archie was dead. Since Saturday, Anne couldn't stop thinking about him. In years gone by, when she'd thought of him, she had envisioned him living a happy life among family and friends, and been comforted by this.

And thus, it was with some trepidation that Anne googled "Obituary—A. McAllister—Toronto." In a matter of seconds, there it was. He had died over a year ago, mid-November 2016. He had been sixty-nine, a few years older than Anne.

As a historian and adept reader of obituaries, past and present, Anne found his obituary somewhat strange. His union membership had been listed first, before citing his family. Archie's father had passed, but his mother was still living. The obit described Archie as the loving and proud father of one son, but no wife was listed. Anne recognized the names of his two brothers, both of whom she had met. The funeral parlour where his body had rested was one Anne knew to be situated in the area where he'd lived when they dated.

I guess he never moved away. It made sense. One of the many things she had loved about Archie was he had been very close to his family.

A black-and-white photo of a much older Archie was attached. She printed it out, trying to remember the laughing young man of her youth. He'd been tall, nearly six feet, and fairly robust, with beautiful blue eyes that twinkled when he laughed—and they had laughed a lot together.

Mostly, Anne remembered how Archie had made her feel— happy and loved, that for him, she was "the one." And the kisses—

well, how could she possibly describe them? No one before or since had ever made her feel like that.

Anne searched the photo for traces of the Archie she had known. His hair had turned white, but his eyes were still blue, and his smile a bit crooked—she'd forgotten that about him. As Anne examined his face more closely, she noticed that while Archie was smiling, his eyes betrayed some sadness, a weariness she had never known in him. And with that, the tears came.

Anne was not a crier—she couldn't even remember the last time she'd wept. When her father had died, she'd shed few tears. So now, she couldn't understand this outpouring of emotion. Her whole life, she had never felt the physical pain of her heart breaking—until now. She simply could not stop crying.

Over the next few weeks, the tears continued to flow. Alone—in the car, in bed at night, watching those Hallmark Christmas movies—she found herself welling up at the slightest thought of Archie. She was having trouble grappling with the news of his death. And this too astonished her. Even though in the years after he broke up with her, she'd had periods in which she had struggled with that loss, for the last thirty years or so she'd been okay, and thought of him only rarely.

The medium had said they were soul mates, but their romance had been brief. After three months together, Archie had broken up with her out of the blue—no fight, no reason. And that had been that.

They'd been so happy. At least, she'd thought so. Anne had never understood why the breakup happened. It had devastated her—not in a dramatic way, but in a quiet way. She'd kept her sorrow private, close within. While Anne quickly put it behind her and married, she had struggled with life for a number of years, never really knowing why. She'd thought she had dealt with the loss and moved on with her life, harbouring no ill feelings for Archie. When she did think of him, on his birthday or Valentine's Day, it was with love. She had met his family and some friends, and knew he was well-loved. He had always been very loving and kind to her. And so, as the years passed, Anne had imagined him happily married with children, living a good life.

Christmas came and went, but Anne's grief remained. Her husband returned to work, and Anne to volunteering at the museum and her writing. She had made no New Year's resolutions, a sign she was neither fully grounded in the present nor vested in the future. Still preoccupied with thoughts of Archie and their past relationship, Anne's mind kept circling around the same unrelenting question: If indeed Archie was her soul mate, why had he broken up with her? In all their time together, they had never had a single fight or disagreement. And what possible reason could there be for his re-entry into her life after more than forty years apart? He was dead. It made no sense, no earthly sense.

CHAPTER 2

Anne and Archie, 1975

Anne met Archie in a hotel bar on the airport strip—an unlikely place, considering she didn't drink and rarely went to bars. It had been a bitterly cold Friday night in early February. After working full-time as a registered nurse at a Toronto hospital, Anne had recently moved back home to attend university. At week's end, she would have preferred to stay home, but her sister Laura and friend Dale persuaded her otherwise.

Her sister was a guy magnet, and knew it. From the time Laura started attending Anne's high school, boys would come up to Anne and say, "Wow, is that your sister?" It was not that Anne felt any less attractive than her sister. They were just different. Both sisters had dark hair and eyes, but that was the extent of the resemblance. While Laura was petite and vivacious, Anne was almost a head taller, quiet and more introverted. She was often told she had a great smile, an infectious laugh. Nevertheless, when she was with her sister, men never really bothered with Anne.

Indeed, Anne was surprised when a man with a friendly face and big smile walked directly up to her and said, "Hi, I'm Archie. Would you like to dance?" To Archie's credit, he was not dressed to impress—Anne liked that. She forgot what he'd been wearing: comfortable clothing, not a suit and tie.

By the time Anne and Archie reached the dance floor, they were already laughing. Archie had learned that she was twenty-one, and she knew he had recently turned twenty-eight.

After they danced, he sat with her at their table for the rest of the evening. Anne had liked Archie immediately, his happy, easy manner and winsome smile. There was an instant connection and a comfort level that she'd never experienced with a man before. When she got up to leave, he did too. Then he asked for her phone number, and whether he could call her to go out sometime. Without hesitation, she said yes.

As they walked out, Archie said, "When I first saw you, you looked like you had just got out of Sunday school." Anne laughed, though she had no clue what he meant by that. Later, Archie would reveal that his initial attraction was neither physical nor superficial. In seeing her, he'd thought that she was someone he wanted to talk to—there had been a depth, a familiarity to Anne he'd been drawn to.

Their first date was on Valentine's Day, ice skating at Toronto City Hall. That was Archie. When they were together, there was never any pretence. He made it clear from their first date that he liked her and was thrilled to be with her. He picked her up on time, coming into the house to meet Anne's parents. Her uncle had been visiting, and he too had come to introduce himself and shake Archie's hand.

As they were getting into the car, Archie pulled out a red heart-shaped box of chocolates. "These are for you—Happy Valentine's Day!"

Until Archie, Anne had dated a bit, but she'd never had a boyfriend, let alone been given a Valentine gift. Astonished and touched, she said, "Thank you."

Archie shrugged. "I was at the store buying my mom a box, and thought I would buy you one too."

Anne didn't say anything; he seemed like he was trying to downplay his gesture so she wouldn't read too much into it. Nevertheless, that a twenty-eight-year-old man had given his mom a box of chocolates for Valentine's Day had impressed her.

Anne remembered the ease of conversation and laughter between them. Not once had there been a moment of silence or awkwardness. On their date, Archie had skated off every now and then to do his own thing. At one point, she had called out to him, and he had stopped and looked at her. After that, he'd skated over to her, took her hand, and stayed by her side the rest of the evening.

Archie was completing his certification to become a steamfitter, and as he drove through downtown Toronto, he pointed out some of the buildings he had worked on. Before they got back to her house, Archie parked the car and turned off the engine.

He's taking me parking, thought Anne. She had never been parking before. Archie turned in his seat so his back rested against the car door, and then put his hands on her upper arms and gently pulled her to him.

As their faces met, Anne could see that his eyes were smiling. Then his eyes closed and their lips touched. The kiss was wow, but at the same time familiar, like she had somehow come home. She had no idea how long they kissed, because as they kissed, she found herself fully in the moment. This was new for Anne. Before Archie, she had never really liked anyone touching, let alone kissing her. By and by, Archie lifted her up and away, setting her back into her seat. As he turned to start the car, Anne saw the smile and soft expression on Archie's face. *That was good,* she thought, as she felt herself smile too.

The next day was Saturday, and Archie called to ask if he could see her, to which Anne instantly agreed. He picked her up in the afternoon. As they were driving along the highway, she asked where they were going.

"To my brother's for dinner," he said, ever so casually.

This startled Anne. "You should have said. I could have made some brownies or something to bring."

Archie didn't respond. Rather, he leaned over and pointed to an apartment building by the highway. "My aunt lives there." As he directed her gaze, his arm brushed up against her midriff and rested there for a moment. A simple gesture, but Anne was struck by the intimacy of his touch, and her response to it.

Archie was the middle of three brothers, and that day they had been invited to his youngest brother's house, a small post-war bungalow with stairs leading up to the front door. As they entered and were led into the living room, Anne was slightly surprised to see both brothers and their wives. She sat down on the couch, with Archie sitting close to her. They all seemed eager to get to know her. Anne could be shy, but that day she chatted easily. Looking back, she attributed her comfort to being with Archie.

Later, someone brought out a Monopoly game and Anne's inner child radiated forth. She loved playing games. However, she took her games seriously, and Archie seemed to take great delight in teasing her, often finding ways to distract her and get her giggling.

During dinner, the brothers talked about a recent hunt in which they had shot a bear. She had never known anyone who hunted. She was not even sure how she felt about it. As Archie and Anne were leaving, the youngest brother, Tom and his wife, Kathy, said she and Archie would have to come back and have roast bear with them one evening. Archie said for sure.

When Archie pulled his little yellow car into her driveway, he turned the engine off and they kissed. In his arms felt like the most natural place in the world to be.

Over the coming weeks, Archie and Anne went about their weekly routines, seeing each other on weekends. One weekend, his parents invited them to the O'Keefe Center to see some kind of British musical-comedy revue. Sitting between Archie and his mom, Anne found her easy to talk to. For the life of her, Anne couldn't remember much of the show. Throughout the performance, Archie would lean in and make some witty observations, and they would both giggle. At some point, Archie's mom looked over at the two of them and shushed them with a single motion of her hand, to which Archie gave Anne a stern look and then smiled.

After the show, all four of them stood outside the theater. Anne could see that Archie got his fair complexion and blue eyes from his mother, and his height and build from his dad. As Anne shook hands with his mother, thanking her and saying it had been a pleasure to meet them both, Anne glimpsed Archie watching her, grinning from ear to ear. After saying their goodbyes, Archie took her hand in his as they walked away.

Over the next three months, their relationship deepened. She met his friends and he met some of hers. The details of what they did and when were hazy now. But through all of that time, it never seemed to matter where they went or what they did, they were happy just being together. While neither one of them talked about feelings of love, their kissing, their joy and delight being in each other's company spoke volumes. Being this happy was a new and welcomed experience for Anne.

At the beginning of May, Archie took Anne to his apartment. Walking into his home, her initial impression was that it was very clean, neat, and sparsely furnished. For some reason, Archie had gone into the kitchen, so Anne sat down in a brown leather recliner and leaned back.

As she turned around to say how comfortable the chair was, she was alarmed to see Archie with a distressed look on his face, his hands clenching the counter as he leaned over the sink. Seeing her look over at him, he straightened, adjusted the towel by the sink, walked quickly toward her, grabbed one of her hands, and led her to the bedroom and his bed.

Unlike the living room, his bedroom was flooded with light. She lay on the bed with Archie beside her. As they faced each other, he smiled at her, and she at him. But then, Archie's eyes quickly sobered.

Without warning, he got up and went to the large window. He asked her to come and look at his view, which, though startled and confused, she did. He stood behind her, one arm wrapped around her, the other pointing out at the Don Valley Parkway and a huge billboard opposite his window.

And with that, they left the apartment and he drove her home. As usual, they kissed a long good night, and Anne gave not another thought to the brief moments of disquiet she had felt in his apartment.

Anne thought it a bit odd when she didn't hear from Archie the next weekend. But as the following weekend approached, Archie called and invited her to a movie, Peter Sellers in *The Return of the Pink Panther*. It was a warm May evening and Anne wore a halter mini-dress, one she had sewn herself. Anne had purchased the fabric, off-white cotton with tiny pale blue cornflowers, because she thought it suited her dark hair and eyes.

Having not seen Archie in two weeks, Anne was brimming with excitement when he arrived to pick her up. She told him, "As of this week, we have been dating three months. I've never dated anyone this long before."

Anne immediately sobered as she saw a look of great angst on Archie's face. She worried, wondering what was going on. Once in the car, however, Archie seemed to return to his usual self. When they reached the theater and were standing in the concession line, he came up behind her, wrapped his arms around her, and held her close. Anne smiled and sighed. And just like that, all was well with the world again.

After the movie, Archie drove her home, and as they turned to each other to kiss good night, Archie put his tongue in her mouth and kissed her more deeply than ever. This surprised Anne. But as the kiss deepened, Anne felt an intense feeling of love and desire that she had never before experienced. Archie leaned over her, until he was almost on top of her. She felt his hand go under her dress and caress her intimately. Anne moaned and arched her back.

And then abruptly, without warning, Archie moved his hand away and said, "You need to get out of the car!"

Hearing the urgency in his voice, she did as he told her, then walked to the driver's side to check if he was okay. Anne was naive when it came to sex, so she didn't understand that Archie was trying to pull himself together before he sped away, without looking at her or saying goodbye. She was totally confused. Had she done something wrong?

The next day though, Archie phoned. Anne was picking raspberries out in the backyard, so her mother took the call. When Anne came in, her mom said Archie had called to say he was coming to pick her up, and that she should bring her swimsuit as they were going swimming at his brother's pool.

As Anne went to gather her swimming gear, her mother called to her, "Anne, Archie's on the phone again. He wants to talk to you."

She happily picked up the receiver. "Hi."

"Anne, I think we should break up."

She was stunned. They were both quiet. He seemed to be waiting for her to respond.

"Can we talk about this?"

"Okay, I'll come over to your house tomorrow night." With that arranged, they said goodbye.

The next evening, Anne waited outside until it grew late. Any hope of changing his mind seemed to disappear as the sun set in the sky. Archie never showed. Worse, he hadn't even bothered to phone to let her know. Finally, she went to bed.

Monday morning, Anne had to be at the hospital at seven. She was scheduled to work the day shift. As she rode the subway into the city, she decided she had to call Archie, to find out what had happened.

After she had made her rounds, she used the phone at the nurses' station, to catch Archie before he left for work. He answered on the second ring.

"Archie?"

She heard him sigh before he replied. "Anne." Silence. "I knew you weren't going to let this go."

"You didn't come last night," Anne said, trying to keep the hurt out of her voice.

"No." And then silence.

Anne exhaled. "So, you want to break up."

"Yes."

Feeling a bit shaky, Anne sat down on the stool next to the counter. She thought, *Is this how it feels when your heart is breaking?* What more could she say?

She stood up, took a deep breath, and said, "Okay. Bye." And she hung up.

She remembered walking toward the corridor, to attend to her patients. As she did so, Anne straightened her spine and set her shoulders back, almost as if she was steeling herself for a life without Archie. And though she saw no one, Anne had the sense that a woman was standing beside her—so much so she had turned her head to look. Later, Anne would come to realize this had been her spirit guide—an early sign of her innate intuition to feel and recognize the energetic presence of spirit. At that moment though, she put her feeling down to an active imagination.

That was it. It was over. She had no idea why. No explanation was ever forthcoming. Anne thought perhaps Archie had met someone else and had not wanted to hurt her feelings. Maybe she had been naive to think he had cared for her. Or maybe, her being so much younger, Archie had tired of her. After all, just when she thought they'd been moving their relationship to the next level, he'd told her to get out of the car.

As she rode home on the subway that day, a deep sadness enveloped her. She missed him already. But Anne didn't remember crying. Upon reflection, she had mourned Archie's absence quietly, silently, never really talking about it with anyone. Anne had tried meeting with him, and he had not even bothered to call to inform her he wasn't coming. When she had telephoned Archie, he had been monosyllabic. She could only assume that they were over and she had to move on. And so, she did.

~~~~~

Two or three months later, Anne received a letter from Archie. That summer, she'd begun dating Jack, a development her mother was not thrilled about. Her mom had liked Archie, in large part because she had never seen Anne as happy and as calm as when they were together.

As soon as Anne arrived home, her mom handed her the letter. She looked at the return address, astonished to see it was from Archie. Jack was with her, but she opened it anyway. The letter was short, a little over one page, hand-written. She could not recall his exact words, but essentially, Archie had wanted Anne to know that
~~~~~

he thought the world of her. It was a kind and loving letter, but that was it.

As beautiful as the letter was, it distressed Anne more than she ever let on. She never knew why, but it had. Perhaps because, in order to move on with her life, she had tried very hard to shut down all memory of their relationship and the breakup. Until the letter, she *thought* she'd been doing pretty well.

And then there was the fact that, in her whole life, Anne had never had anyone write to her in such loving terms. It registered with her heart, her soul. Anne kept the letter for a while. Every now and then, she would take it out and read it, ever amazed by its contents. She could never figure out why Archie had sent it. She thought maybe it had been guilt on his part—that he had felt bad about how he had ended their relationship. But deep within, Anne knew Archie's words were heartfelt. And this made it even harder for her to come to terms with their separation.

A year later, as she was preparing to get married, Anne read the letter one last time. Sitting on the edge of her bed, she came to the decision to let it go, and with that, she threw it into the wastepaper basket.

~~~~~

Seven years later, Anne and Archie met once more. By then, Anne was married to Jack and had a two-year-old son. They were living in an apartment close to her parents' home. It was February or March, and Anne was in the midst of packing, preparing to move outside the city.

Anne had popped into the local grocery store to pick up a couple of items for dinner. After checking out her groceries, she headed to the exit where she saw a man leaning against the wall by the door. He was smiling at her—his blue eyes fixed on hers, his whole face lit up. There was such intimacy and joy in the way he was gazing and grinning at her, it startled her. As he walked toward her, Anne saw his arms open, ready to embrace her. She stopped, and then, like a shot, bolted past him and out into the parking lot.
~~~~~

Only when Anne got into her car and saw it was parked beside Archie's truck, did she realize who the man was. She was horrified. How could she have not recognized him! What must he think of her? *I need to talk to him. I have to go back.* But it was a big store. Would she be able to find him? Maybe she could wait until he came out to his truck. But no, she had to get home. Should she leave a note on his windshield, to connect for coffee later? She needed to do something—she couldn't just leave!

All these feelings were swirling around in her heart when Anne heard a voice, a woman's voice. "He's with someone." There was a pause, and then, "You don't have to go back in."

Anne was alone in the car, so she had no idea where the voice was coming from. It seemed to be coming from somewhere close behind her right ear. Even though she saw no one, Anne never doubted the truth of what it told her. Given that information, she reconsidered. *What's the point of going back in?* She had moved on, as had he. And so, she drove home. Anne never saw Archie again.

CHAPTER 3

Anne, February 2018

For some time now, Anne had been on a spiritual path, and she had come to accept as common knowledge the notion that spirits were a real presence in this world. While she could not see dead people, she occasionally felt their energy and presence.

Anne was never quite sure when her awareness of spirit—active in her life, nudging her along—had begun. Since she was a little girl, she had loved going to church with her family, and she'd always felt comforted with the knowledge that there was a divine being, a God, to whom she could pray and talk, trusting God heard her and felt her love, as she did his. This had filled a void in her life.

Her parents had been very young when she was born, the first of four children. She always sensed that her very being had overwhelmed her mother—possibly because a little over a year after Anne's birth, her sister Laura had arrived. At first, Anne had rebelled, had temper tantrums, to express her anger or get her parents' attention. But the consequences proved less than satisfactory. She was told to go to her room until her father came home, at which time he would spank her.

Over time, she had learned to behave, to forfeit her own needs and wants to care for others—her parents, grandparents, siblings, friends. Whoever was in her life, she became an adept people-pleaser, putting everyone's needs ahead of her own. Anne thought this might have been why she hadn't given Archie a hard time when he broke up with her. It was what he said he wanted, so she had complied with his wishes.

Anne's awareness of spirit as something accessible to her from within had evolved over time. She now saw that spirit had always been there, patiently waiting for Anne to pay attention.

After her kids started school, Anne had returned to university full-time, earning a BA with distinction, then a master's in history. She supposed she had started her spiritual journey in earnest when doing her doctorate. In 1994, she had commenced a doctoral degree in history at the University of Toronto, which had necessitated a daily four-hour commute from home to Toronto, as well as long periods of time sitting at a desk. The study, research, and writing demanded a lot of brain power, and over time the stress began to get to her. On the recommendation of a friend, Anne took up yoga, taking one night class a week. In the beginning she had not been a fan, but the regular practice helped her sleep better at night. She had achieved her doctorate in history, and for the last decade she had been doing some contract work and volunteering at the local city museum, as well as travelling around the world with her husband.

As much as Anne loved what she was doing, she longed for something more, something that fed her heart, her soul. And so, she had begun reading books on spirituality. This was also the time when Oprah was investigating the subject of spirituality on her television show, hosting many guest experts engaged in the exploration of matters pertaining to the soul. Anne found the subject of spirituality endlessly fascinating, and eventually she met other women who shared her passion. For a brief few months in 2002, these friends had come together and formed a goddess circle that met weekly. To be in the company of such amazing women, Anne had considered a privilege and thrill. Though the circle broke up after only nine months, she still cherished the magic and joy of that experience.

Since Anne's dream of Archie riding up to her on a Howdy-Doody horse, she had a powerful sense that he was around, as if he had decided to stay with her for a while. Little things were happening, like her desk light clicking on in the middle of the night while she slept. One day, the reading glasses Anne always kept by her computer had been moved to her bedside table. And she just felt him around her. Archie had always seemed to emanate solidity, a solidity of nature, of character. Anne had loved that about him. He'd grounded her, made her feel safe—given her a sense of peace she had never known. And now, especially at night, his presence—his solidity—was unmistakable. She sensed Archie was trying to get her attention, but she had no idea why.

For the past ten years, Anne had been seeing a life coach. She had first heard of Jane through Clare, a long-time friend. One day as they were leaving a yoga class, Clare mentioned that she thought Anne would really appreciate this woman she'd been seeing. "I'm surprised your paths haven't crossed. Like you, Jane was older when she returned to university to earn her doctorate. I think you would really connect with her." Shortly thereafter, Anne booked an appointment.

At their first session, she felt an instant rapport. Since then, Anne had seen her on a fairly regular basis, usually every four to six months. Anne always looked forward to her appointments and felt Jane's insight and wisdom supported her as she navigated the myriad of life changes and challenges.

Anne was overdue for a session with Jane; 2017 had been a rough year. She'd been feeling anxious, stressed, and generally unwell, which she had attributed to her father's recent death, her mother's ill health, and Jack's mother's advanced dementia. Anne had been seeing a naturopath who was helping her resolve her persistent cough. Nevertheless, even before Archie's arrival on the scene, Anne felt as if she were closing down. Physically, mentally, and emotionally drained, she felt challenged with accomplishing even the simplest of tasks. But she just kept going, pushing through—not saying anything to anybody.

Within a week of her first encounter with Archie, Anne emailed Jane to set up an appointment. In all the years she had been seeing Jane, she had always focused on the present, on what was going on at that moment in her life—so "Archie" had never come up. Anne explained in her email to Jane that her "soul mate"— someone she had once dated—had returned.

"To be honest, Jane, I have no idea what he wants, but he doesn't seem in any hurry to leave. And since you can see and converse with those who have crossed the veil, I thought he could come to my next appointment. Would it be possible to set one up for the New Year?"

Jane responded quickly, and an appointment was scheduled for February 22.

In the meantime, Archie continued making his presence known to Anne. It had been thirty years since she had really given him any thought; she had been so busy with life. But with Archie's return, long-buried memories of their time together were resurfacing, and with them came feelings of the joy, the love they'd shared. How she had felt when they kissed. How happy she had been with him. And then waves of grief would inundate her. In the middle of her last yoga class, she'd felt the emotion about to burst forth. *I have to get out of here! Now!* She'd barely made it to the bathroom before breaking down in tears, sobbing.

Archie never would have imagined that Anne had kept the heart-shaped box he'd given her on their first date. Stored in a box marked ANNE'S MEMORIES, the heart had accompanied her through all of her various moves and life changes. Only recently had Anne finally let it go. In preparation for major house renovations, she had conducted a massive decluttering campaign. And not just a physical clearing of rooms—for Anne, there had been a spiritual component to it. Her life coach had asked what she most wanted in her newly renovated surroundings, and the first word that popped into Anne's mind was *space.* She had been feeling constricted and knew that her soul needed room to breathe. Thus, Anne's goal had been to clear out all those things that no longer served her, in order to have space to just be.

Anne had been tackling the upstairs hall closet when she came upon the empty heart-shaped box. Holding it in her hands, she remembered Archie giving it to her on their very first date, Valentine's Day. But that had been more than forty years ago. *Really, Anne!?* Why was she hanging on to it? She needed to let the box go—and so, with that, she had tossed it into the blue bin.

Now, Anne couldn't help but wonder at the fact that Archie had come to her a year after she had relinquished the heart box. Had her letting go of the heart created space for more love and joy to come into her life, in the form of Archie's spirit?

Valentine's Day was fast approaching, and for some reason Anne felt she wanted to do something for Archie. Jack and Anne had never really made a big deal about Valentine's Day. Jack was of the mind that he demonstrated his love for Anne all year round. He didn't need a special day to profess it. Nonetheless, he had been quick to honour Anne's wishes, and they always exchanged cards.

Anne did not want to give Archie a card. She thought perhaps she would write him a letter, a belated response to the one he had written her so long ago. And so, one night before turning out the light, Anne put pen to paper.

Dear Archie,

Forty-three years ago today, we had our first date and you gave me a heart-shaped box of chocolates. I was so moved by your gift, as no one had ever given me anything like that before. I kept that box until September 2016 (two months before your death). I guess it was the only thing that connected me to the brief beautiful time we shared together.

Forty-three years later, it seems we (our souls) have found our way back to each other. Not sure how long you will be with me—last time you left without so much as a goodbye. Hopefully, I will be stronger now, knowing we are soul mates. I am still not fully certain what that means. However, it does explain the deep feelings of love I felt for you. You probably never knew this, but as a child I never liked to be held. And up to the time I dated you, I was uncomfortable with my dates kissing or touching me. But with you, it felt so natural and easy, like somehow I had found a kindred spirit.

It was a tough time when you ended it. Looking back now, though, we each had our own soul journeys in this life, ones that did not include each other. And so, I guess I should thank you for ending our relationship, doing a job that had to be done. I could never have done it myself.

On December 9, you revealed to me that you were my soul mate. And then, you came to me in a dream and I learned of your death. I guess you know how much that news shook me to my core. It was a huge physical reaction. All those emotions I had safely secured away when we parted came flooding out. Long-suppressed memories of you and us resurfaced with many, many tears shed. I am still dealing with the emotion and love I hold for you. Again, you have touched my heart. I think this is the only love letter I have ever written, ironic because it is one I will never send.

I must say, I remember your cocky confidence, easy smile and great laugh, your friendly face, your warm and gentle touch and embrace. We shared much joy and laughter together. I loved that you were close to your family, and I loved your heart.

And so, I want to wish you a Happy Valentine's Day, and say that your presence in my life forty-three years ago was a blessing that I carry with me today. That you have come into my life again is almost beyond belief. But, as you probably know by now, I am a spiritual woo-woo and your presence is very real to me. I feel so privileged to know your soul energy is with me. It is the greatest gift I could receive at this time in my life. Thank you.

Love,
Anne

P.S. I will do my best to honour your presence.

Early Valentine's morning, sitting on the side of her bed, Anne informed Archie she had written him a Valentine's letter, in honour of the anniversary of their first date. As she read it aloud, tears ran down her cheeks as she imagined him sitting beside her. Still, wherever he was, she trusted he would hear her words.

Archie *was* sitting next to Anne, and was moved by her heartfelt words. What truly surprised him was that, without any explanation of why he had broken up with her, Anne had simply embraced him and taken him back into her life, as if no time had passed—something he had not expected. However, in truth, it was what he had loved about her—her loving heart and generous spirit.

When he first returned to let Anne know he was dead, he had been nervous. After all, she was married and had a full life as a wife, mother, and grandmother. He had been more than a little distressed by her outpouring of grief, and worried his return was too hard for her. He said as much to his spirit guide, who assured Archie that Anne had had to shut down all memory of him in order to move forward with her life. The overwhelming emotion she was feeling was long overdue. Anne was grieving Archie's death, but more significantly, she was finally allowing herself to grieve their breakup all those years ago. She had never cried, never mourned that loss of her experience of great love.

CHAPTER 4

Archie Explains

One week later, Anne and Archie headed to Jane's for their appointment. As she parked the car, Anne explained to Archie that Jane was psychic, had been her entire life, as was her mother before her. "She will see and hear you. I have been seeing Jane for over ten years. I trust her. So, if there is there is anything you need to communicate to me, you can tell her.

Walking to the open garage that led to the office, Anne suddenly bent down to pet a feral grey cat. "Well, hello again. How are you doing in this cold? How kind of you to come and greet me and my friend." She then straightened, walked to the office door, and let herself in.

Archie smiled. They had only dated for three months, but he had fallen fast and hard for Anne. Since his return, he loved being with her. And he welcomed the opportunity to learn things about the woman she had become. One thing he knew: she loved animals and talked to them readily; people less so.

Sitting in the vestibule to remove her boots, Anne called, "Hi Jane."

Hearing Anne, Jane rose from her desk and headed to the door. Over the years, Jane had come to know her quite well. For her doctoral dissertation, Jane had studied soul ages. Just as people had different ages, she argued that souls did as well, and each soul age had different characteristics and lessons. From their first meeting, Jane pegged Anne as an old soul whose interest in spirituality paralleled her own. Though Anne had no major issues, Jane had to admit that her email had sparked some concern.

As Anne was taking her time with her boots, Archie decided he might as well go on ahead and introduce himself.

"Hi, I'm Archie."

Jane, ever vigilant in the monitoring of the sacred space of her office, was disconcerted by the sudden intrusion. The male spirit who had just entered her office looked to be in his early to mid-thirties, and was tall and robust, with light brown hair. What struck her most was his face. He had a very kind face, with sparkling blue eyes and a friendly smile. Nonetheless, she was unsure about whether he should be there.

Upon entering the office, Anne was a bit taken aback, as she had never seen Jane look confused—or, well, displeased. Usually, Jane greeted Anne with a big wrap-around hug. Today, however, she stood in the middle of the room, looking back and forth from Anne to an empty space beside Anne.

Archie, Anne thought. "I brought my soul mate with me."

"What's his name?" Jane asked.

"Archie." She guessed she'd failed to mention that in her email.

Jane nodded to him and said, "Okay, you can stay." Turning to Anne, she explained, "I had to make sure he was with you. I have had spirits come in here uninvited, and not always welcome."

Anne apologized. She hadn't realized Archie would go in without her. As memory served, though, that was so him. He had always been very outgoing and confident.

Anne took a seat in the comfy lazy chair reserved for clients, as Jane sat in the identical chair facing hers. Anne sighed. She loved Jane's office. If a mother's womb were a room, this is what it would look and feel like, at least for her. In the colder months, Jane always had the space heater going, so it was toasty warm. The walls were covered in bookshelves, floor to ceiling, filled with volumes ready and waiting when needed. Both Jack and Anne were bibliophiles and they had bookcases in almost every room of their house, so this added to the comfort factor. And if there was such a thing as a personal embodiment of Goddess Earth Mother, Jane would be it. Her hugs alone were one of a kind.

Jane quietly assessed Anne's energy as she let her settle in. Anne was a compulsive journal-writer and note-taker, so she needed time to get out her reading glasses, journal, and pen. Jane had to admit, she'd been rather surprised by the turn of events in Anne's life. She'd known Anne a long time, both as a client and as a student of the spiritual workshops she facilitated with her friend Olivia. Jane liked and respected Anne, and always looked forward to their sessions, perhaps because they had so much in common. As long as she had known Anne, however, she had never heard her mention any other man in her life besides Jack. This session would definitely be interesting.

Jane observed Archie checking out the room, while hovering close to Anne. He clearly had things to say, but was respectfully waiting for them to take the lead.

Jane initiated the conversation. "So, Anne, tell me what has been happening for you since I last saw you."

Having come prepared, Anne handed her a copy of Archie's obituary, which included his photo. Jane examined the photograph. It depicted a much older, almost unrecognizable version of the Archie in her office. He was likely presenting himself at the age when Anne would have known him. Jane guessed that to be around thirty, maybe slightly older.

Anne spoke of the astonishing return of Archie, a man she had dated in 1975, when she was twenty-one and he twenty-eight. They had met in a hotel bar on the airport strip and she had been quite surprised when Archie had asked her to dance.

"If I hadn't gone that night, we would never have met."

Jane reiterated Archie's words to Anne. "Archie says if you had not met there, you would have met elsewhere."

"Oh. Well, anyway, he asked for my number and our first date was on Valentine's Day. And so last week, it was the forty-third anniversary of our first date. I wrote him a Valentine's letter, which I'd like to share with you."

Jane watched Archie gazing at Anne as she read, beaming. In all the years she'd known Anne, she had never seen her glow like this.

After reading the letter, Anne said, "We dated for three months, and during that time, we never had a fight or spoke a cross word. He introduced me to his family. That's how I discerned that was his obituary—by the names of his brothers. I thought we were very happy, but three months later he called to say he wanted to break up. He wouldn't meet with me to talk about it, and when I phoned him he was uncommunicative. I said, 'So you want to break up.' And he replied in the affirmative. That was it."

Archie needed no prompting. As he explained what happened, Jane echoed his words. "Archie says near the end of your relationship, he started hearing a voice, a persistent thought in his head that told him, 'You and Anne cannot continue. You have to break up with her.' He says when you met and were dating, he thought he was done—he had met his girl. And so the voice was very distressing for him. Archie says, at the time, he thought he was going crazy."

Anne interjected, telling Jane about the evening Archie had taken her to his apartment. He had gone directly into the kitchen and had seemed so upset, then had grabbed her hand and taken her into the bedroom.

From Anne's perspective, he broke up with her abruptly and unexpectedly. One minute he was inviting her to go swimming at his brother's pool, and the next he was breaking up with her. All these years, she had never understood what happened.

Today, Archie said he didn't meet with her after he broke up with her on the phone because his resolve would have crumbled upon seeing her.

"So that was it," Anne said, finally understanding. "Seven years later, I ran into Archie in a grocery store. That was the last time I saw him. I was alone and had checked my groceries, and as I headed to the exit Archie was there, waiting for me, just beaming at me, the way he had when we dated. It took my breath away. He was walking toward me, his arms open, ready to envelop me. I had this feeling of panic, and I booted past him and out of the store. It had been such a shock, I'm not even certain I recognized him at a conscious level. It was only when I got to my car and saw his truck that I knew who he was—I had parked my car beside his. That was the last time I ever saw him. It still kills me that I didn't go back to talk to him."

Prompted by Archie, Jane said Anne's walking past him in the grocery store had been very, very difficult for him. He had seen her wedding ring and the image of a little boy, and knew Anne had moved on. That she was a wife and mother. Up till then, he had hoped that one day down the road they would get back together. That had been a very tough day, but a wake-up call.

"He says he had a hard life."

"No! I wanted you to have a good life!" Anne cried out.

"Archie says it was a very physical life, and when he died, he was ready."

Jane continued, "After you, he lived his life..." She stopped and looked to Archie to hear the specific word he was using. "'Practical' is his word. He loved your Valentine letter. He's pleased you felt the same way, as he always considered you his Valentine, and this past Valentine's Day was special because of it. He says he couldn't get in touch with you after his death because his guides wouldn't let him. But he wants you to know that you and he are twin flames. You have spent many, many lives together, some not so good. But there has never been so much love as in this lifetime. It was very special."

With this, Anne felt tears coming, and swallowed.

"He wants you to know he saw you one day at the University of Toronto."

Anne and Jane both looked at each other in amazement.

"That would have been fairly recent." Anne had attended U of T in the late 1990s up to 2004. "Why didn't you say hi?"

"He says you looked like you had purpose—not that you were happy, but that you seemed to be living a life of purpose." He said if she had looked fragile, he would have approached her. But he saw she was okay and thus didn't.

Anne had no memory of seeing him and was perplexed, but said nothing more.

Archie said that when he died and met his spirit guide, he realized it had been this guide's voice telling him to break up with Anne.

Jane seemed intent on observing Archie, when she broke into a huge grin. "Anne, Archie's singing to you—your song. It's 'I'll Always Love You' by the Spinners."

"I didn't know we had a song."

Dumbfounded, Anne looked over at Jane, who seemed to be completely captivated. She was now repeating the song's lyrics for Anne's benefit. "So, you're breaking my heart, taking my sunshine from me, knowing that I'm to blame....'Cause in my heart, I know that I'll always love you, I'll always love you, baby."

"Anne, I wish you could see Archie. He's dancing, gesturing, as he's serenading you."

It was enough to observe Jane as she tried to keep pace with Archie, her head turning—seemingly to follow his energetic body, all the while trying to discern the words he was singing. "Sometimes a man has too much pride to see, but losing your love, my darling, has opened my eyes for me...."

As Anne sat there, she couldn't help but think that when spirits from the other side came to speak, it was often with a message like "I love you." And then they left—at least that had been her experience. But not Archie! According to Jane, he was moving around the room while he was singing. *Singing!? Had he been like this when we dated?*

When he broke up with her, Anne had wanted to talk with him. Now, forty years after the fact, now that he was dead, Archie wanted to talk. Seriously, what was going on here? Anne found it all a bit heartbreaking—earth-shattering, perhaps.

After the song, Jane continued to relay Archie's words.

"Your guides were kept busy trying to keep you apart as you lived and travelled in the same geographic circles. Archie says, next time, if you live a life apart, you will have to choose to be on different continents. He couldn't handle another life knowing you and not being able to be with you."

"If I have my way there's not going to be a next time apart."

"Archie wants you to know he has no plans to reincarnate any time soon. He will be there when you cross," Jane said. "Oh, Anne, he's waiting for you. Your next lives will be spent together!"

"Really?" For some reason, she had felt he would withdraw his energy at some future date, and she had actually been quite worried about it. She let out a sigh of relief. The idea of his leaving her was like waiting for another breakup. She didn't think her heart could take it a second time.

"Archie is asking if you have any questions."

Anne felt like she'd been hit by a Mack truck. Questions? She was certain she did, but at the moment she had nothing. Anne confided to Jane, "This is a lot to digest. Until today, I had no idea of his feelings." And then to Archie, she said, "It's a good thing you're dead, because if you were still living you would be in serious trouble."

"Archie's laughing. He says your story could be a Nicholas Sparks novel."

"We could co-write it and maybe after my death it could be published." While Anne laughed too, she was thinking—*Seriously?! We dated three months, and then nothing. He must be joking.*

As Anne was leaving, she thanked Jane for all she had done.

Jane nodded. "You have another appointment in May, but if you need to see me sooner, just call. I'll find a way to fit you in." And with that, Jane hugged her goodbye.

That night, Anne had trouble sleeping. *Great!* Her mind was teeming with questions, now that she had no way to get answers. She found herself struggling with Archie's revelations that he had loved her, had never stopped loving her, and that his life had been hard because she had not been in it. What was she supposed to do with this?

She still couldn't understand why Archie's spirit guide had told him he had to break up with her, especially when they were twin flames and loved each other so. It made no sense. *They better have a good answer for me when I cross over.* At the moment, however, no explanation seemed adequate to ease the overwhelming pain she was feeling. Anne was pretty sure there were no self-help books out there for this kind of relationship. As she drifted off to sleep, Anne made two notes to self: 1) find out about twin flames; and 2) look up "I'll Always Love You" by the Spinners.

The next morning, Anne went to her desk and switched on the computer. Her mission was to find out about twin flames. But first Anne googled "I'll Always Love You" by the Spinners—a group she had never heard of. Apparently, they hailed from Liverpool, England, and the song was released in 1965. Anne would have been eleven years old. No wonder she'd never heard it before. Archie would have been eighteen, though, and the song had clearly held meaning for him after their breakup.

The lyrics spoke about a girl breaking a boy's heart. Anne was a bit dumbfounded. Is that what Archie thought all those years ago? *He* had broken up with *her*! He'd broken her heart! The song ended by saying the fellow would love her till he died. *Okay, enough!* Upset and bewildered, she closed the page.

She then typed "twin flames" into the search engine. She was astonished to find so much information about a subject she knew nothing about. Apparently, twin flames were unique, different in nature from all other relationships—kind of like twins. Twin flames were one soul split in half, into two bodies——and as such, represented a deeper bond than even that of soul mates. The relationship, spiritual in nature, was marked by unconditional love, often deeply respectful in nature and one that honoured each other's situation and choices, even if they did not understand them.

Because twin flames were each other's half, when they met there was instant recognition and intense attraction, like there was a magnetic pull that drew one to the other. They were openly demonstrative, touching each other often. *Well, that was certainly true for us.* While there was immense comfort found in the other, it could also prove deeply confusing.

Anne was genuinely surprised to discover an entire website devoted to questions and answers about twin flames and the challenges arising from these relationships—characterized by deep love, emotional turmoil and upset, all at the same time. The nature of the questions spoke to the deep, intense love shared by twin flames. A common thread seemed to be that the twin flame bond could be so intense, it proved challenging and confusing to both parties—so much so that they often ended up parting ways. But once parted, it seemed many twin flames were obsessed with "union"—getting back together with their other half. Nonetheless, the experts suggested that rather than obsessing over one's twin flame, one needed to surrender to self and look within.

An adept researcher, Anne picked up what she perceived as a major running theme present in the forum—spiritual growth. Since twin flames were basically each other's mirror, their purpose in meeting, coming together on earth, was always about each other's personal soul growth. It was a soul journey that couldn't be shared with anyone else on earth. Someone described the meeting of her twin flame as an alchemical experience. While emotions of deep love and connection were amplified, so too were feelings of insecurity, doubt, and fear. Hence, meeting one's twin flame, being in a relationship with him or her, was ultimately about spiritual growth—to release old emotional wounds and fears, ultimately leading one to self-love, self-acceptance, self-mastery.

Interesting, very interesting!

As Anne scrolled further down the list, she stumbled upon an online course about twin flames, soul mates, and hard soul helpers. *Sounds perfect!* It was offered by an intuitive, whose name and reputation Anne was familiar with. Twenty years ago, as part of Anne's efforts to develop her intuition, she, along with her good friend Ariel, had taken a three day in-person course directed by this same woman. She remembered how both she and Ariel had been impressed by the instructor and the course itself. It had been the beginning of Anne's discovery and appreciation of her own innate intuitive wisdom.

Without hesitation, Anne signed up. Since the course was pre-recorded and online, Anne could listen to it at her leisure. That was good, because at the moment she was feeling a little overwhelmed.

CHAPTER 5

Embarking on a Journey to Self-Love

riday morning, Anne got up early and went to yoga. She needed to do something physical. She kept thinking, *What's done is done. Archie is dead, and our breakup caused enough grief, both then and now.* Still, she struggled to understand *why* Archie's guide had told him to break up with her—something to ask Jane at her next appointment.

In the meantime, she faced the problem of how she would move forward in her life with this new awareness, plus the fact that Archie still seemed to be hanging around. Anne could feel his energy with her during the day, but most particularly at night when she closed her bedroom door and climbed into bed.

After yoga, a few women from her class gathered for tea and talk. Today, the topic under discussion was self-love. A friend, Eloise, said something profound, at least for Anne.

"Would it not be wonderful to love oneself first, and then enter a romantic relationship? Instead, we tend to do the opposite, fall in love with a partner before we look to loving ourselves."

When Anne was growing up, self-love had never been on her radar. Rather, her parents warned her against being selfish or self-centered, so Anne had learned to put others' needs first. But lately, Anne had been feeling tired, and physically unwell. Even her body seemed to be urging her to focus on self-care and self-love. Jane, her life coach, distinguished between being selfish and self-love: "To love and care for oneself first is not self-indulgence, but self-preservation." If Anne was empty, spiritually and emotionally, she had nothing to give. Anne often wondered if her emotional outbursts and depression that had plagued her at various times throughout her life had come from not loving herself, not caring for herself.

In the past year, Anne felt she had embarked on a spiritual journey of discovery about self-love. She thought it might have started with the decluttering and renovation of her physical living space. And now with Archie's return, possibly she was undergoing an emotional decluttering, ridding herself of old emotional baggage that no longer served her.

After her father's death, and her own breathing issues, Anne had looked up "lungs" and "coughing" in the Louise Hay book *You Can Heal Your Life*. According to Hay, lung problems were related to depression, grief, fear of taking in life—not feeling worthy of living life fully. Hay suggested that the new thought pattern or affirmation for this would be: "I have the capacity to take in the fullness of life. I lovingly live life to the fullest." Perhaps Anne was not only mourning the loss of her father, but the loss of herself as well.

Feeling depleted, worn down, she had lately come to the decision to leave the local museum where she volunteered. She had been there eleven years, but the last little while she had been feeling empty, like she didn't belong there anymore. So she knew it was time. In the back of her mind, she thought maybe once her history book was completed, she might return; but intuitively, she knew she wouldn't.

Her other thought was that maybe after she was finished writing her book, she herself would go, would die. Two or three months ago, hoping the night air would ease her breathing and cough, Anne had gone out for a walk. Feeling at the end of her tether, she'd looked up to the night sky, and said aloud to God, Source, spirit, angel, whoever was out there listening, "Just so you know, I can't do this anymore. I am done. I AM SO DONE!"

When she arrived home, it was late and she went up to her room. Sitting on the bed, Anne felt two hands placed firmly on the top of her head. There was no one there, at least not that she could see, but she felt magnificent energy pour into her, and was calmed, her spirit soothed. She had no idea whose hands they were, possibly those of her angel or spirit guide. At the moment, she didn't care. It felt absolutely blissful, so much so that she hesitated to move lest it stop.

At breakfast the next day, she described the incident to her husband. Jack laughed. While he thought it was fine if Anne wanted to travel the spiritual path, he had always made it perfectly clear that it was not his thing.

But lately, things like this had been happening to Anne. Things she couldn't explain. The past summer, she'd awoken one morning to feel someone holding her hand. She opened her eyes to look. No one was there, but a hand was definitely holding hers, and was not letting go. She felt someone, some energy sitting beside her. She was not alarmed, but curious. Whoever it was, the energy felt loving and supportive.

The last couple of years had been difficult and Anne had been feeling lonely. Possibly the presence holding her hand was her spirit guide, letting her know she was not alone. Eventually, she felt the hand release hers and, with that, it seemed the energy or spirit left as well.

Again, Anne shared what had happened with Jack. Since before they were married, Anne knew they thought very differently about life. Nevertheless, she was trying to be more open with him about her spiritual experiences. She had no idea why, what she expected. His response was, "Seriously, Anne? You were probably dreaming."

Shortly thereafter, she had spoken to Jane and asked if she had any sense as to who had been holding her hand. Jane said she had no idea, and reflected the question back to Anne. "Who do you think it was?" Anne had no idea either, but felt it had been a loving presence.

The rest of February and March, Anne felt that spirit, God, the universe, were sending her little messages of self-love. She was still reeling from all that Archie had disclosed to her. In her mind, she kept revisiting the moment she had walked past him in the grocery story. He had smiled at her with such joy and love, so much so that she had panicked. Yet, after realizing who it was, she could not make herself go back in. She realized that she would never be able to change that moment and take away the pain she had caused him. She had to forgive herself, even if she didn't understand. She reminded herself, *I have to be kind to me, and have courage to move forward and love myself first and foremost.*

Anne had seen Jackie Kai Ellis, author of *The Measure of My Powers: A Memoir of Food, Misery, and Paris,* interviewed on television, and was so moved that she bought the book. Upon reading it, Anne was especially drawn to the author's account of a phone conversation that took place between her and a dear friend. Ms. Ellis expressed her fear that she might once more suffer the overwhelming pain of depression. Her friend's response was that, over the course of Ellis's journey through the pain and sadness, she had come to love herself. And for that, she should be proud.

As Anne contemplated this, she thought about how loved she was by her parents, her husband, her children, and friends—and now, it would seem, by Archie too. But did she love herself? What would that look like? How would it feel?

Maybe this lifetime was about Anne learning and actualizing self-love—to love herself, without judgement. If successful, she could then be fully present in her wisdom, her being, and her relationships. Anne found it somewhat ironic that just as Archie came back to profess his love, her attention was directed inwards to self-love and self-care. And her body appeared to be telling her the same thing. Anne had read in *Re-member: A*

Handbook for Human Evolution, by Steve Rother and the Group, that there is but one true relationship: the one you have with yourself. That your relationships mirror self, one's own magnificence, the God within you. The answer to all relationships was to love oneself first. Love of self comes before all others. And unity consciousness speaks to the idea: "We are here to love you until you learn to love yourself."

Was this why Archie had come back, to love Anne until she learned to love herself? As her twin flame, was he the mirror of her divinity, her magnificence?

As all these thoughts were whirling around in her head, Anne finally took the time to watch the online course about twin flames, soul-mates, and hard soul helpers, the one she had signed up for a month ago.

She was very curious to get a professional's point of view. The intuitive talked a bit about each of these relationships and how they differed. Anne had always thought each person just had one soul mate, but she learned that in fact, one has many. Thus, in addition to being a possible romantic love interest, soul mates could be dear friends and/or family members. In contrast, hard soul helpers were those people, often family members, one would describe as difficult, challenging. Hearing this, Anne could think of a couple of family members who fit that description, but she had learned from them as well.

Addressing twin flames, the instructor described this relationship as a deeper connection than that shared by soul mates. For the most part, she seemed to echo what Anne had already learned in her online research. The bond shared by twin flames was unique in that, energetically, they were each other's half. As such, the feelings of love went so deep that when they met, there was instant recognition, as well as a compelling, intense need to be near the other, openly displaying their affection for each other. They often entered one's life at inconvenient times—perhaps when one or both were married—and this too added to the confusion. Again, the instructor's advice was similar to information Anne had gleaned from the twin flame website—step back, go within, and do some deep soul searching. In other words, the answer to twin flame relationships was in one's personal soul wisdom and growth. Only then could one make an informed decision about the twin flame bond, about whether it was possible to be together or not.[1]

Why is it that the more I learn about twin flames, the more depressed and discouraged I feel about my relationship with Archie? Reflecting on his recent revelations, Anne thought that, in some ways, the twin flame bond could be felt as a hard soul helper connection, but within one's own soul-self.

---

[1] Lori Wilson and Grandmother, online course: "Twin Flames, Soul Mates and Hard Soul Helpers," www.inneraccess101.com

CHAPTER 6

Anne's Mother

The phone was ringing. Dead to the world, Anne didn't reach the phone in time. She looked at the clock on her nightstand—two in the morning. No message. Anne crawled back into bed.

As she started to doze off, the phone rang again. It was Max, her brother.

"Mom passed."

"What?"

"Mom passed."

Anne heard his words, but could not process them. *Mom?* Anne had just talked to her. She held power of attorney for her mother's personal care—they would have called her, not Max.

After her father's death a year ago, Anne's mother had declined considerably. In a wheelchair and on continuous oxygen, she had pleaded with Anne, and anyone else who cared to listen, that she simply wanted to go to bed one night and not wake up. Her pulmonary specialist had said there was little he could do, and had referred her mother to palliative care. And in the last couple weeks, Anne had been working with a palliative care doctor from hospice.

As a former nurse, she was fully cognizant that his treatment would result in her mother's death. Nonetheless, she had been unprepared.

It was close to three a.m., and Anne worried about driving the one and a half hours to Toronto. She called Max back and they arranged that she, her two brothers, Max and Joe, and sister Laura would all meet up at nine in their mom's room at the retirement home. After all, there was little they could do now. Mom was dead, and they would have to wait till morning to contact the funeral parlour to make arrangements.

Having settled that, Anne went to Jack's room. He was asleep, but Anne nudged him until he stirred and opened his eyes.

"Mom died."

Jack stared momentarily, and then closed his eyes again. She wondered if he'd heard her—he didn't have his hearing aid in.

"Mom died," she repeated.

Anne climbed into bed beside him. She was feeling the need to be held. Jack, a deep sleeper, was clearly dead to the world and rolled away from her. She would have to tell him news of her mom's death in the morning. For a minute, Anne just lay there, looking up at the ceiling, feeling alone, bereft.

Returning to her room, Anne crawled into bed. Lying on her side, she became aware of an energetic presence—Archie—at her back. It felt like he was spooning her, holding her. Anne sighed. Feeling soothed, comforted, she quickly fell fast asleep.

Waking up in the morning, Anne could still feel Archie. He'd stayed with her the entire night.

"Thank you, Archie," Anne softly whispered.

Over the following days as she and her siblings planned the funeral, Anne was overcome by the great outpouring of love and support from family and friends. This was especially evident, given that Jack didn't really "do death."

Anne always considered herself incredibly blessed to have Jack as her lifelong partner. Throughout their years together, he had always been caring, loving, and supportive, as both husband and father. Lately though, since Jack's father's death, Anne had become aware of his inability to deal with death, to handle grief. But then, how could he? He had grown up with parents who had not "done death." Years ago, Anne had been genuinely taken aback by her mother-in-law's lack of sympathy when Anne's grandmother had died. And there had been no memorial after Jack's father's death, as per his wishes. Still, as much as Anne tried to be understanding of Jack's discomfort around death and dying, she found it especially difficult now with her mom's death.

Prior to her mother's visitation, Alex, their son, had taken his parents out for dinner. He'd insisted Anne order a huge strawberry daiquiri, and over the course of the meal, Alex uplifted her spirits with conversation about the happy times they had shared with her mom and dad, his beloved grandparents. At the funeral parlour, Alex had stood beside Anne as she greeted the friends and family who'd come to offer their condolences. His ease of conversation and being with people made it easier for Anne to get through what proved to be a long night. By the end of the evening, however, Anne found herself laughing and enjoying the company of old friends and family who reminisced with her about both her parents.

Two girlfriends from Anne's school days had seen her mother's death notice in the paper. She had been so touched. Each had come to see Anne, to reconnect with her.

Her best friend, Kat, had written Anne a beautiful note in which she described the experience of losing her own mother as one of the most eventful and profound times in her life. Still, she assured Anne that while her mom was no longer there in body, she would continue to live, love, and support Anne, in spirit. That she knew this to be true.

With the visitation, funeral, and burial, the next week was a blur. Family and friends came and went. Her siblings asked Anne to give the eulogy, which would not be easy. Anne knew her mother had loved her, and she had loved her mother. Yet the best way to describe their relationship would be to say it was complicated. As the first-born, she knew she'd been a difficult child. Her mother never failed to remind her.

Just a month ago, her mom had again reiterated to Jack how much Anne's hyperactive nature and big emotional outbursts had tried her patience. She'd had trouble understanding why Anne was like that. It was then that her mom disclosed her long-ago attempt to contain Anne, to suppress her big energy.

Sometime after Laura was born, Anne's mother had asked the pediatrician to prescribe medication to "calm" Anne down—after which her *own* father, Anne's maternal grandfather, had severely criticized her for taking Anne's spirit away. He loved that when Anne smiled, her face was like the sun, radiating love and warmth to everyone around her. And when she was mad or upset, her face was like a storm cloud. Being that way himself, he appreciated his granddaughter's sensitivity, her authenticity of being, her way of expressing her feelings, her truth, even before she could talk—a rare quality in one so young.

Seeing Anne become so quiet and subdued had unnerved her mother as well, and the medication was stopped. Anne had no recollection of this, but at times she had wondered if she actually did suffer from mental illness as her mom had suggested.

She knew her parents loved her, that they had done the best they could. She also had known that as soon as she was able, she would have to get out of the house. At seventeen, after high school graduation, Anne moved away to attend nursing school, which had been heaven-sent.

It turned out she had a gift for nursing. She would never forget how wonderful it was to feel accepted and liked for who she was. In her first year of training, she remembered one palliative patient to whom she had been assigned had informed her nursing instructor that Anne exemplified a wisdom beyond her years. She had been genuinely touched by his comment—it was in stark contrast to her mother's assessment of her.

Near the end though, a couple weeks before her death, her mother had said "I love you" to Anne. She thought that might have been a first. In their family, love was not something talked about or expressed. Rather, it was something assumed to be understood. Her mother telling Anne that she loved her was so monumental that Anne had included it in her eulogy. And Joe, her youngest brother (fifteen years her junior), came up to her later and said that her experience of their mother as not openly loving and affectionate had been his as well.

Whereas Anne's mother had been a devoted daughter to her own mother, she had clearly struggled with motherhood. Even so, Mom had been the heart and centre of their family, the glue that held it together. She'd done the best she could for all of her children. And as a grandmother, her mother had excelled. Once Anne had Alex and became a mother in her own right, she had come to appreciate her mother's support, seeking it out often. It was hard for Anne to imagine a world without her mom in it.

A couple of days after the funeral, Anne received flowers from her friend Clare, with a poem attached entitled "Mother Root" by M. Awiatka. She and Clare had met when their kids were young, and their friendship remained. They continued to meet regularly for coffee and conversation, to discuss life, family, books, and most important, their spiritual journeys. In her sympathy note, Clare wrote that she was sending energy of ease of well-being, peace, and spaciousness to her in the coming days.

Anne was amazed by the poem, given that she had entitled her eulogy *Motherlove*. Over the first couple of days following her mom's death, she'd sorted through boxes of old photos and papers, collecting pictures for the video and memory book. At the bottom of one box, Anne had discovered an Easter card that her mom, then a teenager, had sent her own mother. Below the printed greeting, her mom had inscribed the words, "Motherlove, your only daughter." Anne had never seen "Motherlove" written as a single word, but she loved it. She was sure her mom had intended it as a term of endearment. However, as a noun, as a subject, it meant so much more. For Anne, her mother was the personification of motherlove; indeed, our mothers are our first teachers about love and self-love.

And if Anne were to be completely honest, she had not fully appreciated her mother until she herself had become one. She had learned how challenging it was to be a loving wife and parent, all the while trying to be more, to feed your soul. And now just days after her mom's funeral, Clare sent her a poem titled "Mother Root." What were the chances?

But it was not only the poem's title that resonated with Anne, it was the image the poet had poignantly drawn through her words. The poem spoke of two hearts, one the root—the mother, the other. The flower, when it blooms, "affirms a heart, unsung, unseen." Had Anne's mother felt frustrated, angered by the limited opportunities available to her while being a wife and mother? Had she felt unsung and unseen?

At the funeral service when the minister had spoken, he'd had little to say about Anne's mom—though he'd known her for decades. What he did say was that in searching for something to say about Marilyn, Anne's mom, he couldn't think of her without thinking of Anne's dad, George—"George and Marilyn, Marilyn and George." For good reason, Anne had found his cursory appraisal considerably lacking. As a historian and student of women's history, Anne was sensitive to, and critical of, the old patriarchal paradigms that disregarded women and their influence. Her mother had been so much more than just a wife, as Anne's eulogy went on to profess.

The day of the funeral, Jack had been quiet, distant. Anne recognized his unease as he struggled to navigate what, for him, was a foreign emotional terrain. At the luncheon following the burial, Anne was thrilled to see familiar faces she had not seen in a very long time. Rather than sitting down to eat, she went around the room, connecting with family, friends, and neighbours whom she wondered if she would ever see again.

At some point, Jack came up to her and stated his displeasure that he was sitting alone at a table where he knew no one. Anne was startled—disappointed. A deeper sadness, a deeper grief engulfed her.

As requested, though, Anne joined Jack. Her uncle and cousin, both of whom she loved and saw rarely, were at the table, and so Anne enjoyed sharing some time and memories with them.

Her cousin reminded Anne that at a family reunion, she'd taken him out in a rowboat on the lake. It had been a first for him. She would have been seven or eight at the time—her cousin maybe four or five.

"Really? I have no memory of it. You were taking your life in your hands—to let me take you out in a boat!" And they laughed. *Hard to believe—I must have had more self-confidence way back then.*

Later, while Jack went out to the car, Anne gathered the photographs of her mother that were scattered throughout the room. Now that everyone was gone, Anne was feeling desolate. Without thinking, Anne got her cell phone out to listen to a message her mom had left her a couple of days before she died. She needed to hear her mom's voice.

Two weeks later, Anne found herself in a local furniture store, on the hunt for a chair for her newly renovated office. She loved this store and all its offerings, from the very biggest of furnishings to the smallest of accessories. As Anne tested a chair for comfort, she spotted a small wooden heart laying on a nearby end table. She placed it in the palm of her hand. It fit perfectly. She turned it over to check the price. Eleven dollars. She reminded herself she was there for a chair, and set the heart back down.

As Anne moved through the rest of her day, she couldn't get the heart out of her mind. The next day, Anne returned to the store to find it still there. Had it been waiting for her? She thought so, and immediately purchased it. Taking the heart home and placing it in her bedside table, she wondered if Archie had sent it to her to replace the heart-box she had thrown away.

A couple weeks later, another gift appeared. Anne and Jack loved going to antique markets—they both loved old books and things that had history. And so while their house was largely contemporary in design, antiques, old books, and art could be found scattered throughout. Jack often joked with Anne that it was because of his love of old things that he kept her around. History, he said.

One gorgeous spring Sunday, Anne and Jack were at one of their favourite haunts, the Aberfoyle Antique Market. On this particular day, Anne walked into a unit she rarely visited. On a bookshelf at the very back of the shed, Anne was delighted to find A.A. Milne's *The Complete Tales and Poems of Winnie-the-Pooh* in perfect condition. She loved Pooh. She loved his wisdom, and that he possessed a great heart.

As Anne leafed through the pages, she noted no name had been inscribed in the space "This book belongs to." But author Milne had dedicated the book "To Her." Somehow, on reading this, she knew it was from Archie, that he had wanted her to have the book because he loved her, and because he had loved her eulogy, especially the ending in which she had cited Pooh telling Piglet: "If there ever comes a time when we can't be together, keep me in your heart. I'll stay there forever."

CHAPTER 7

Coach Session after Mother's Death, May 2018

A couple weeks after the funeral, Anne went for her appointment with Jane. When she had booked the appointment, she'd had no idea that her mom's death would be a topic of discussion—talk about divine timing.

Anne had invited Archie to come with her, but was unsure if he would. Throughout the days following her mother's death, she had been acutely aware of Archie's presence. From that first night when he had spooned her as she'd sought comfort and sleep, she had felt him near.

When Anne arrived, Jane was busy at her computer and told Anne to sit and make herself comfortable.

"How's everything?"

"My mom died," Anne said softly—so much so, Jane seemed not to have heard.

"My mom died."

Jane turned and moved to the comfy chair opposite that of Anne's. As she did, she checked Anne's energy.

"Your energy is very closed and narrow around you. Not surprising, given your mom's death. Tell me about it," she invited.

Anne appreciated Jane. With no platitudes, present in the moment, Jane was there to listen to her. Anne talked about her mom and the funeral: how surprised she had been by her death, even though she shouldn't have been. How she was pleased that her

65

mother had died as she had wished—just gone to bed in the evening and not woken up.

Jane knew Clare, and so Anne talked about the flowers and poem Clare had sent. How she had been struck by the poem, entitled "Mother Root." That it had so resonated with Anne's eulogy on "Motherlove." And how writing her mother's eulogy had caused Anne to reflect and ponder her mother's life with more appreciation, more compassion.

When Anne spoke about the synchronicities of all of this, Jane simply said, "Anne, there are no coincidences. You have travelled a spiritual path for some time now. You know that."

Anne nodded. She went on to say that she was feeling anxious, depressed, and frankly overwhelmed by everything currently going on in her life. One evening, Anne had meditated, asking to meet with her spirit guide. She described the meeting to Jane.

"I found myself in a garden, sitting on a bench under a tree. My spirit guide, a woman, stood facing me. I explained my situation—my mom's death, Archie's re-entry into my life, and my efforts to finish my history book and find a publisher—and requested some wisdom, some guidance."

"She responded with a question: 'What did you say to your daughter when she was feeling anxious that she had not yet met her significant other?'"

Anne remembered the moment very clearly. "I said that this was her time, and to enjoy it. One day when she was happily married with children and crazy busy, she would long for the time when it was just about her."

"That is what I am telling you now, Anne. This is *your* time, time for self-love and self-care."

As Anne related this, she was struck by how these words resonated. She had also been astounded by her guide's question, indicative of how intimately she knew Anne and her life.

"It was remarkable, because lately I have been thinking and reading about self-love and care. It feels as if I'm receiving reminders from spirit, Source, God, and/or the universe in the form of books, conversations with friends. The theme is making its presence known, loud and clear."

Jane then spoke about herself—how in the last few years, she had made a point of getting away on her own for three or four days. Twice a year, she would rent a room in a quiet location, out in nature usually. Like Anne, Jane kept journals, and on these trips she would pull one of her old journals from the shelf to take with her. She also took a book to read. She would walk and, sometimes, book a spa treatment or a reading (medical intuitive or psychic) from someone she trusted.

Anne thought about the idea, and said she didn't think Jack would take kindly to it. Although, as soon as she said this, she thought perhaps she wasn't being fair. Jack had proved, time and time again, his unwavering support. When Anne was doing her doctorate, she had won a national award that had enabled her to go to London for four months to conduct research at the British Museum and Library. At the time, her kids were teenagers, and Jack, while not thrilled, had stepped up and been Mr. Mom in her absence. Anne was very aware of how challenging her being away had been for him. He'd missed her.

Jane said, initially, her husband had felt the same way. But when Jane came back from these mini-sabbaticals, he saw her happiness quotient had risen, and this made life better for them as a couple. Recharged, Jane simply had more to give to him, and her family.

Anne thought her decision to leave the museum in January and focus on the completion of her manuscript was a major act of self-love—to prioritize her work and herself. However, she would give serious thought to Jane's suggestion about getting away, and see what opportunities might open up.

She looked down at her list of subjects she wanted to address, the next and final one being Archie. His disclosures at her last session, when he had revealed his love for her and the reason for their breakup, had shocked her.

"If we, as twin flames, were not meant to be together in this life, why did we even meet and have a relationship? Did our spirit guides go on a coffee break?" Anne looked to Jane and asked, "Is Archie here?"

Jane smiled. "Archie's here now. But before he answers your questions, he wants to give you a big hug."

Anne sat still, unsure how one hugged a spirit. When dating, they had spent a lot of time wrapped in each other's arms. Anne sighed. Just the thought of Archie wanting to hug her was so sweet, so tender, loving, and kind. At times like this, she felt constrained in her physical body. At night, when Anne felt Archie's energy around her, she sometimes hugged her pillow, pretending it was him, as she conversed with him. Crazy, she knew, but the situation she found herself in was a bit crazy. She had no idea what she would do if it weren't for Jane validating that Archie was indeed present and not a figment of her imagination.

"Archie wants you to know he loved your eulogy to your mom. He says it was beautiful, and that throughout the whole death and funeral process you showed yourself to be all that he knew you to be." At this, Jane raised her eyebrows and nodded to Anne. "Archie understands that Jack was not supportive in perhaps the way you needed him to be. And that he, Archie, was with you pretty much the whole time, offering his love and support. But he's concerned for you. Archie feels you are close to the edge."

Anne asked what he meant by that.

"He feels you're burning the candle at both ends." He stressed the importance of rest when she was tired.

Jane continued, "So, to get back to your question. Archie says that before this life, 'We were very old souls who had been together on the other side for two centuries. As a result, both of us had forgotten how hard it was here on Earth, how long Earth time was. In planning our individual lives apart, we had decided to come together early in our lives for a short period. Our guides had advised us against this, but we were insistent. Neither of us had been prepared for how strong our feelings would be. How hard it would be to part. During our lives, each time one of us searched for the other, we honoured our soul contract to be apart.'"

Anne listened intently. This was the first she'd heard of a soul contract.

"Is it okay that we're together now?"

Archie apparently nodded and said that with his death, the contract had been successfully completed. He said that, in the many lives he and Anne had shared together, Anne was most often the man, and he the woman.

Dressed in her customary jeans and T-shirt, Anne grinned. "Well, I guess that makes sense. I've never really been a girlie-girl. And I cannot remember the last time I wore a dress." Indeed, she had worn a tuxedo to her son's wedding.

"That goes for me as well," Jane laughed, gesturing to her own sporty attire.

"Archie wants you to know he is happy you are remembering the joy you and he shared during your time spent together."

Anne acknowledged this to be true. Lately, Anne was recalling more details—especially how much they had laughed, as well as the amount of time they had spent kissing in his car. When their lips locked, she had been totally lost in the moment, feeling him, them, together.

"One Sunday afternoon, we dropped by one of his friends' house. They had just had a baby boy. I loved babies—still do. While Archie was talking with his friend, I went further into the living room where the new mother and baby were. The baby was nestled in his bassinette. After conversing about her experience giving birth and being a new mom, she asked me if I wanted to hold her son. Immediately I said yes. I remember sitting down in a chair and the woman placing her baby in my arms. And for a short while, I held him—my attention fully focused on the newborn babe and his perfection."

"'Don't get any ideas,' I heard Archie say. I looked up to see Archie smiling at me. Very soon after, we left, and as soon as we climbed into his car we were wrapped in each other's arms, kissing happily."

In a nutshell, that was how they'd been together.

"I imagine we would have had kids if we'd stayed together."

Jane said, "Archie is nodding." Jane echoed Archie's words, "If we'd had sex, we would have stayed together, and the babies would have started coming. I don't think contraception would have worked for us."

Hearing this, Anne quickly sobered, remembering Archie was dead. Through Jane, she asked Archie, "How did you die?"

Archie said his death certificate listed heart attack as cause of death, but truly he had died of a broken heart. He'd had the opportunity to pass ten years earlier, but had chosen not to. Looking back, he thought he probably should have. Ultimately, he died alone in hospital. Archie explained that in past lives, he had been a strong person, out there accomplishing great things, and thus, this most recent life had been a challenging and humbling experience for him. Jane clarified, "He says that according to social mores and norms, he had been a loser."

"You were never a loser!"

"That's why I loved you! You saw and knew the beauty of my soul."

There it was again. He said he loved me. Something he had never said in life.

The appointment was nearing an end, and Anne wanted Jane to balance her energy on the table. As she lay down, Jane asked her if she wanted a pillow placed beneath her knees and a blanket over her. Anne said yes. Jane noted that there was a lot of energy that needed to be released. Not surprisingly, Anne's heart chakra was a pale green, rather than the deep emerald green indicative of a heathy and strong heart chakra.

Anne wanted to ask Archie one more thing.

"He's gone, Anne. But before he left, he kissed you on the forehead."

Had she felt it? No. Anne began to feel emotional. "I'm sorry."

"This is all very hard, isn't it?" Jane said, as she saw tears well in Anne's eyes. "Archie's back. He's telling you, if you need him, you should just say, 'Archie, I need help' and he will be with you. Archie, in spirit, is your safe person, your soft place to land." Anne felt his words significant since she'd recently confided to him that she felt safe and soothed when in his presence.

This calmed Anne. She was fully aware that Archie had work to do, as did she. Still, she marvelled at their love for each other—his love for her, but especially the depth of feeling she held for him, not just emotionally and spiritually, but at a physical level.

As Jane was finishing up, clearing her energy, she said Anne's heart chakra was bright green now. And then, the spirit of her mom came—"very hesitantly," Jane noted, as manifesting in physical form after having crossed was new to her, and she could not stay long. She sent Anne her love.

"I love you, Mom, and I am very happy you're Home."

Once the chakras were clear, Jane asked her body what it wanted. It picked a flower essence called "Mother-Daughter Essence" that nurtured creativity, self-love, and love of mother and daughter. How perfect!

As Anne scheduled her next appointment for September, she spoke briefly about how, with her mother gone, she needed to mother herself—self-love and -care, just as her guide had instructed her.

Jane asked, "Think about what that means for you, and we'll talk about it next time."

Driving home, Anne pondered the question. *What* does *self-love and self-care look like for me?* No one (with the exception of Jane) had ever asked her this. She asked herself, "What do I need?" Anne had no idea *how* to love herself, but she knew she needed to make space in her life for more joy, more love.

She wondered if she could last until her next appointment with Jane. Reflecting on how supportive Archie had been lately, Anne recalled how kind, tender, and loving he'd been when they dated. What they had missed—what she had missed. *How did I move on, knowing our great love for each other?*

Anne had read somewhere that an open heart is a broken heart. It felt true for her. With the loss of Archie, her dad, and now her mom, Anne was feeling fragile. At various moments throughout the day, she would experience waves of exhaustion and would need to lie down and rest. Perhaps this was what Archie had been talking about, about her being close to the edge.

That night as Anne settled into bed, she felt Archie's energy around her and said, "I am speaking to you from my present experience and life as Anne. If we had never met and been together, I would not have this gift of you now, which is precious to me. I don't mean… How do I say this? It breaks my heart to learn of the pain you suffered. If I had known, I would have found a way to ease your grief and pain. And yet, now that you have crossed over, I know this was something we could never have done for each other, due to our soul contract."

CHAPTER 8

A Memory Surfaces

Near the end of June, on one of her regular research treks to the University of Toronto's graduate library, Anne wondered if she would ever walk onto this campus again without thinking of Archie. Ever since he said he'd seen her at U of T, Anne was mystified as to when and where that could possibly have occurred. She had never asked Archie about it; it was her feeling that if he wanted her to know something, he would tell her. Otherwise, Anne honoured and respected his privacy. That was how they had been when they dated, and it was how they were now. But today, as Anne entered the library, an image resurfaced in her mind.

The last two or three years of doing her PhD—fifteen years ago—Anne would typically arrive at the library around 8:30 in the morning and promptly head to the cafeteria. She would buy a Starbucks coffee and muffin, and then sit, not in the main seating area, but rather in a small alcove off to the side where there were only four tables. Rarely, if ever, was anyone else there, and Anne relished time by herself before heading up to her tiny office on the eleventh floor. A creature of habit, Anne chose to sit at the table on the right-hand side by the wall, from which she could look out the floor-to-ceiling window.

One particular morning, she recalled seeing an older gentleman fixing the coffee vending machines. He had been crouched on the floor near the stand where she had grabbed some cream, and had looked up at her as she did so. A couple of minutes later, he took a seat at the table directly opposite hers, choosing the seat facing hers. Anne figured he was taking a break, while keeping an eye on his tools. Nonetheless, she had felt slightly disconcerted that her solitude had been breached.

Anne had looked over and taken note of him as he drank a coffee from the machine he'd been repairing. Once, he looked over at her and smiled. It was the familiar yet searching way he made eye contact with Anne that caused her to think, *Do I know him?* She looked again and thought, *No.*

Anne was quite reserved when it came to strangers, so she turned away, drinking her coffee and looking out the window. She had been self-conscious of him observing her, but each time she glanced his way, he looked down or away. She was uncertain how long he remained, but there was a moment when she saw his legs turn as he rose to leave. As he did so, she looked at him, and their eyes met again. This time, his eyes seemed sad as he smiled at her. And with that, she heard him quickly gather his tools and take off in a rush.

Had that been Archie? Anne was feeling anxious, to the point of feeling sick to her stomach, because her intuition was telling her that this was the meeting Archie had spoken of.

That evening, as Anne settled into bed and felt Archie's energy, she recounted her memory and asked if that had been him sitting at the table in Robarts' cafeteria. When Archie said he'd run into her on the university campus, Anne imagined he had seen her in passing as she moved from one building to another—not that they'd been sitting alone together, three feet across from each other for a period of at least ten minutes.

"What was that?! Why would you not have come over and said hi? Would that have been so difficult?" Anne was trying to make light of it, but inside she was feeling hurt and angry with him, with herself. Why had she not recognized him? Archie would have been in his mid-fifties. His hair was still the same, had not yet turned grey. He had looked thinner and sadder than the Archie she had known. She guessed they had spent too much time kissing, and not enough time looking at each other. If he had just come up to her, said "Hello, Anne," and embraced her—now, that she would have remembered.

"You are so lucky you're dead, because right now I could wring your neck!"

Anne was at a loss. Why had she not known Archie? Her question was met with silence. Nor was her higher self forthcoming with an answer—high self being Anne's soul or spirit that connected to divine consciousness, wisdom and love. Over the last few years, Anne was trying to pay attention and heed this inner knowingness or wisdom that manifested in dreams, meditations, or often just as intuition.

As Anne continued working on her history book, she found herself obsessing over her recent recollection. There had been no other people sitting at the tables, just the two of them. She kept replaying the situation over and over in her mind. When he first sat down and she looked at him, he had looked at her with a tentative smile, then looked down at his coffee. Had he been waiting for her acknowledgement? She could only imagine how disappointing it must have been for Archie. Anne was upset with herself that she could have caused him pain, however unintentionally.

Anne tried to place the meeting in the context of what was going in her life at that time—not that it mattered. She was both appalled and confused by the memory. And what seemed to make it worse was that Archie had recognized her on first sight, and had come to sit at the table next to hers. Why had he not come over and said something? It would have been late fall 2002, or early 2003. She would have been forty-nine and he fifty-five. Surely their guides could not have cared about their connecting at such a late date in their lives.

She was feeling a little broken-hearted about the whole thing, but Anne's spiritual wisdom reminded her, "This is water under the bridge." She could not change what had passed. She needed to get beyond the hurt and upset, to stop taking it so personally.

And then, in the early morning hours as Anne lay somewhere between sleep and wakefulness, she heard a voice. "It was a gift—for him."

~~~~~

Another morning, as Anne was waking, she felt Archie's energy and heard his words: "I wish you could see yourself as I see you."

Anne was thrilled that she had heard his words so clearly in her head. Her response surprised her. "If I ever write our story, everyone is going to fall in love with you. You know that, don't you?"

While Anne felt gratitude and joy to have Archie in her life again, she still found herself feeling fragile, a word she had never before used to describe herself. She struggled with the memories that had resurfaced: the kindness in Archie's eyes and his quiet, gentle manner; him moving his legs as he turned to rise from the table, and then gathering his tools and leaving in haste.

A week later, Anne could not sleep and took to her journal at two in the morning. Anne was clairsentient, meaning she felt and heard messages from spirit as voices in her head. Though admittedly, she didn't fully trust this knowingness that was inconsistent at best.

But this morning, Anne could feel Archie's gentle presence, and her heart opened to his words. He was talking to her about their meeting at the university coffee shop. He wanted to explain his side of things. It had been early morning and he was repairing the coffee machine when he heard her voice ordering coffee. He knew it was her.

"I watched as you walked toward me, and then turned to sit at a table in the alcove. You seemed oblivious, wrapped up in putting your two bags on the chair, and fixing your coffee. When you finally sat down, I just watched you sip your coffee and look out the
~~~~~

window. In my mind, I was weighing my options. Considering your strong reaction at the grocery store thirty years ago, I was nervous.

"I decided to get a coffee from the machine and sit down at the table kitty-corner to yours, in a chair where we could see each other, where I could see you. When I sat down, you looked over, and our eyes met. I thought I saw a glimmer of recognition at first and smiled. But then you took a sip of your coffee and looked out the window. I knew then that you didn't recognize me, but I was okay with it. It felt so good to just sit and be with you. Every now and then, I would glance over at you. I could see you were aware of this and were trying to figure out if you knew me.

"Dearest Anne, I cannot begin to tell you the array of thoughts and possibilities that were going on in my head and in my heart. When we dated, you had always been so full of joy, and that day, for the first time, I saw the unhappiness in your eyes. Nonetheless, you had an air of confidence about you, an assuredness. I thought perhaps you had become a professor. I want you to know that if you had, in any way, looked distraught, I would have approached you. However, in the end, I just relished those few minutes we shared together."

It had been so long since Anne had felt Archie's tenderness that it was hard for her to process—to register. These last few months knowing and feeling their deep love for each other made it hard for Anne to accept the rare and missed opportunities when they could have connected while he was still living. That Archie would sit beside her and not speak with her.

Though Anne knew she should have been grateful to be able to hear Archie, instead she was annoyed.

"I love you Archie, but this hurts me. Both occasions when we met, you could not once have said, 'Hi Anne, remember me? I'm Archie. We used to date.' Or even just 'Hi Anne'? We could have sat together and had a conversation. That would have been kind.

"Clearly, this meeting had been orchestrated by the guides as a gift for you. It was your gift, so I guess I have no right to say anything. Nonetheless, I am still in body and vulnerable. And I am trying to have a meaningful conversation with you. You said that it's because we parted when we did that we are now able to have a relationship. If this is the case, then I have to talk with you in a real way. I do worry about our ability to communicate. Since you no longer walk the earth and we can't go parking, it would seem we have to resort to this channelling and talking. Believe me, I would much rather be kissing, but this is our option at the moment."

Was that laughter? "Are you laughing at me?"

More laughter—and then Archie said, "Yes! And me too—kissing I mean!"

Anne sighed. She'd so loved this man for his kindness, humor—and kisses.

Since she was not due to meet Jane for a couple of months, Anne decided to meditate and talk to her spirit guide. Maybe she could help with all the emotion Anne was feeling. Her spirit guide reiterated to Anne that the meeting was a gift for Archie, to let him know Anne was okay, and that he had made the loving and correct decision to break up with her all those years ago. The gift was meant to give him some peace of mind, so that he could go on.

Anne then remembered when Archie rose from the table. He had given Anne a smile, and when their eyes met, his had radiated kindness and love. Her spirit guide also said that Anne was not meant to recognize Archie. It was certainly Archie's choice whether to speak to her or not, and he had chosen not to. As such, Anne must honour and respect his decision, knowing it had been made with love, and in love.

As Anne reflected on the last few months since Archie's return, she felt a shift taking place within herself, and tried to make sense of what was happening—to step back, take a breath, and look at the situation from a higher perspective. Both as a historian, and as a nurse, she had learned to do this as a way to understand a person or a situation more fully. In her reading on spirituality, Anne had read many definitions of love. In *Re-member: A Handbook for Human*

Evolution, Steve Rother had defined love as the opposite of fear. Whereas fear was the lack of wisdom and understanding, love was the abundance of it.

Later that evening, Anne wrote a message to Archie in her journal: "And so, Archie, in this life, you were abundantly understanding and wise. Therefore, with gratitude, I can only love and honour you and your choices with regard to us."

~~~~~

As all of this was transpiring, Anne was living her life. She had finally left the museum and now directed her time and energy to completing her obituary book—but Anne was experiencing limitations. All of her mentors and supervisors had recently died, or were seriously ill. How could she create spaces of light in her own life and move beyond her feelings of restriction? It was causing her to not like herself, to feel that she had somehow failed.

Still, she knew that it was the soul's journey to self-love and wisdom, not the destination that mattered. Somehow, in 1975, in shutting down memories of her relationship with Archie, Anne had closed part of her heart, part of herself. She felt Archie's presence was allowing her heart to open, herself to open.

One night, Anne dreamed she was alone in a locked room. She could hear someone outside, someone coming with keys to unlock the door. And Anne felt fear. Fear of the unknown. Was the person on the other side of the door Archie? On waking, Anne realized that Archie was opening her heart and that, while she was excited about this, she was also anxious, afraid of what that might mean. What that would entail.

When Archie had broken up with Anne, she now realized, her emotions had been triggered. Old childhood wounds resurfaced, affirming her inner child voice that told Anne she was not enough, not good enough. As a young child, Anne's father—as loving as he was—had been relatively absent, either working, taking courses, or out playing sports, and her mother had been emotionally distant and critical.
~~~~~

As a young teen, Anne had suffered from anorexia nervosa, around which she still carried a lot of shame, attributing it to vanity and/or mental illness. Anne's weight had plummeted to eighty-two pounds before an aunt had noticed, and called Anne's mother—her mom had not seen her daughter's advancing disappearance.

One day in the mid-1990s, Anne had heard Princess Diana comment on her personal experience with eating disorders, saying that it was not vanity but emotional abandonment that was the root cause of this disease. Thus, these individuals needed compassion and love, not criticism and body shaming. At the time, though, it had not really registered with Anne, in part because she had shut all memory of her eating disorder down years before. And throughout her life, Anne had never talked about it with anyone, had never shared that painful experience with family or friends—not even with Jack.

With Archie's return and her mother's death, however, Anne was, bit by bit, putting these pieces together. In 1975 when Archie left without saying goodbye, Anne had had to shut down that geography of her heart, all memory of him, of them. It had been a matter of survival. But, now with his return and their deep love remembered, these other less-pleasant memories, feelings, were coming forth as well.

Anne knew that her soul needed space to breathe. She had thought that leaving the museum and focusing on her writing would have given her more space—but it hadn't.

On Jane's recommendation, Anne was reading *Rising Strong* by Brené Brown. Brown stated that "owning our story and loving ourselves through the process is the bravest thing that we will ever do." Anne had been thinking about Margery Kempe, an English secular mystic who had been the subject of Anne's undergraduate thesis. Kempe had lived in England circa 1370 to 1430, and her *The Book of Margery Kempe* has been credited as the first autobiography to have been written in the English language. Kempe had owned her story by writing it down. Not an easy feat for a woman of that time and place. More than anyone, Kempe had taught Anne in a very real way about history, its study, and creating spaces for understanding those individuals different from others, from herself.

In writing about Kempe, to whom Anne had taken an instant dislike, she learned that history was not about judgement, right or wrong, liking or not liking someone, but understanding. Previously, Anne, as a student of history, had always avoided writing about anyone she felt she might not be able to do justice to. *Do no harm!* Anne took those words to heart. But she realized that trying to understand someone or a situation was not maligning anyone, past or present. In placing Margery Kempe within the context of her community—a community bound by the ties of kin, trade, and piety—Anne had come to appreciate Kempe's being and the tremendous courage she had exemplified in her willingness to follow love and her soul path, regardless of all the cultural and social challenges working against her at the time.

Brené Brown also wrote, "Vulnerability is not winning or losing: It's having the courage to show up and be seen when we have no control over the outcome. Vulnerability is not weakness; it's our greatest measure of courage." In other words, one's vulnerability is the basis of one's strength. It is a key to growing self-awareness. And Jeshua, in *Your Soul's Gift,* stated that any self-awareness is about self-love.

Anne appreciated Brown's wisdom and courage, her willingness to be frank and open about herself, her feelings, to bare her soul to all. At the same time, however, all this wisdom overwhelmed Anne. She felt fear and anxiety, but had no idea what to do with it.

CHAPTER 9

Session with Jane, Autumn 2018

It was the first week of September when Anne met with Jane, a session she had long been anticipating. Lately, Anne feared she was losing it. While she talked to Archie every night, she wondered if he was the best check on her reality, given that he was invisible, and she could only feel and occasionally hear him. Anne had no idea what she would do without Jane because, in truth, she was the only witness of Anne and Archie as twin flames, as a couple, one in body and the other in spirit.

Upon arrival, A

nne was greeted with a gentle hug.

"So, how have you been managing over the summer?" Jane asked.

Anne shared the news of her memory of Archie on campus. As she read her journal entry about the encounter, Jane informed her that Archie was here and requesting permission to speak. Anne had not been aware of his presence, but was eager to hear what he had to say.

Archie agreed with the words that had come from spirit—their meeting at the university had been a gift for him. "Just to be with you was such a gift, to see that you were okay and to spend that time with you was lovely. It carried me through a long time."

Then, Jane said, "Archie wants you to know that you are still beautiful."

Anne was speechless. When they dated, Archie had never said that to her. Interestingly enough, she had always felt beautiful when she had been with him—and still did.

Archie continued. "It was my loving choice not to speak with you. I don't think I could have taken it, to have to say goodbye again."

"Anne, what would you have done if he had spoken to you?" Jane asked.

Anne really didn't know. "What struck me was when we first made eye contact, his eyes looked at me with such love. I felt it—so much so, it threw me off, as it was so intimate and yet I didn't recognize him. I had to look away."

"Archie says he's glad you remembered that—that the love registered in your memory bank."

Anne still wished that they could have talked and connected. However, knowing the love she felt for Archie, she conceded, "It *would* have been hard to say goodbye again. Although we never really did say goodbye, did we?"

Archie explained that prior to incarnating, he and Anne, in planning their lives apart, had established that they would come together for a short period. After this, they would each move on to fulfil contracts and agreements they had entered into with other souls. Their hope was that after their breakup, they could perhaps continue as friends.

"Archie is laughing and says, 'To think we thought we could be friends! There was no way, Anne. Our love ran too deep. It was like the grocery store all those years ago, when you couldn't bring yourself to go back in, once you realized it was me. The good news is that one of our tasks in this life was to let each other go, and we accomplished that.'"

Anne was still not clear as to why they had contracted to do this—possibly to learn the lesson of self-love, and for each of them to stand in their own power? She had no idea.

"Archie wants you to know that he is still around you and will continue to be, until you tell him otherwise. If you asked him to leave, he would honour that."

"That makes me happy to know you are here. And I love feeling you with me, Archie."

Anne revealed to Jane that she had been reading a book entitled *My Life After Death: A Memoir from Heaven* by Erik Medhus, a young man who had committed suicide. Strangely, she'd learned of it in an email, and, interested about Archie's life on the other side of the veil, started reading it. She was surprised to learn that Erik, though dead, had a home base on Earth. It was the home in which he had grown up, and where his family, his parents still lived. He visited his mother every day, and made a point to be there when she woke up. And his mother, Elisa Medhus, always greeted him with "Good morning, Erik."

"On reading this, I offered Archie my home, especially my study/bedroom, as a home base on Earth. I'm sure he has a home base with his mother, but I thought perhaps he could have a second home base with me."

"Archie loves that you are reading this book, and says yes, and thank you."

"May I ask: What do you do on the other side?" Since it was coming on two years since his death, Anne was curious.

He responded, through Jane: "Believe it or not, I am doing life review. I thought I would be finished with all that and planning my next life. But no, I'm still in life review."

Anne smiled. "That sounds like you. You were always so cocky and confident."

"Besides, you're here and have not passed yet."

"He's waiting for you so you can plan your next life together," Jane said.

"At this very moment, I am reviewing our relationship, our time together. It was a beautiful love from beginning to end. What I am learning is that I saw everything in black-and-white terms. You saw everything in shades of grey. I loved that about you." Archie said that, in life, he had been very rigid and controlling.

"I never felt you to be that way," Anne interjected.

"I was, in how I lived my life. I was very rigid and controlling about myself. I feel now I should have relaxed and had more fun."

As Anne listened to Archie's words, she was thinking that possibly she too was that way in how she lived her life. While still here, maybe she needed to relax and have more fun.

"Archie wants to know if you wish him to stay for the rest of the session."

Without hesitation, Anne said, "Yes. He probably knows me intimately now anyway."

Anne was not sure how long Archie stayed, but there were a couple of times when she could feel his loving energy around her head and crown chakra. His energy seemed to seep down through her entire body.

Jane certainly had dealt with a lot of "across the veil" moments between loved ones. Even so, Anne's and Archie's story was remarkable, and unique. But as their relationship was slowly unfolding, she was concerned for Anne and how she was managing, with one foot in this life and one foot in the other world, the spiritual realm. "You have had a lot to handle in the last few months. How are you dealing with all of this, Anne?"

Anne sighed. She confessed that lately she'd been feeling emotional, and experiencing waves of exhaustion. She attributed this to a combination of things: learning of Archie's death and his love for her, her mother's death, and not really moving forward on her book. Anne thought she might be ill, but she'd had a complete physical and been given a clean bill of health.

Anne looked out the window, pausing to reflect upon another time—a time when she'd felt similarly unsettled, unmoored, and anxious. It had proven to be a turning point in her life. Bringing her attention back to Jane, Anne shared her thoughts.

"I keep thinking back to 1988, when I feel I had an opportunity to go, to die."

Jane had heard this story before, but clearly Anne felt the need to revisit it.

"A rapidly growing tumour, the size of an orange, had been discovered on one of my ovaries. My gynecologist had serious concerns that it was malignant. At a deep level, I had been okay with the diagnosis. I remember thinking, *I would be okay dying.*

"At the time, I'd wondered why I wasn't more distraught about the prospect of having cancer. For all intents and purposes, I lived a perfect life. I had a husband who loved and adored me, and two amazing children. Jack and I had just moved into our dream home. In fact, as I contemplated my upcoming surgery, I had been enjoying my morning coffee by the kitchen window, overlooking a forest of trees in our backyard."

Over the years, Anne had periodically suffered from bouts of anxiety and depression, and so she was stunned by her calm realization that she could die, and it would be okay.

"In my mind, I asked myself why I felt that way. I was a responsible and loving wife, mother, and daughter. Even so, I could not remember the last time I'd laughed, truly laughed.

"And then this small voice asked, 'But where is Anne?' Hearing this, I came to the profound awareness that, in all my great efforts to be a good mother, wife and daughter, I'd somehow, somewhere, lost me—Anne."

The day of the surgery, Anne was alone. Her husband had had to work. Jack was a caring husband, but when it came to matters of illness or death, he struggled. Thus, Anne had long come to accept that in these situations, she was best left on her own.

"Just prior to being wheeled into the operating room, I felt an angel or spirit beside me, supporting me. And in that moment, I made a promise to myself, to spirit: that if the tumour proved to be benign, I would change my life. I had no idea how I would do it— just that I would. Even so, I knew I had to do something for me, me alone."

Reflecting back now, though, Anne felt she'd known this had been a wake-up call. That somehow she had to get her life back on track: to find the "Anne" she had somehow lost along the way to becoming a wife and mother. And so it was.

"The surgery was in March, and in September of that same year I registered as a full-time student at the local university. And the rest was history, in more ways than one.

"I feel somehow I am in a similar place now, thirty years later. How can that be?"

Jane replied, "Instead of asking, 'What have I not healed?' ask 'What have I not allowed in that would bring me joy?' What gives you joy, Anne?"

"If I'm honest, I really would like to finish the history book I'm writing. I'm not sure it would give me joy, but it would give me a sense of relief, of completion of the academic cycle. I love my family and friends, and I take joy in being with my granddaughters. Truly, I feel I have accomplished all I ever wanted and more. I'm not sure taking a sabbatical would help at this time. Some days, I feel ready to go. Archie is lucky because he got to go first. I'm still here."

"You can go at any time, you know."

Without thinking, Anne said, "But I have things to do, my book for one." The rest of the appointment was a blur. Anne had no memory of what they talked about.

It wasn't until late evening, as Anne was getting ready for bed that she felt someone say, "Did you hear what Jane said? You can go anytime." Was the universe making sure Anne knew this was a possible exit for her? Her grandmother had lived to be a hundred, and Anne had simply assumed that she would be around for a long time too.

But I can go anytime. With this new possibility, Anne thought, *Yes, fine.* And then, a huge wave of relief washed over her. She felt gratitude and joy. She could go anytime and Archie would be there waiting on the other side. As Anne closed her eyes, she felt Archie, his energy. There was such sweetness to the merging of their energies—an intimate coming together. He took her breath away.

"Are you relaxed and having fun yet?" Anne asked. She heard laughter, and then it all started again. Laughing too, Anne said, "I guess so."

CHAPTER 10

Staying or Going

While contemplating the latest turn of events, which begged the Shakespearean question—to be or not to be?—Anne emailed Jane. "You were looking over my shoulder when you said I could go anytime. Who were you looking at? Who said that to you? I'm curious because that same night, spirit, High Self, Source (not sure who) directed this to my attention. I guess they wanted to make certain it had registered."

Jane's reply was brief. "I think the context was that you had commented that you thought you'd gotten the tougher end of the contract that you and Archie had made. That he got to cross over earlier. Archie's response (with a smile) was that you could go any time you want—to be with him. Is that helpful?"

So, it had been Archie who had asked her not once, but twice, if she wanted to go.

Anne realized that over the years, she'd easily adopted the spiritual language around living and dying. For her, being alive and living on earth was "staying"—staying in this life. The opposite of that was "going"—leaving this life, crossing the veil, going Home.

Over the next few weeks, Anne became aware of spirit sending her information to support her in the decision she was now being asked to consider. One evening as she was preparing dinner, she happened to come across the movie *The Shack*. At the end, the protagonist was given a choice to stay with his daughter (who had been murdered) and God, or to return home to his wife and remaining children. God, played by Octavia Spencer, told him there was no judgement, either choice would be right.

If Anne were being honest with herself, she was feeling tired—depleted—much like she'd felt before her cancer surgery. Earlier this year when her mom died, Anne realized that, in many ways, a weight had been lifted from her shoulders. She had helped both parents receive hospice care so that their deaths would be well supported—so their suffering would not be prolonged. Her children and granddaughters were all well, as was Jack. Perhaps she had actually been ready to go for a long time, but with the death of her parents she felt the burden of familial responsibilities lift. Her father had called her "the rock of the family." Being the eldest, she had always felt responsible for her parents and siblings, ensuring they all got together on holidays and birthdays.

But with her parents gone, Anne realized she didn't have to do that anymore. She had done enough for family, friends, and community. Both of her children were adults, and Jack—well, they had enjoyed a loving and supportive relationship for more than four decades. Jack was a wonderful man, a caring husband and father. Still, for some time, Anne had been feeling lonely in her marriage, in her relationship with Jack. In the past, whenever this had come up, Anne had sought out new endeavours and interests that kept her busy. But lately, even as she pressed on to write her history book, she was struggling. Anne felt done, that there was nothing really keeping her here—nothing more that she wanted to do or be. Still, she appreciated that this decision was not to be made lightly.

Anne asked for divine wisdom, but it seemed no answer was forthcoming. Earth was the realm of free will. It was her choice, and either choice would be right. There was no judgement, only understanding and love.

Giving the matter serious consideration, Anne wondered if all her soul contracts in this life were complete. She jotted a note to self as a reminder to ask Archie this at her next session with Jane. Though it made sense that all her soul contracts would be completed, otherwise why would she have been informed of this as a possible exit point? Still, she had to make sure.

At lunch as a break from writing, Anne would often watch old reruns of *Oprah.* One particular day, Oprah was interviewing Elizabeth Gilbert, author of *Eat, Pray, Love,* a book and movie Anne had loved. Gilbert was speaking about one of her journal entries in which she'd asked, "What if I just quit?" And the answer given was: "It's okay to quit. I will still love you. I will still support you." Oprah asked Gilbert who she thought had provided the answer, and her response was that she'd been unsure, but felt it had been informed by God, the wisdom of Source. Anne was pretty sure she'd seen the episode before, but today it resonated deeply.

Did Anne think that in going, she would be quitting? Yes! *But why?* Perhaps because, in part, Anne thought she had to publish a book based on her doctorate. That it was important. Before his death, her PhD supervisor had encouraged her, saying people needed to read her book. And now, for whatever reason, Anne was thinking about writing another book, a novel about the love and relationship of twin flames—based on Archie and herself—one that transcended death and the physical world.

Conversely, Anne was feeling that she wasn't a good fit for the Earth plane, and it might be her time to go. Anne felt her love for Archie was deepening and longed to be with him.

Anne found her quandary somewhat paradoxical, considering that, in 2005 when deeply depressed, she'd badgered God or spirit to please let her die. And then one night, Anne had a very vivid dream. She dreamt her spirit guides met with her—at least she assumed they were her guides. The meeting took place in the eat-in kitchen of an old apartment she and Jack had rented when Alex was a baby. There were three individuals seated at the table by the window. One was a male in his mid-thirties, who had escorted her into the meeting. She remembered sitting down, and then being ushered out into the apartment's larger living area, while her guides remained in the kitchen to further deliberate on her request.

The room in which she waited was full of people milling about. Finally, the same man who had led her to the table came out to her, looked into her eyes, and said, "No."

Anne now wondered if she would have to meet with that group again to plead her case as before, or if now that her soul contract with Archie had been completed, the decision was her own to make.

As Anne continued to mull this over, she had another session with Jane, at which Archie was again present. It seemed Archie still wanted to talk about the breakup, as well as the letter he had sent her shortly thereafter. Anne shared more details with Jane about the breakup. When she mentioned sensing a woman beside her after saying goodbye to Archie on the phone in the hospital, Jane said it made sense that Anne's spirit guide would be with her as the contract to be apart took effect.

Regarding the letter, Anne said, "While I can't remember the specifics, it was a beautiful letter. Nonetheless, I found it confusing. I wasn't sure if Archie expected me to respond. There was nothing in the letter to indicate that."

In the midst of the session, Anne recalled something she'd never shared with anyone. She herself had forgotten it till now. A little over a year after the breakup, Anne had married Jack, and for the first few months she'd had a very hard time. She'd struggled. A couple of times, she'd phoned Archie. She wasn't sure why.

"I think I simply needed to hear his voice. The first time I called, Archie answered and he sounded very up. As soon as I heard him say hello, I intuitively knew I couldn't speak to him." Since Archie had made it clear he had not wanted to be with Anne, she assumed he would not be happy that she was calling him. It was so opposite to contemporary norms and values that said, "If you love someone, you search them out, and once you find them, never let them go."

"When I called him a second time and he wasn't home, I knew it had to stop. I was married and couldn't do this anymore."

Anne found it so interesting, in reviewing all of this, and throughout their lives apart, that she had seemed to have a sense that she could not speak with Archie.

A decade later, after Anne became a full-time university student, she was so busy that she rarely, if at all, thought of Archie. At the grocery store, when the voice had told her he was with someone, it comforted her to think of him well and happy, married with children.

"What is your take on twin flames?" Anne was interested to get Jane's take.

"Twin flames—there is a deep richness to their bond, even deeper than that between soul mates. Kind of like twins. Not everyone has one." Jane said they are basically each other's half.

Anne then shared what she'd learned. "Shortly after discovering Archie and I were twin flames, I took a course about twin flames, given by an intuitive who channelled the spirit of her **Shoshone** grandmother from a past life in the fourteenth century. Grandmother had spoken of the historical origins of Earth as a teaching planet for love, and how twin flames had come to be——how they had chosen to energetically split apart, to sacrifice their unity for the Earth's integrity. Because twin flames are each other's half, there is instant recognition when they meet and they have a constant need to touch each other, be near the other. The course reiterated what I had already discovered in my online research—that the twin flame relationship was intensely felt, so much so that it often proved confusing and challenging for both parties.[2]

"We were like that, you know. I never liked being touched by anyone, but with Archie it felt like the most natural thing in the world to be touching and kissing him. Whenever we stood in line or sat next to each other, we would lean in close to the other, or have our arms around each other. I never had that feeling with anyone,

---

[2] Lori Wilson and Grandmother, online course: "Twin Flames, Soul Mates, and Hard Soul Helpers." www.inneraccess101.com

before or since. I struggled for a number of years after the breakup, never fully understanding why."

Having listened to more details of Anne's story, Jane said, "Twin flames are like that. They are the thread that weaves through each other's lives."

Anne thought that was why she had shed so many tears when she learned that Archie had died. The realization that he was no longer on the Earth plane had hit her hard. All the memories and love she'd blocked came flooding back, and with them, torrential grief.

At this point, Archie entered into the conversation. He wanted to talk a little more about their soul contract. "When making our soul plan for this life, we had been together on the other side for a very long time. Our last lifetime, we were brothers living in the jungles of Africa. We studied the big cats, and were totally self-sufficient. We could talk to the animals and never once feared for our lives. It was a very happy lifetime. Nevertheless, it was in the 1780s, so our guides were concerned for us. Before we incarnated, we had a meeting with all of our guides—yours, mine, and those we shared. Seated at a round table in a large room, our guides stressed that this life was going to be very, very difficult. They kept asking us if we were sure we wanted to go ahead and do this. They then exited the room, leaving the two of us alone to make our final decision. We knew this life was the last piece of the contract, which had us coming together early in life for a short period and then separating. Both of us were anxious to get it over and done with. And so, we agreed to move forward."

"Archie says that after agreeing, you had looked at each other, wondering how you two were going to get through being separated."

While Anne felt sorry for herself, as Archie was across the veil and she was still in-body, she acknowledged that he'd had a much tougher time than she had. After all, he was the one who had to break up with her because the voice of his guide told him to. Tough to do when he loved her and had anticipated the two of them spending the rest of their lives together. In addition, Archie thought he was going crazy because he heard voices. On their last date, when they were kissing in the car, he had thought, *This is so awesome!* It was no wonder that, after he had heeded the voice's directive to get Anne out of the car, Archie drove home, sure that he must be certifiable. Who did something like that?!

For Anne, it had been easier. From her perspective, Archie had broken up with her because he had not cared for her, not loved her. She simply thought he no longer wanted to be with her.

"I was twenty-one and I never asked why he was breaking up with me." Perhaps Anne's soul had been making it easy for him. Or, as she would later come to appreciate, her respect of Archie's decision was a mark of the unconditional love she held for him.

In the last bit of the session, Anne addressed the possibility of her going, about the choice facing her, as well as the fact that she continued to grapple with grief—a lot of it, she knew, based on her growing awareness of the great love she and Archie had shared all those years ago, that they continued to share. And because of their soul contract, they had sacrificed, missed out on a beautiful love and life together.

"Firstly, I need to know if I have finished all my soul contracts for this lifetime. Are they, Archie?" asked Anne.

Archie confirmed that, yes, all her major contracts had been completed. She did have some remaining agreements, but these were not essential, and she need not stay for them. He explained that, unlike soul contract, agreements were not binding. They were more flexible.

While Anne should have been relieved learning this, nevertheless, there was something more. Deep in her soul, Anne felt she was grieving for herself, that she still had to do something— some soul growth—but was unsure what.

In her readings on death and grief, Anne had come to learn that grief was a journey unto itself, and one that would not let her go until she moved through it. Anne had to accept grief as part of her journey and honour her feelings. Recently, Anne had heard a moving definition of grief: "Grief is love with no place to go." But if that was true, she wondered if grief was something that ever left you.

"I have been contemplating another book, Jane. During our first session with Archie, he mentioned our love story would read like a Nicholas Sparks novel. However, I will not write it alone. If I stay to write our story, Archie will have to help me."

As Anne lay on the table for balancing of her chakras and energy, she could feel energy around her head, like she was receiving an electrical charge.

Jane returned from washing her hands and asked Anne if she could feel her third eye pulsating. Anne nodded yes. "That's Archie communicating with you. He says he has been trying to do that through your heart, but has had trouble. He wants you to know, Anne, that this is how he communicates with you—how you will know he is around you."

Jane seemed to be conversing with Archie. Anne heard her say, "If I was trying to find Anne, it would be through her crown chakra."

As per usual, Jane asked her body what energy it wanted for support. Today, Anne's body requested dog medicine. Jane read from her book that the dog has been considered the servant of humanity—a guardian, ever loyal to the trust placed in its care. As a totem or spirit animal, dog bestows the gifts of unconditional love, loyalty, courage, and protection.

As Anne listened, she recalled her dog, Susie. In her happiest childhood memories, Susie was there, playing in the backyard with Anne and her friends, running alongside her, sleeping on her bed, sitting beside her at the dinner table. But woe to any adult whom Susie saw as a potential threat. She became fierce, barking uncontrollably until the perceived predator had left the property. Anne had been heartbroken the day Susie had been taken to the vet, never to return. More than any family member, Susie had taught Anne about unconditional love, what if felt like to love and be loved unconditionally.

As Anne was leaving, she told Jane about the wooden heart she'd purchased a few months ago. "I think Archie sent it to me to replace the empty heart-shaped box I'd thrown away when I was de-cluttering."

Jane observed that this——what Anne shared with Archie——was an experience of grace in her life. "Cathleen Falsani states: 'Justice is getting what you deserve. Mercy is not getting what you deserve. And grace is getting what you absolutely don't deserve—benign good will, unprovoked compassion, the unearnable gift.'"

The unearnable gift! How wondrous! A gift and trust that Anne must honour and cherish.

CHAPTER 11

Thinking Outside of the Box

"If we are going to make our relationship work, we need to think outside the box." Anne had said this to Archie shortly after his return. At the time, she had no idea what that meant or would look like. Nevertheless, she trusted that somehow, together, they would figure it out. While she was so appreciative of Jane helping them communicate with each other, Anne was anxious to converse with Archie privately, on a more regular basis. The problem she faced was how to make this happen.

Archie wanted this too. Initially, the easiest way for him to communicate with Anne was through dreams—and within the first year, he had gifted Anne with a number of dreams. While they varied, they had often allowed Anne to know the enormous love they held for each other, not only in this life, but through the ages. It thrilled him when Anne acknowledged these dreams by recording them in her journal. In the first dream, when he had ridden up to her on a horse, he had been so impressed that she'd described his steed as a Howdy-Doody horse. It would have been incongruent if he had come to her as a knight on a white horse. Throughout their many lives together, they had never been that kind of couple.

In other dreams, he had tried to communicate the depth of their love, and the size and nature of their relationship. Even so, both he and Anne were eager to communicate more directly.

When Anne slept, her spirit left her body and travelled to the astral plane to be with him. In life, he didn't have the language to talk to Anne about what happened, but since being on the other side, he did. Anne was truly delighted to learn that Archie and her soul were having better conversations on the other side—but she had no conscious memory of them. She had to figure out a means to converse with Archie when she was in-body and conscious.

At the beginning, Anne had felt Archie's energy in various ways, throughout her day. At night before sleep, she would sit and talk to Archie, but over time these one-sided conversations frustrated her. When Anne shared her feelings with Jane, Jane said Archie had laughed and said their conversations were not one-sided. He talked to her; she just wasn't listening. Knowing Archie talked to her left Anne feeling both saddened and frustrated that she could not discern all he was sharing with her. Sometimes, Anne did sense what he seemed to be saying. Nevertheless, without Jane, they were connecting at a basic level, and it was sporadic and inconsistent at best, at least from Anne's perspective.

As Anne contemplated the challenge of listening, she had a dream in which she heard Archie's actual voice speak clearly to her. The setting seemed to be a basement, a rec room of a house. As she entered, Archie was standing in the doorway and their bodies brushed against each other. He smiled and held her to him for a moment. His body felt very solid and real, and recalled to her how wonderful it had felt to be in his arms.

On entering the room, Anne found herself in the company of Archie and his friends. Archie was speaking about his childhood and the freedom he experienced living in Scarborough, where he would hop on his bike and explore the surrounding environs with his buddies. And then he addressed Anne directly, calling her "hon."

"I can hear you, Archie! You called me 'hon'!" Anne was over-the-moon excited, both in the dream and when she awoke. When they dated, Archie had never used any terms of endearment. And so, for Archie to have said he loved her, and now to have called her "hon," was incredibly moving for Anne.

Shortly after this, Anne began to imagine writing a novel, a love story about Anne and Archie. She knew Archie was still busy with his life review, but perhaps he could help her. Anne was very aware that she needed to make space for the love, frustration, anger, and grief she was feeling. She could not push the emotions away, as she had done after their breakup. She had to acknowledge her feelings, and perhaps having a separate journal was the most appropriate place to process them. She also recognized that she needed to know when to walk away from her writing and do something else, grounding activities such as yoga, walking in the woods, gardening, spending time and playing with her granddaughters.

Anne had always journaled, but she decided to create a separate journal in which to record her journey of grief and love, related to Archie. So much was going on in their relationship, she felt the need to document their spiritual reunion in a sacred space. Yet, at the same time, she was nervous about putting it down on paper, where her husband or children might discover it.

Anne had another session with Jane scheduled for mid-December, almost a year to the day from when Archie first made his presence known to her. A year later, Anne's life had undergone significant changes. The most amazing was her awareness that Archie was a very real presence in her life, her safe person, whose love recalled the joy and laughter they had shared together. Every day, but especially at night, when Anne closed the door to go to bed, she felt Archie's energy enfold her. She felt him as an energetic presence, often as a kind of beautiful tingling around her head. At night, they were together in a sacred place that no one knew about. Not even Anne in-body had an awareness of it.

A couple years back, in one of the spiritual workshops facilitated by Jane and Olivia, Anne had learned that spontaneous writing was an effective way one could communicate with spirit (High Self, angels or spirit guides)—and have a record of what was said to review later, as well. As a meditative exercise, Anne and the other participants had had an opportunity to practice having a conversation with one of their guides or angels. While everyone confirmed their experience of meeting with their guide or angel, all

Anne received was an image of being on a bridge. As hard as she had looked, no one showed. When she'd looked down from the bridge, she did see a couple of men wearing yellow hard-hats, but they had not so much as looked up at her.

When Anne shared her disappointment with the group, Jane had suggested that perhaps her guide's message to her was "bridge under construction"—whatever that meant. Consequently, up till now, spontaneous writing was something Anne used rarely, in part because she never really trusted what was being said to her, as if she was making the conversations up in her head. But, anxious to move their relationship to the next level, Anne determined to try again— to try spontaneous writing with Archie. Hopefully, it would be easier with him.

One February evening, Anne set out to converse with her High Self. Olivia had explained that when speaking with High Self, one should voice a welcome, and then ask to be told what one's strengths are. Anne closed the door to her bedroom and took out her journal. She felt Archie's energy and made him aware of her plan to invite her High Self to speak with her, and use spontaneous writing to record it. If this proved effective, she suggested that she and Archie might give it a go.

And so, with pen in hand, Anne welcomed her High Self and began the conversation. "From my wise heart, I ask that all information from my High Self may serve gently and easily for my highest and best good." And then, as per Olivia's instructions, Anne asked, "Please, what are my strengths?"

And then, without thinking, Anne felt her hand writing down the words that came into her awareness. She just seemed to know the words as she simultaneously recorded them on the page.

High Self:
Courage
Kindness
Generosity
Perseverance

A Generous Heart
Loyalty
Warmth of Spirit

Anne: Is there a message you wish to convey to me?

High Self: You need to focus on your work, and self-love and self-care. By writing your book, you are loving and caring for yourself, your soul. If you do, all will be well.

Anne: I'm so happy that Archie is with me now. I feel so supported.

High Self: You two have successfully completed your soul contract. Your love for each other has moved many here on the other side, more than you could possibly know. But, in addition, you have both learned much wisdom in being apart. We are pleased.

Anne: So, I have a question. When Archie sat beside me at the University of Toronto coffee shop, why did I not know him?

High Self: This is complicated, to be sure, yet simple as well. I, your High Self, was very aware, and had agreed ahead of time that this meeting would take place. Archie had been going through a difficult time in his personal life, and the meeting was a gift for him. For whether you knew it or not, you are a light in his life. Archie, as your twin flame, saw and felt it immediately on your first date on Valentine's Day. As your High Self, I cast a veil of forgetfulness on you at the coffee shop. Although more than a couple of times when your eyes met, you were conscious of his spirit. Archie certainly had free will to speak to you, but because there was no recognition on your part, he chose not to approach you.

Anne: Still hard for me.

High Self: Let it go. Archie is with you now, and you are with Archie, loving and being with each other. Soon you will be writing a book together. I, for one, am very excited about it, as is Archie— a story full of love, but of humour too amidst the pain. It is a book that will be enjoyed by many souls.

Anne: Thank you, High Self, for your loving wisdom and insight, in love and appreciation. So, may I connect and speak with Archie at this time? I would like to practice listening to him.

Anne could feel Archie's energy then, at her crown chakra. "Archie, when I said our conversations were one-sided, you said that wasn't true. That I simply wasn't listening. So, tonight, with spontaneous writing, this is an exercise for me to pay attention to your words. And so, please talk with me."

And with that, Anne turned to her journal and began to write—again, without thinking but being open to whatever came to her. As she did, she felt more than heard his laughter as she wrote down his words coming into her conscious knowingness.

Archie (laughing and then serious): First, I love you, and am thrilled with this step forward. And yes, you are a lesson in patience for me. Everything over here is fast. One has a thought and then you are there. Although I must admit, I just love being with you. I was touched by your offer of your study/bedroom as my home base. Of course, it has been a home base for me, almost from the time I began connecting with you over a year ago. Nevertheless, your invitation was beautiful to me, proof of your loving and generous nature. I love that you are reading about the other side to understand my life here. The Erik Medhus book is a good one. It was no accident you received an email about it. There will be more books to come.

Anne: So interesting. I had a bad week. I think I'm still grappling with grief that you're not here, and I'm missing you. I'm just trying to take one day at a time, and focus on finishing my history manuscript.

Archie: Yes, please. You have a lot to accomplish, but remember to shower some love and attention on yourself. At the same time, know I love you and shower you with my loving energy. You are getting tired. Let's wrap this up for now. We'll talk tomorrow.

Anne: Thank you. Will you be at Jane's on Thursday?

Archie: It's our anniversary. How could I not!

—Anne Jeffrey, *Anne & Archie's Journal,* Vol.3
(February *11*, 2019)

From that day forward, Anne used spontaneous writing to converse with Archie. Every evening, without fail, when Anne closed her bedroom door, Archie knew it was *their* time. Sitting in bed, Anne pulled out her journal, and she and Archie would talk as she recorded their conversations. With the spontaneous writing, Anne was trying very hard to listen to Archie's words. Anne thought that it was not so much a matter of not knowing the words. It was more about trust, trusting herself and her intuitive nature—something she had struggled with throughout her life. And she knew it was also a matter of trusting Archie, their twin flame connection and conversation. Had she heard correctly when Archie said that he had the same wooden heart with him on the other side, a replica of the one she had purchased for herself? If that was true, she loved it.

"Did you just say, 'Too many words'?"
"Yes! See, you do hear what I'm saying to you."

CHAPTER 12

Valentine's Day 2019

---

*T*he year before, Anne had written a Valentine's letter to Archie to mark his return into her life, on the forty-third anniversary of their first date. Anne had cried when she'd shared it with him. Her twin flame and the love of her life had come back to let her know that their soul contract had been completed. The news had been bittersweet, as Archie's return also disclosed news of his death. A year later, Anne was still dealing with her grief about this. According to Archie, every night Anne's spirit left her body and they were together on the other side. Anne, however, still had no conscious memory of it.

She had mentioned this to her friend Helen, who was spiritual and quite intuitive in her own right. Helen had recently moved nearby after her husband's death, and Anne felt their friendship to be a gift. They had met at one of Jane's and Olivia's spiritual workshops, and since that time had formed a kind of satellite group of their own. Anne, Helen, and four other women who had all attended the spiritual workshops met monthly to talk about spirituality, in light of their lives, relationships, and personal soul journeys. Anne had yet to be forthcoming with the group about what was going on with Archie. Nonetheless, she felt a spiritual bond and kindred spirit with these women who now graced her life.

After some thought, Helen suggested that perhaps the reason behind Anne's amnesia was protection. If Anne were to remember her time with Archie on the astral plane, she would choose to exit. To Anne, that made perfect sense and she decided to let it go.

Anne still suffered bad days. Only last week, Jack had been dumbfounded when she'd started crying at the dinner table and had to excuse herself and lie down. Reflecting back, she had no idea what had triggered her.

Since Jack never ate during the day, he was always famished and liked to have dinner around 5 or 5:30, when he got home from work. And that day, Jack had come home earlier than usual—or perhaps, Anne had been later than usual in the meal preparation. She'd been in her study the entire day, wrapped up in reviewing eighteenth-century newspaper and periodical obituaries, in an effort to more clearly pinpoint the time when there had been a shift in their function—from domestic news/advertisements to commemorative tributes.

"Sorry, Jack, I got so engrossed in my writing, I lost track of time." She guessed it was a little late to make the chicken she had planned. She opened a can of soup and made some egg salad sandwiches with fresh bread.

Jack loved egg salad, so he was just as happy with that anyway. Jack was pretty easy that way. For the most part, no matter how hard his day was, he tried not to bring work home with him. For him, home was his haven. Now that it was just the two of them, he quite liked the structured solitude that was theirs in the evening.

"How was your day?" Anne asked.

"Okay. You know, same old, same old. How was yours?"

"Slow-going." In so many ways, Anne was in awe of Jack, his genuine caring and compassion for his patients, as well as his ability to manage his staff and the business end of his dental practice. His skill and professionalism were renowned in the community. And his staff had been with him since the beginning.

"Do you see an end in sight?" Jack asked, looking up at her. Jack knew how hard Anne had worked on the book.

"I don't know. I feel like it's going on forever. And lately I feel so weary—exhausted."

"Anne, just get it done and send it out. It doesn't have to be perfect."

Anne knew Jack was right, but nevertheless, she started crying.

"Anne, what's wrong? Tell me."

"I'm missing Mom, I guess." With tears streaming down her cheeks, she excused herself from the table. Upstairs in her room, lying on her bed, Anne sobbed.

This Valentine's Day, Anne wrote Archie another letter in which she acknowledged her gratitude for his continuing presence in her life, something she'd not expected a year ago.

Dear Archie,

It is with great love and joy that I write this Valentine for you. I get very emotional to think you agreed to stay with me because I asked you. This past year, having you in my life has been incredible, to say the least. I love that we have a relationship that spans the veil. In many ways, we have become this old married couple, but in other ways—we are like explorers discovering and forging our "out of the box" relationship. When I said to you last year, if this relationship is going to work, we need to think outside of the box, I never could have imagined what we share now—a deep love and intimacy, something more than we had all those years ago.

I finished reading the Erik Medhus memoir, Life after Death. It has given me glimpses of the possibilities of your life on the other side. He speaks to the fact that his relationship with his mother is closer now after his death. My hope is this will remain true for us as well. His mother wrote that she still has hard days of grief. I'm grateful she shared this, as I do too.

The intense love connection we experienced all those years ago—I have never had that again in my life and when I grieve, I grieve that loss. But I also mourn the loss of simple pleasures we never got to share with each other: falling asleep and waking up in each other's arms, cooking a meal together, walking on the beach, hand in hand. I miss you, but even more, I miss us when we were both in-body and in love.

With our first kiss, it felt like I had come home. And of course, I had. And so, dearest Archie, Happy Valentine's Day.

Love,
Anne

Anne read the letter aloud, knowing Archie heard it. Today, she was missing the man who had held her in his arms and kissed her deeply. She missed his laugh, his teasing, but mostly she just missed him, his tender touch, his kisses, and his humour. One of Jane's first comments about Archie was that he had a great laugh. And he did. Anne only wished that she could hear it once more.

Anne spoke to Archie of the unique nature of their connection, so different from her usual efforts to distance herself from outward demonstrations of affection. She recalled Archie's deliberate touching from their early dates, as well as her response to it. In her memories, the two of them were constantly touching each other, hugging and kissing each other, and always next to each other, leaning into the other, whispering in each other's ears. She had asked Archie if he had remembered him touching her in the car.

Archie had forgotten. Regardless, from the very beginning, Archie shared that both he and Anne experienced an immense comfort with each other on all levels. "We were more comfortable touching each other than not touching." It had freaked Archie out, but it had also intrigued him. On seeing Anne in the bar, he had felt drawn to her like a magnet. He thought, *I want to talk to this girl,* and that was very unlike him. And after their first kiss, it just escalated from there.

~~~~~

On this year's anniversary of their first date, Anne had scheduled an appointment with Jane. Just before leaving home, Anne decided to bring a photograph of her aura, taken a couple of weeks ago at a psychic fair. Glancing at the photo before placing it in her bag, she noticed something that, until now, had escaped her attention. Someone was standing behind her left shoulder. Was that Archie?

On arriving at Jane's office, Anne immediately handed her the picture and asked what she thought. Jane examined the photo closely, taking in both Anne's aura and the mystery figure behind her.

"Archie's here. Let's ask him. He's laughing. He says he was with you at the psychic fair. As you were getting the photo taken, he thought, *Okay, I will be in the photo with Anne.* Archie says this is his Valentine's gift to you."

"I love it. Thank you! It *is* unique, as I have come to think of us as a couple. I will treasure it." On more than one occasion, Anne had bemoaned the fact that they had never had a picture taken of the two of them together. She was very moved that Archie had thought to do this for her, as a gift for their anniversary. From that day forward, Anne kept the photograph, along with his obituary photo, at the front of the journal recording their conversations.

Anne then shared with Jane the spontaneous writing conversations she'd conducted with High Self and with Archie.
~~~~~

Since Archie was present, she asked him about the difficult time Anne's High Self had referred to.

"Were you going through a tough time in your personal life? It would have been late 2002, early 2003."

Archie explained that there had been stretches in his life where things had gone well, and he had not thought of Anne. But in his mid-fifties, he began having vivid dreams of her.

Jane said, "Archie says he would wake up devastated. And then he would get angry with himself, knowing you each had a life. He spiralled into a deep depression. He had no empathy for himself. He felt like a loser. There had been times in his life when he could let it go, let you go. But then it kept resurfacing."

Hearing this, Anne was visibly upset.

And then out of the blue, Jane said, "Archie wants you to know he loves your grey hair."

Thrown off-balance—Archie was good at that—Anne was speechless. Compliments always made her feel somewhat uncomfortable, and she wasn't used to Archie's compliments. He had never really been like that when they dated, at least that she could remember. Was he trying to distract her from his heart-wrenching revelation?

"Thank you, Archie. I loved yours too, in the obit photo."

Jane continued, "Archie says that finally one of his brothers said, 'Hey bud, you need to get some help.' But he never did. The dreams reawakened the feeling he held for you and it made your separation harder. And so, he took the gift of you at the university coffee shop. It carried him through for a long time."

About four years later, at the age of fifty-nine, Archie spoke of having had the opportunity to go. He was in a car with another person—the other person was driving—when a big semi came through the intersection and veered, missing them by an inch. He had been very aware of that missed opportunity and grieved after that.

"Why didn't you go then?"

"After the accident, the longing to go Home kicked in for me. I stayed because I thought I could learn more, but I really didn't.

Ten years later, I developed pancreatic cancer. Very painful, but the good thing is, it was fast. I died alone in hospital. I was on so many drugs for pain, in the end I didn't care. I hoped there was something after death, but I really didn't know. In those last ten years, I didn't care enough to care that much."

Anne was quiet. Later, when she'd had time to fully contemplate Archie's deep grief and depression, her heart broke. The contract ensured that she could not have done anything to help him.

Anne wanted to talk about the notion of unconditional love. Not long ago, she'd accidentally come across an online interview with a woman—she didn't catch her name—who discussed her personal relationship with her twin flame. They had gone steady in high school. She described their relationship as one marked by respect, integrity, and unconditional love for the other, typical of twin flames. At graduation, he informed her that he was going away to university and wished to break up. She had gone along with it. There was no fight, no disagreement, just an honouring of his wishes.

The woman went on to marry three times. In her words, her husbands had all been wonderful, but throughout her marriages she'd experienced a deep loneliness. She did meet up with her twin flame a couple of times, but each time one or the other was married and they honoured the other's situation.

Finally, they did reunite and marry when her children were grown. But even then, her twin flame had said to her that if she didn't want to move away from her children, he understood.

Everything this woman had to say about her twin flame and their relationship of unconditional love had resonated deeply with Anne. Given her feelings for Archie, she'd never fully understood her ready acceptance of his breaking up with her.

"For the first time, I understood our relationship and what unconditional love meant and looked like. When Archie said he wanted to break up, and after not meeting with me to talk about it, I quietly said 'Okay, bye,' and hung up the phone—no muss, no fuss." Despite her love for him, she'd never challenged him about his decision. She had respected and honoured his wishes and moved on with her life.

Archie came in then to say that the notion of unconditional love was a big piece for him too. Once he got to the other side, the dichotomy of his life was: "Why did I break up with her?" versus "That was unconditional love in action."

Jane said, "Archie loves the notion of unconditional love. However, there are two parts. One part is unconditional love for the other person—you, Anne; the second part is for one's self. After the breakup, Archie says he was trying to discipline himself not to obsess about you. His worst fear was that you were alone and miserable. He kept thinking, *I just want to see Anne, to know she's okay.* He felt he was being led, and then he saw you at the grocery store.

"He says that when you brushed past him, he knew you were a wife and a mother and had moved on. Archie wants you to know, his initial instinct was to run out after you into the parking lot and take you into his arms and tell you, 'We can figure this out.' But he didn't, because of his unconditional love for you. He honoured you and that you had moved on. And as hard as it was, he knew he had to as well."

Anne nodded. It had just been too hard for her to go back into the store and speak with him. And that decision had been supported by the voice she'd heard, letting her know Archie wasn't alone.

She asked about the spontaneous writing, how accurate she'd been in recording his words.

"Archie says you got it spot-on." Jane copied Archie's motion with his thumb and index finger, the tips forming a circle to indicate "perfect." "He says it's not that you don't listen. It's just that you are so close, you hear immediately what he says. The spontaneous writing is excellent, because it makes you slow down and pay attention."

Archie wanted to go back to the subject of unconditional love for a moment. "Now that I'm on the other side, I see how extraordinary I was. I heard the voice telling me I had to break up with you. And even though I didn't understand, I did listen." Archie said that the whole thing was orchestrated and planned on the other side, and part of the plan was that he would do the breaking up.

Anne conceded that Archie had the more challenging part of the contract—the breakup—and thus, she credited its successful completion to him. She herself could never have done it.

The session was nearing an end and Anne reiterated to Archie how happy she was to learn that he had agreed to stay with her.

A year ago, Archie had originally intended to connect with her a couple more times and then withdraw his energy. "Archie thought his staying would be too difficult for you. Your grief at the time was so profound. But after that, you really connected. Archie wants you to know that across the veil, there is nothing you have not shared with each other."

Archie wanted to talk about their first kiss. "He is telling me to tell you, Faith Hill." Jane was bewildered and looked to Anne for clarification.

Anne smiled. "'This Kiss'—it's a song by Faith Hill." She had always loved that song and the video that went with it.

"Archie says he knew from your first kiss. He never felt anything like it. He felt the kiss before your lips touched."

Over the past few months, Anne had often thought of that kiss. If she concentrated, she could still feel the feeling and see his smile after as he gently placed her back into her seat.

"Archie wants you to know that he is very serious now. He is asking you for the last time, 'Do you want to go?'"

Anne felt immediately torn. When at Jane's office and interacting with Archie, she felt a tremendous, heartfelt pull to go. Archie's presence in her life recalled the great love they held for each other. However, along with that came Anne's awareness of her authentic being, the beauty of her soul, something she'd lost or forgotten. With that consciousness, she somehow knew she wasn't done yet. She had a story to tell—theirs. Of course, it would be fictionalized.

Anne was excited about the possible book she and Archie would write together. The very thought of the two of them collaborating on this project filled her with enthusiasm. The yearning to be with Archie was nevertheless drawing her to go. Put simply, she missed him.

"What will you do if I stay?"

"I have my stuff to work on. Don't worry about me."

The next morning, Anne awakened to a bright sunny day. Sitting on the edge of her bed, she looked out the window overlooking the park dotted with snow-covered trees. She was seriously considering the question Archie had posed to her yesterday. Did she want to go? What kept coming to her mind was his assessment of the last ten years of his life. Archie felt he should have gone at fifty-nine, when he'd had the opportunity. Those last years had been extremely challenging and painful for him. Last night in spontaneous writing, she'd asked Archie what he thought she should do. His response was that it was her decision. He did say phase one had been their reconnecting across the veil. Phase two would be their book, which would help a lot of people.

Anne knew from *My Life after Death: A Memoir from Heaven,* that Erik Medhus and his mother, another across-the-veil relationship, had created a blog about suicide—one that had given tremendous support to many individuals. Anne also recognized that, if Archie would have had the resource of their future novel when he was alive, he could have had the language to communicate to others what he was experiencing, and perhaps not feel like he was going crazy. If their book could help just one person move through the devastating experience of loss of love, Anne realized she wanted to stay. Still, she felt some resistance, reluctance on her part.

As she continued to gaze out onto the wintry morning, she heard Archie say, "Anne, think of this book as the child we never had."

Okay, now she was a puddle.

CHAPTER 13
Staying

Anne: So did I hear you correctly this morning? I thought I heard you say, "Think of this book as the child we never had." Did you really say that?

Archie: Yes, and I meant it.

Anne: That was incredibly moving and romantic.

Archie: Ours is a great love story and I would very much like it to be told. Anne, as much as I would love to have you here with me, we have a wonderful opportunity to give this lesson in love—love doctors, that is us. Ironic, is it not? During life, I felt like such a failure in love. However, once I crossed over, I realized we had both excelled, not only successfully completing our soul contract, but also in our relationship and love for each other. It was unconditional love in action. And now, completed, we are together again, loving each other. A different take from the fairy tales. Our love story is real and shows the possibilities of love that span the veil and transcend death. It will be fun, lots of love and joy. Feel good about your choice. It was made in love. Anne, don't fret too much about it. I will be your co-author.

Anne: Are you saying you will be my ghost writer?

Archie: Yes!

Anne, feeling lightened, laughed.

—Anne Jeffrey, *Anne & Archie's Journal,* Vol. 3
(February 19, 2019)

And so with that, Anne chose to stay. She would simply have to take it one day at a time. Anne was continually in awe of how she and Archie seemed to have seamlessly picked up their relationship, as if no time had passed. As if they had never been apart. For this she felt blessed, graced. Anne fully recognized that she was deeply in love with Archie, even more so than when they had dated. That was why it was so hard to stay—definitely bittersweet.

When contemplating the New Year 2019, Anne had wondered how the year would manifest, especially with regard to Archie. Of late, Anne had been bitchy to live with. She knew it was her and had nothing to do with Jack. And for that, she really didn't like herself much. *Is this what married people feel when they have an affair?*

The night before, Jack had gone to bed early and Anne put on the movie *The Notebook.* Archie had come and they had watched it together on the couch. Anne had always found this love story to be a tearjerker. Now, viewing it with Archie, it affected her even more. When Allie said "I thought it was over" and Noah responded

"It was never over—it still isn't over" and then took her into his arms and kissed her, Anne was moved to tears. *Would their book ever be able to convey the deep love she and Archie held for each other then and now?* She wondered.

Anne recalled an incident that had occurred when she'd been a young girl, aged nine or ten. It had been an indoor recess, and she and a friend were in the girls' washroom. While washing their hands, her friend asked Anne what she wanted to be when she grew up. Anne paused to think, and then answered, "I'm not sure if I want to be a nurse or a teacher, but I do know I want to help people." Throughout her life, Anne had used this as her guiding principle, but for some reason she always felt like she'd somehow fallen short.

Archie was now telling her that their novel would help people—show readers the possibilities of love that cross the veil. That relationships could continue to evolve and deepen after death.

That night, Anne informed Archie of her commitment to stay and write their story, but only after she'd finished the history tome she was working on. At the same time, she revealed some self-doubt about her decision.

Archie knew all about Anne's self-doubt. "Trust yourself. I know you have talked to me about your feelings of being Home-lonely—something I can relate to and have talked about with you. Your feelings are valid and I honour them, sweetheart. Even so, I also think you are feeling overwhelmed. You are giving this history book your all, and yes, you are tired. Once it is completed, you will feel a weight has been lifted. I for one am thrilled you have chosen to stay and write our story.

"I know you have asked me when phase one happened. There is no time here, but trust me when I say, it was very powerful. I had forgotten just how connected we were and are when we are Home together. Actually, I had probably not forgotten, due to the depression I suffered because you were not in my life.

"In my physical life, Anne, I spent most of my life rushing around; I could not have imagined the relationship we share now— the quiet moments of being together, going for walks, reading poetry, talking, cuddling, laughing, and intimate moments of simply being together. Not that we haven't had our challenges to get to this point—of course we have. Nonetheless, when we connected, it was—well, there are no words.

"Remember, there is no time here, so for me, we are Home. We are together. Don't cry, hon, everything is great. And through it all, your beautiful soul made the tough decision to stay and write our book, the story of this amazing relationship. Don't think I'm not aware of how difficult this choice has been for you. Of course, knowing and loving you as I do, I anticipated it. You are very brave and have a wise heart. Know that when our work is completed, you will cross over quickly. Your wish to do the book and exit has been noted, and will be honoured. As for your body, take care of it."

"Will I be aware, as you were, of the missed exit?"

"Yes. But Anne, feel good about your decision. It was made in love. Just be present and take one day at a time. And yes, we will help a lot of people."

His whole life, Archie had been fascinated with Anne, and now that they could be together, he loved being with her. Truth be told, when they first connected Archie found it difficult to be away from her, even for a short time. He had loved watching her sit and write, cook dinner, or drive in the car listening to the music she played. Anne played a lot of music.

The other night, he had loved cuddling with her on the couch as they watched the movie. Anne said it had reminded her of the time when they had been watching an Elvis Presley movie at her parents' house (and no, he couldn't remember the title either). If asked, he probably wouldn't have even remembered that it had been an Elvis movie. He only remembered Anne's lips, their kissing, wrapped up in each other's arms. He had never felt anything like it, ever. Anne didn't like to admit the same when Jane was present. She was reserved that way. But he knew she felt it too, and that was why she cried sometimes.

"Don't get me wrong, Anne. I'm thrilled to have Jane mediate our conversations, at the beginning, and still now.

Nonetheless, I prefer when it's just the two of us. Be confident that anything I need or want you to know, I will tell you. You are scribing our conversations perfectly. And even when you don't share your thoughts, I know them. For example, today you were thinking about when you extended an invitation to use your home as my home base on Earth. And then you thought, 'Home is where Archie is.' For me, Anne, you are home. You are my home base. Hence, wherever you travel to, I go too, because it's home for me if you are there. I have said this, but it bears repetition: 'We could have made our home anywhere. We were just happy being together. Still are.'"

Anne nodded. For some reason, Archie's ability to read her heart, to know her thoughts, didn't freak her out. Rather, it soothed her. That Archie knew Anne fully, her shadows and her light—that she could be a brat, and that he loved her still. That she was enough. Perhaps it was the twin flame thing—that they were each other's half. This was his unconditional love for her. How she wished she could love herself so completely.

In contrast to her personal self-doubt, Anne had always viewed Archie as confident in his being and doing. "I guess I always took it for granted that you did everything well: kissing, dancing, driving. You seemed to move through life with such ease—at least, that was my sense when we were together."

"I did. The key there was *when we were together.* Remember, darling, you and I have successfully finished our soul contract that called for our separation. That was no mean feat. I know you have conceded that I had a harder time with it. However, don't underestimate yourself, and remember this was never a competition. After my life review and the review of our past lives, I'm fully aware of how challenging it has been for you. Yes, in life, I must admit that at times I was angry with you. I questioned whether you had ever cared for me, loved me as I loved you. How you had moved on, and so quickly. Though once Home, Anne, all those feelings left, and I felt only love for you. I know your heart and what this contract cost you."

ACT II:
RECALLING ANNE

CHAPTER 14

Remembering Anne, the Reluctant Goddess

With Anne's commitment to continue living, across the veil, the council of guides reconvened to oversee the last piece of the soul contract: the writing of the book, which, in essence, would be the final testament to the test of eternal love that Anne and Archie had undertaken. And a special council now stepped forth to supervise the project. This council had three aspects: wisdom, support, and questions. Archie was in a very unique position, in that he was assigned guides to support him in the enterprise.

Mid-March, the council called a meeting and asked Archie to be present. Anne's primary guide was there, as was Archie's, as well as the guides they shared. The council said that they felt things were progressing well, and that they were pleased with how Anne and Archie were conducting this last part of their contract.

They asked Archie how the spontaneous writing was coming along. Anne's recording of their conversations would certainly make the telling of their story much easier.

"She is recording our conversations with accuracy, but I do have a minor concern. Anne sometimes questions what she's doing, what she's writing. She wonders if she is making up our conversations. She has greater trust in her dreams."

Anne's spirit guide stepped up to speak. She felt Anne was emotionally and spiritually vulnerable. "While she has agreed to stay for the book, I fear she might descend into a renewal of grief. I think we need to be proactive and take steps to remind Anne of who she is. She has forgotten that piece of herself. While she has met with me a couple of times in meditation, presently Anne trusts you, Archie, and your relationship, first and foremost. Let her know we are granting you and Anne the relationship, officially recognizing it. And that your book is a gift for others. Has Anne made the connection between your dreams and her time as a goddess in Ireland?"

"No."

"Well, it's time for her to remember that aspect of herself. Anne kept a journal of her time in Ireland. Ask her about it. Perhaps she'll read it to you. You, yourself, might find it most enlightening."

~~~~~

Anne: Just looking at the date, and we are three-quarters of the way through this journal in less than a month—a journal that, by the way, has 192 pages. I don't think we talked this much the entire three months we dated.

Archie: No, we had better things to do with our mouths. I think this is mostly you. I'm not that gabby.

Anne: Do you want me to do a word count?

Archie (Laughing): No, you don't have time. We communicated perfectly...still do.

—Anne Jeffrey, *Anne & Archie's Journal,* Vol. 5
(April 16, 2019)
~~~~~

How does one become a goddess—or more to the point, how did Anne become a goddess? That was a very good question, one that Anne often pondered, given that she had once been part of a goddess circle.

Initially, eight women met for a celebratory feast to mark the 2001 winter solstice. Dressed in goddess garb, they each brought a favourite dish, and hostess Ariel observed that they had put together a perfect meal, from hors d'oeuvres to dessert. After making flower garlands for their hair, they all wrote down their intentions and wishes for the coming year, and then burned them in the fire.

From that day forward, they formed a goddess circle, gathering together weekly, holding circles, conversing, eating, and attending various spiritual and crystal workshops. At one point they rented a space outside of Guelph, where they facilitated a goddess workshop to share the joys of holding circles with other women.

After months of their communal practice, six of the goddesses, including Anne, planned a trip to Ireland for the last week of August 2002. At Ariel's suggestion, they had even found accommodation in a castle for their sojourn. The castle was an old tower that had originally guarded one of the five roads leading to Tara, the inauguration site and seat of the High Kings of Ireland. That week had been incredibly magical for Anne, so much so she had documented it in a journal.

~~~~~~

Anne was never sure why Archie asked her to read her Irish journal. His interest seemed to come out of nowhere. Perhaps it had been Anne herself who had sparked Archie's curiosity.

As Anne woke one morning, a thought came to her mind.

"Archie, you mentioned that in your mid-fifties, you went through a very challenging time. When I asked, you said you started having dreams of me, and then would wake up devastated. Anyway, it got me thinking about what I was doing in my life then. In 2002, I belonged to a goddess group. We met weekly to hold circle. In
~~~~~~

these circles, we each poured our individual heart energy into the circle's centre, and then expanded it, sending it to various locations: people, places, and animals in need around the world. Archangel Michael oversaw the circle and protected it. The energy we sent out varied. Sometimes, it was very gentle, and other times immensely powerful, depending on why and where we directed it."

Anne wondered if Archie, being her twin flame, had possibly felt or picked up on her heart chakra energy she'd been sending out into the world. At the time, Anne had definitely felt this to be an initiation of sorts, for each and every one of the goddesses. For her, she felt it was the universe encouraging her to step into her own power.

"The culmination of our goddess circle came in the form of a trip to Ireland. But it was what happened before the trip that truly amazed me. Two days before I was to depart for Ireland, Merlin— of wizardry fame—came to me in the middle of the night and insisted I get up to write down his words to me. Somewhat dazed, I went to my desk, but the only paper I could find was a small notepad, three by five inches. And thus, Merlin's message had been recorded on five small sheets kept together with a paper clip, now tucked away in my Irish journal.

"The circle broke up after the Ireland trip, and a few months later, Ariel, one of the goddesses, said that an angel had come to her in a dream. Apparently, the angel said that she noticed our goddess group had stopped doing the circles. That they were missed.

"So, my point is, Archie, I wonder if your dreams of me were, in some way, connected to that time when I was sending my heart energy out into the world."

Archie had always found Anne enchanting, and when the dreams of her came in his mid-fifties, that enchantment returned. He had no idea where Anne was, but found what she was doing to be wondrous. "You know you are a mystic, Anne. However, to answer your question, I'm being told yes."

"That's incredible."

"Actually, it makes sense. We're so deeply connected. Of course, I would pick up your heart energy." Archie asked Anne to read Merlin's message. And so, she did.

Merlin came.
I thought it odd.
'Twas in a cave he stood.
Why me? I said.
I'm only small and you are a star so big.
[Merlin then opened the cave to reveal a wall of fire blazing.]
You are not so small,
your heart is big and shines brighter than this fire.

If you see me big, know I speak wise words.
I don't lie, but tell you truth.
You are bigger than you know.
Though you may not know it, you are a star.
And like a star in the night,
your light shines bright,
so bright other universes see your brilliance.
You are special—
there is no other quite like you.
And I have come, I need your help.
There is war coming, hunger and strife.
I need your light to render.

"The wall of fire turned out to be real." Anne explained that the great hall of the castle where they were staying had a massive stone fireplace. And in the evenings when the fire was lit, it looked very much like the wall of fire Merlin had revealed to her.

The morning after their arrival, Merlin returned. After breakfast, as the six friends gathered to hold circle, Maeve, a true seer—she could communicate with her guides and the spirit realm—said that an older gentleman had woken her during the night, several times in fact. He was most insistent, telling her that when he came to circle to speak, she, who usually led the circles, was to turn to Anne. Anne was to channel his words.

Anne was unnerved by the turn of events; she didn't do this sort of thing. Maeve and her sister Ariel—that was *their* comfort zone, not hers. Still, Anne trusted Maeve and her intuitive wisdom. And considering she'd recently channeled a personal message from Merlin, she thought maybe she could do this.

At first, Anne didn't recognize the speaker. She thought possibly he was from the church, but then hesitated. Suddenly, she asked if he had a long white beard. She felt a smile and heard yes, and she knew it was Merlin from Glastonbury. What was fascinating to Anne was that she'd never disclosed anything of her dream of Merlin to the group—so Maeve couldn't have known. And so, for the first time ever, Anne channeled a message for the goddesses. Merlin wanted them to know that this circle would mark a great shift in their lives and that, in the future, people would seek them out.

"No wonder I was having vivid dreams of you. Your energy was so high, it was easy to tap into." After hearing Merlin's prophecy, Archie asked if he had been correct.

Anne reflected on this for a moment. Immediately following the trip to Ireland, the goddess circle, a group of friends once so close, broke apart and dispersed. At the present time, she really had little to no connection with any of the goddesses.

"I think it did mark a shift in all our lives, and for some, they have become healers of various sorts: one a shaman, another earned her doctorate and works as a medical intuitive, a clinical nutritionist, and a practitioner of energy medicine. As for me, it did mark a shift of consciousness, but in a more subtle way—I don't have people coming to me to be healed, to be sure.

"Two years later, I completed my doctorate and went into museum work. Neither has given me a voice or platform of success in the way the world defines it. I have continued the pursuit of my true passion, spirituality, in various ways. As you recently shared with me, however, all the time, unbeknownst to me, I was gathering the pieces in anticipation of your return and the writing of our book.

That was helpful, Archie, to learn that I was being led or guided by a higher soul purpose. Thank you."

She continued. "For so many years, I felt like a failure. It seemed nothing ever really panned out for me in terms of career." Anne had had this discussion with Jane more than once. Jane had suggested that, being a very old soul, this lifetime for Anne was perhaps her last, and it was about wrapping up various loose ends. Knowing this had given Anne some semblance of peace. Nonetheless, she had suffered periods of depression. It seemed no matter how hard she worked, nothing ever came to fruition, and this had deeply saddened Anne. She felt somehow, somewhere, she had lost her way.

"Sometime, I would like you to read me your journal of your Ireland trip with the goddesses."

Anne agreed, and over the next week, each evening, she shared daily entries recorded years ago.

On the other side, Anne's guide was pleased. Not only would this be important to help Archie understand the goddess aspect of Anne, but it was time for Anne to remember who she was and why she'd stayed. Revisiting Merlin's wise and prophetic words all these years later would help her to do both.

The next night, Anne read an excerpt of their second day, a day that held particular interest for Archie. He had never shared with Anne any details of his dreams of her, nor had she asked, in an effort to respect his privacy. But this day—where she'd been, what she'd done—he had dreamed of her there. He had seen her joy, her childlike exuberance, her laughter. She had shone so brightly for him.

Anne's Irish Journal (Day 2: Sunday, August 25, 2002)

We set out early for the long trip to the west coast and the Cliffs of Moher. We had rented two cars and today, I was in the car with Joyce and Gabby. Along the way, we stopped at the Burren Centre in Kilfenora, Co. Clare. Kilfenora is known as the City of the Crosses, due to its historical significance as the religious center of the region. Leaving our cars in the parking lot, we entered the building. While the others immediately went in, I made a detour to the ladies' room.

As I exited the loo, I noted in the foyer a small- to medium-size dog who, upon seeing me, trotted up to me, his tail wagging. Bending down, I gently stroked his head, and asked how he was doing, and where his person was. All of a sudden, a female security guard barged into the vestibule and began shouting at the dog, ordering him to get outside. He looked sad, but did as he was told. At the time, I thought no more of it, thinking the dog was likely waiting for his master to come out of the center.

Our group took some time to tour the exhibit and the gift shop. Nonetheless, on exiting, I observed the same dog, sitting on a grassy knoll to the right of the door. He still seemed to be waiting. I was a bit worried, as it concerned me when people left their animals unattended for any length of time. On closer examination, I noted that the dog looked a bit unkempt and distressed. I went over and conversed with him. While he acknowledged me, he continued to sit.

Adjacent to the Burren Center was St. Fachtnan's, a medieval cathedral. We walked around the cathedral and then looked at the crosses in what I assumed had once been a small graveyard. Whereas tradition maintained that there were once seven Celtic crosses, only the remains of five still exist, three of which now stood in this hallowed ground. Near the gate that led to the church and burial ground was a simple Celtic cross, around which we had all congregated. It was then that I saw "my" dog coming through the gate.

Like a man on a mission, the dog came directly to me and looked up expectantly. Maeve was standing beside me and I shared my concern for the dog. He seemed upset, but I was unsure what to do. Maeve paused, tuning in to her intuitive wisdom and/or guides— I was never quite sure about the source of Maeve's knowingness, but I did trust it.

Maeve explained that his master had died, and the place in which they had lived had recently been torn down. Since that time, the dog had been searching for him, unaware of his death.

"Can you communicate this to him?"

Maeve shook her head. Her guides were telling her no. "The dog has made an emotional connection with you, Anne. It's your responsibility."

I was nervous, but decided that maybe I could do some reiki for him. I had taken the first two levels of reiki a couple of years ago, though I had never really used it, too busy doing my PhD, commuting, and being a wife and mother.

I knelt down beside the dog and placed my hands not on, but around his head and shoulders, sending the reiki energy to his High Self, with the intent that it would serve his highest and best good. While doing this, I communicated with him telepathically that his person was dead and no longer walked on the Earth plane. All the while, the dog stood very still. And then, without warning, the dog's head lifted. He barked and took off toward the cathedral ruins.

I stood, feeling somewhat bewildered.

"Where's he going?"

Maeve said that the master's spirit was there, and the dog was running to him. I asked her what would happen now. She said he would have to decide that for himself, to stay or go Home with his person.

After gazing upon this ghostly and happy reunion, we headed to our cars. As we were pulling out of the parking lot, I saw the dog running toward us. Did he hope I would take him home? I desperately wished I could, but having three cats, I knew it wasn't really possible.

Joyce said, "Anne, he's coming to thank you for your help. How sweet is that!"

I will never know what happened to him, what he decided to do. I would like to think he found some kind person to take him in. He truly had such a beautiful spirit.

Something happened at the Cliffs of Moher that I couldn't put my finger on. I felt tension between the two sisters, Maeve and Ariel. As we regrouped at our cars, we agreed to meet back at the beach by Kilfenora, and then head to the Ceilidh in town after dinner.

Arriving at the beach, Joyce, Gabby, and I took off our shoes and socks, rolled up our pants, and waded into the ocean, playing in the waves. At one point, Joyce said she still wanted to go to County Clare.

I turned and said, "This is County Clare! We're in it!"

We all started laughing and continued to jump over the waves. As the sun set, we carried on, playing and giggling. I even took a photo of my feet in the ocean. For that brief moment in time, it felt as if we were children again, so much so that I observed a group of young boys staring from the shore. They seemed transfixed by us.

When it grew dark, we walked up to Vaughan's Barn, where the Ceilidh was taking place. I looked for the dog, but he was nowhere to be seen. We were told Kilfenora was the home of the Ceilidh, and that here, Anna instructed people from miles around in this form of dance. Young men and women even came from Italy for the month of August to seek her instruction.

The barn wasn't huge, and looked to be relatively old. It had stone walls, and the wide-planked wood floors were well worn. There were two rooms or spaces in the barn, but the wide opening in the connecting wall made movement between the two spaces easy. At one end was a bar, around which many people were mingling. Beside the bar was a raised platform for the small band.

While clearly strangers, we were immediately embraced by all there. We met Anna and spoke with her for a short while. She encouraged us to dance, even though we had no idea how to dance the Ceilidh. It didn't matter. One group of her students grabbed us and said not to worry, they would show us what to do. And so, we danced and laughed until well past midnight. The fellows with whom we were dancing asked us to come back to their place. However, we knew we had to get back. As it was, I worried the others might be a little cross that we would be returning so late.

On our way home to the castle, the three of us were laughing, high on life, all the while wondering what had happened to the other three goddesses. We arrived late, around two in the morning. Since we had two bedrooms, I was bunked with Maeve and Karen, both sound asleep. Maeve roused slightly and said they got lost and returned early.

That night, I dreamt of Merlin and the Philosopher's Stone. It was such a magical day and I truly felt as if my guides were trying to nudge me along my path, to step into my power, into the fullness of my being.

~~~~~

After reading the entry, Anne said, "Seventeen years later, rereading these words, I'm struck by the fact that I have recently been faced with a similar decision to the dog, with regard to you, Archie—my twin flame. Do I stay here, or go to be with you? Also, it seems my guides are still trying to help me step into my full potential. If that's the case, I admire their tenacity for not giving up on me."

As Anne had been reading, Archie was imagining her that day. He had dreamed of her in the ocean, splashing in the waves, playing and laughing. He had seen her dancing, free and full of joy. "That day, when you felt free and happy, you seemed very much like you felt when we dated, but even lighter, brighter. I definitely think that was a night when I dreamt of you. I felt your energy all the way from Ireland. I know you often call yourself the reluctant goddess, but quite frankly, that day there was nothing reluctant about you."

"I guess you're right."

"Anne, sweetheart, I felt you all the way from Ireland! I'm not sure you fully appreciate the magic, the majesty that was you that day, that week. And I'm here to remind you who you are."

It had been so long since Anne had thought about her goddess experience and the wonder of their Irish trip. As she shared it now with Archie, she was quite astounded by her journal account.
~~~~~

The next evening, Anne and Archie continued their discussion and reading of her Irish journal. Anne had piqued Archie's interest in the goddess movement. In their lives spent together on Earth, he had usually been the woman, and Anne, the man. Thus, he was amused by Anne's dubbing herself the reluctant goddess. She was unquestionably exploring her feminine side in this life. And going by his dreams of her at that time, she was sincerely enjoying it.

"I have to say, Anne, I'm endlessly fascinated with your earthly journey. I cannot tell you how much I look forward to our next life together."

"You have already said that I will be the man."

"Yes, believe it or not, your soul is most comfortable in the male body."

"Will you still love me?"

"Oh, yes, very much so and more."

"I find it hard to imagine, as I quite love us in this life, you as Archie and me as Anne."

"Our souls united in this life to feel the intensity and depth of our love. That same feeling and connection will be there, but this time we will be free to act on that feeling, no holds barred. That's why I'm so excited."

"It sounds like you are already planning our next life."

"Yes, but Anne, you are involved too, even though you have no memory of it."

Anne said nothing, but admittedly she found the idea of her High Self, or soul, planning another life when she was still working on this one somewhat worrisome. *Confusing and challenging— weren't those the words that were used to identify twin flame relationships?!*

"Archie, do you ever miss me now that you are on the other side?"

"No, because when I feel the need to be with you, I go see you. Sometimes you are busy, and I just check in to see how you're doing. If you're having a bad time, I sense it and check in, let you know I'm here with you. I love what I have come to know as 'our time,' when you close the bedroom door at night. I'm truly surprised by it; it gives me great joy."

"It gives me great joy as well. Often, I'm hesitant to turn out the light, as I don't want our time to end."

"Anne, I don't leave when the light is off. You feel me with you."

Anne nodded and sighed. "I was telling a friend that if someone gets a hold of my journals, they will think I have gone totally crazy."

"That's their problem, not ours. We know this is real."

On the first Monday of the month, Anne met with her "On the Spiritual Path" group, and spoke about her plan to write a novel with her deceased twin flame. While Anne had kept Helen informed of her developing relationship with Archie, this was news to the other three ladies present. Over the past few months, Anne had come to view their meetings as a safe and sacred space in which all could speak freely. She trusted that what was said in group never left the room.

At one time or another, all of them had shared individual experiences of connecting with loved ones across the veil. So when Anne explained her relationship with Archie and her decision to write their story, they all listened respectfully, with loving care—no judgement. When Anne was finished, only then did others speak.

"How are you feeling about all this?" Joan asked. Joan was the youngest of the group. She impressed Anne with her curiosity as well as her old soul wisdom, her open willingness to share where she was on her life path; what challenges she was working on and how she was dealing with them. She would often give critical reviews of books, courses, and healers that supported her growing spiritual awareness.

"To be honest, I'm feeling a little overwhelmed, given I'm still working on my history of obituaries. Lately, I have been feeling pain in my left chest area. I'm not alarmed. It's more of an ache than a sharp pain."

Talia, a medical intuitive, directed her attention to Anne's left chest area. "Firstly, it's not important for you to know the cause of this. What I am seeing is crystal stones with colours streaked through it—'Opal.' I'm getting the word 'opal.'"

"That's my birthstone. But how is that connected to the pain?"

Jessie, also highly intuitive, said that under the stone, fire was coming into Anne's heart to cleanse and purify it. "Give it time. But you should feel an easing of the heartache that has solidified over time."

And with that said, Anne passed the "talking feather" to Helen, to signal that she was done and it was Helen's turn to talk.

The next day, Anne had a major meltdown. She was struggling with having a foot in both worlds. Poor Jack! How could she possibly explain what was going on?

The day had started out well enough. Her sister Laura and a friend came for lunch, and she thought the visit had gone well. Nevertheless, when they left, Anne felt a wave of grief inundate her. Jane called it "Home-loneliness" and perhaps it was. Anne thought it also was a deep missing of Archie. Though they connected, he was in spirit, and sometimes she just wanted him back in his body, to feel his arms around her. *Archie is dead,* Anne had to remind herself.

When Jack came home from work, Anne set dinner on the table. She'd made meatloaf, his favourite. Anne was unusually quiet as Jack talked about his day. Then he asked how her writing was going. She wasn't even sure why his question had set her off. Maybe because she was feeling challenged with the chapter she was working on, which examined the depiction of women as both subjects and authors in obituaries—more complex than one would imagine.

How am I going to write a novel when I can't even finish this history? The grief and Anne's angst that she wouldn't be able to fulfil all that was expected of her caused her to break down crying.

"Anne, you have to get a tougher skin about this. Just finish it and move on to the next thing. You're spending way too much time on it. Get it done already."

"It's easy for you, Jack. When you come home from work, you're done for the day. With writing, it's like a cloud over your head that never leaves you." Feeling defensive, Anne heard her voice escalate. She knew she wasn't being fair, that Jack faced challenges every day, either with patients, staff, or equipment breaking down. His patients were often very anxious, and Jack was sensitive to their needs. It was what made him especially good at what he did. Nevertheless, it was a stressful profession, and over the years Jack had had to find ways to manage the stress. Anne appreciated how hard Jack worked to support his family, but sometimes she wondered if he saw or appreciated who she was, and all she did.

"You don't have to yell. I'm not yelling." Somehow Jack always made her feel that it was her fault if they had a fight or disagreement. Maybe it was.

"I don't want to talk about this anymore. I can't."

"That's why you never get anywhere, Anne. As soon as things get hard, you drop them."

"That's not true, not fair, and you know it. And I shouldn't have to apologize for my feelings!"

After her outburst, Anne went for a walk to calm down. For Anne, walking was often a meditative experience, and tonight she heard her High Self speak the words *self-love* and *self-care*. Jane and Olivia were holding one of their workshops on Saturday. Anne emailed them to say she'd been having a rough week, and asked if there was space for her.

Jane replied right away, saying there was always room for her.

Later that night, Anne conceded to Archie that she was feeling challenged, overwhelmed.

"I love you, even if you were a total brat tonight." Archie suggested that perhaps she should see this as an opportunity to love herself unconditionally. "Be gentle with yourself, as you were to Alex when he was a toddler having temper tantrums."

Anne was glad somebody loved her unconditionally, because just now she wasn't feeling the love for herself. Still, she knew that when one's emotions are triggered, as hers had been that night, it was the soul's way of talking to oneself, to her.

"It must be easy to love yourself unconditionally on the other side."

"Yes, because you have all the information. There is no judgement here, only understanding and love. Nonetheless, it's important to know that, if your soul task is to learn about unconditional love for others and for yourself, you will draw experiences into your life that will test you in that lesson. Your guides don't want to make it easy for you. Without challenge, great love can't grow. Do you understand this, Anne?"

"Are you telling me to forgive myself, and love me?"

"Yes. When you're not being a brat, you're very lovable and loving. Still, I love all of you, and I want you to love yourself in the same way. You were, and are so loving of me, unconditionally."

"I never stopped loving you, even though I didn't understand."

"So, it would seem the drama is finished for now."

"Yes." And with that, Anne opened her Irish Journal to day four of her goddess trip.

Anne's Irish Journal (Day 4: Tuesday, August 27, 2002)

Day four, the magic continued. What manifested today astounded each and every one of us. Before we left for Ireland, someone had suggested that we might try to have tea with the "head witch" of Ireland, Lady Olivia Robertson, who founded the Fellowship of Isis. However, never in our wildest dreams could we have imagined that it would truly happen.

When sharing the suggestion with Grace, the owner of the castle where we were staying, she said that Lady Olivia was a good friend of hers, and she would be happy to call her up to see if she would consent to a meeting. The following morning, Grace came over to say that the goddesses had all been invited to Lady Olivia's castle, on the condition that we first take her out for lunch.

On our way to Huntingdon Castle, Grace regaled us with her stories about men, fairies, the castle, and various other Irish tales. I had no idea what to expect. But, upon arrival at the castle, a little sprite of a woman, with long black hair flowing down her back, ran barefoot down the castle steps to greet us. Though she was eighty-five years old, she moved like someone half her age. Grace had informed us that Lady Olivia was very eccentric, as were all her friends. I found this fascinating, given that I found Grace to be a bit out there herself. Nevertheless, I discovered Lady Olivia to be absolutely delightful and most gracious.

At Grace's suggestion, we took Lady Olivia to lunch at a beautiful restaurant, and sat in a garden where supposedly Charles Wesley had preached a sermon around a large well. At the table, I found myself seated next to Lady Olivia. Reluctant to talk about herself, she wanted to hear about us and our goddess circle. We mentioned that, just the day before, we had visited Kildare and Brigid's Cathedral. Lady Olivia said she, herself, had seen Brigid of Kildare in a dream once, two years before.

After lunch, we returned to the castle and Lady Olivia led us into the basement, hallowed ground where she'd constructed altars and chapels to various goddesses of the world. Since Brigid was the goddess of Ireland, Lady Olivia conducted us to the Brigid chapel for a ceremony. She instructed each of us to take water from the font to anoint ourselves. She then opened the well in the floor and anointed us with water from it, after which each goddess went separately up to the altar to voice her intent.

When it was my turn, I stated, "It is with humility, love, and gratitude that I stand here. I am thankful to you for helping me to remember my divinity, and hope I may help others remember their own."

By way of conclusion, Lady Olivia came to each goddess with words from the Oracle. To me, she said, "You will be—you are—a teacher. You stand on dry ground while others around you are sinking into the bog. Hermes and Mercury are with you and guiding you."

Following the ceremony, Lady Olivia gave us a tour of the other chapels and then took us to a room on the main floor, her study, where she sold her books and tapes. After viewing a short film entitled Women with Wings, *we, the goddesses, took a brief walk around the castle grounds and gardens. Before we knew it, it was five p.m.*

As we were taking our leave, Lady Olivia gifted us with a certificate in honour of our goddess circle, which she named The Brigid Merlin Lyceum of Healing. During lunch, I had shared my encounter with Merlin, and Lady Olivia had clearly seen him as a significant presence for our goddess circle. As she presented us with the certificate, she thought it needed something more, and proceeded to draw figures of Brigid and Merlin on the certificate, paying close attention to colour and detail. As she coloured, she reminded me of a child, so delighting in her own creation.

On our way home, we stopped at Morrissey's pub for a beer. The pub was still in its original form; it had been both a grocery store and pub, and had won all kinds of awards for its historical decor. When someone mentioned going home Friday, I felt a cloud of sadness descend over me, and the others as well.

As I write about the day, it's nine p.m. and we still have not eaten. We invited Grace to join us for dinner, and the girls are downstairs cooking. My final note for the day is something Lady Olivia disclosed to me at lunch. She noted that this week was the celebration of Isis, and she'd wondered what special thing would happen to her that day—and it was a goddess circle overseen by Brigid and Merlin.

It was late when we went to bed. "Barry the bat" that had been unnerving my friends in the other bedroom for a few nights, was back, so we decided to sleep all together in one room. Tomorrow we are heading to Dublin via the 8:50 a.m. train.

<center>~~~~~</center>

After reading, Archie was quiet. It was Anne who broke the silence.

"Wow, I had forgotten all that. My intent was remarkable. I can't believe that came from me. I feel better, Archie. Thank you."

Over the next couple of days, Anne finished reading Archie her journal.

Anne's Irish Journal (Day 6: Thursday, August 29, 2002)

The last day, the mood of our circle was very subdued, as if we all felt the winds of change coming. Maeve confided to me that she would be leaving the circle after the Ireland trip. For me, I know that both Alex and Lizzie will be moving away from home, the very weekend I return from Ireland. And it seems the guides, angels, and spirits recognize the shift in our mood, honouring our need for space and gentleness. As we moved through the day, we each remarked on feeling this orb of loving kindness that seemed to surround us.

Our last goddess circle was held at a stone circle, newly constructed by a man who owned a sandstone quarry. As we walked among the stones, the energy felt to be very much swirling in the air. Maeve led the meditation and said that our purpose was to ground the circle's energy into the earth. When the meditation ended, I said a blessing, "May the white light of divine love and protection surround this stone circle, sealing out all negative thoughts, energies, and experiences." Gabby added, "Gently and easily for everyone's highest and best good." And then, in unison, we all said, "So be it, and so it is." And with that, Maeve said the energy moved from air to earth, and the circle felt to be very much grounded.

Merlin came to our last goddess circle and imparted the wisdom, "One voice can make a difference."

~~~~~

Anne explained to Archie that shortly after their return from Ireland, the goddess group dispersed. "Ariel and Gabby began shifting into shamanic work and wanted me to join them. However, it somehow just never called me."
~~~~~

In some ways, Anne had been disappointed in herself. It was three or four months later when she ran into Archie at the university. Jane had recently asked what Anne would have done if she'd recognized him, or he had spoken to her. She really didn't know. She was certainly feeling the winds of change and wasn't particularly happy, possibly because she had no idea what she was going to do after completing her doctorate.

Shortly thereafter, though, Anne and Jack began to rediscover the joys of being a couple, flying solo, safe in the knowledge that their children were well and happy. Anne had always loved Jack's sense of adventure, his willingness to venture forth and learn new things, always with enthusiasm and attention to detail. And the next few years were truly a golden time, filled with new activities: horseback riding, scuba-diving, and travelling extensively to places afar.

One Christmas Eve, Anne found herself, Jack, and a friend, Jean—just the three of them, riding camels in front of the Giza pyramids in Egypt. On Christmas Eve! Anne had burst into song, "We Three Kings of Orient Are"—lyrics she knew by heart because, when eight years old, she had played the third wise man in a Christmas pageant.

As Anne reflected back, she appreciated that her life had been richly blessed with family and friends, full of love and adventure. Nevertheless, keeping busy, always on the go, had been Anne's way to push down the emptiness and loneliness she'd felt most of her life. No wonder she was feeling confused and challenged by the turn her life had taken at this late stage. She loved Archie deeply and was so grateful for his presence. That they could be together was a gift, a joy. Still, Anne couldn't fully comprehend all of it. She felt she was missing a piece of the puzzle. Maybe it was just the historian in her, always seeking more information to get to the bottom of things.

CHAPTER 15

Staying's Not Easy

In life, Archie had a brevity and clarity of expression that Anne somehow lacked. Perhaps her hesitance, indecisiveness, and self-doubt came from her seeing the shades of grey in life, in people. Archie, on the other hand, had, in his own words, viewed everything in black-and-white terms; he seemed to exude self-confidence, at least in Anne's eyes. Archie knew all about Anne's self-doubt, which often manifested in her perfectionism, something he had never been aware of while they were dating. Nevertheless, in writing *their* book, he finally had to tell her that she'd have to stop with the perfectionism. It was interfering with her ability to move forward and finish her history on obituaries. He wanted her Home sooner rather than later.

The very next session, Anne shared with Jane that, since Archie's comment about her perfectionism, she was trying to let go of some of it.

For Anne, there was no one like Archie. He was the only person with whom she could truly be herself, and feel safe and cared for. Hence, as the months passed, Anne found time away from him to be increasingly difficult—she felt a deep loneliness within. As they contemplated the writing of their story, their connection was strengthening. At one session with Jane, Archie had said that, upon first connecting with Anne in 2017, he found he couldn't be away from her for more than four hours at a time. Anne found it to be the opposite: the longer Archie was with her, the more she yearned for him.

When she said this, Archie was there to explain that this was the nature of their twin flame soul connection. It was an ebb and flow, give and take, like the flames of two candles burning.

One evening, Anne and Archie conversed more about their upcoming project.

Anne: I'm excited about starting our book.

Archie: I know. I look forward to our collaboration. We have collaborated before.

Anne: Did you ever think that our love story would one day be written?

Archie: Heavens, no! But I was a sucker for those sappy books and movies.

Anne: That truly surprises me. You never struck me that way, although you were very loving and affectionate. The only movies we saw were an Elvis Presley movie, and Peter Sellers in "The Pink Panther." On second thought, however, our first date was on Valentine's Day, and you gave me a heart-shaped box of chocolates.

Archie: You changed me, Anne. Before I met you, I was a little gun-shy when it came to women. So, I had never told anyone I loved them before. And then you came, and from day one and our first kiss, I was a goner. If I was not so controlling, I could have said "I love you" after the first couple of weeks. I certainly felt it. And later after we broke up, I knew I *loved you*, because being apart from you was agony. When we parted and you weren't there, a part of me/my heart went with you, never to return. It was a really tough time. I couldn't stop thinking about you. Your absence was palpable. Physically and emotionally, I ached for you, for your touch, your kiss, your laugh. And now I'm aware, I spiritually yearned for you.

Anne: I so wished you would have said all this then. I had no idea. Being with you, Archie, was my first experience of what joy felt like. I recall one date when we dropped by a local bowling alley. Sitting on a bench, I watched you talking with the man at the counter—all the while, I was thinking, "I'm happy, I'm really happy." And this was new for me. But I had low self-confidence. It was easy for me to believe that you didn't want to be with me. Now, your selection of "our song" makes sense. The lyrics in "I'll Always Love You" talk about the man having too much pride. Did you? I never felt that to be true.

Archie: It is very complicated. But you, sweetheart, brought me to my knees. I never knew I could ever feel what I felt for you. I loved you so much. I never wanted to hurt you. Once I saw you had moved on, it was hard, very hard.

Anne: I'm so sorry. But you realize that if I had known any of this, I would have come to you and our soul contract would have been null and void.

Archie: Yes, and to be honest, as difficult as it was, the very thought of having to do another life to get it right would be my idea of hell.

Anne: So you're a hero.

Archie: As are you, Anne. WE BOTH ARE! We proved unconditional love for each other.

Anne: Why does our contract's successful completion feel less than celebratory? I'm not sure you know how happy I am that we can be together now.

Archie: We see each other at night while your body sleeps.

Anne: Is this why I'm so tired some days?

Archie: Yes. I did suggest you cut back, but you were vehemently opposed to that. You said our *time together nurtures your heart and soul. And since I feel the same way, I won't fight you on it.*

—Anne Jeffrey, *Anne & Archie's Journal,* Vol. 4
(March 17, 2019).

When Anne experienced another wave of grief, she asked Archie, "Is it too late to change my mind and go?"

Archie was anxious for Anne. He felt she was stretching herself too thin. Since his return and their reconnecting, she'd insisted on being together every night. However, she'd made little accommodation during the day to compensate for that. Most days, she was exhausted and running on empty.

Over the first few months they had tried different things, but in the end Anne refused to compromise their time together on the other side. They had been apart long enough. To their council of guides, Anne had been very clear as well: if she stayed to write their story, she could not, would not do it alone. She needed Archie to help her, and it was non-negotiable.

Additionally, her history tome was proving to be a source of great stress. Because she had not pursued a career in academia, she was basically doing this book on her own. She had no professional mentor supporting her. And besides this, Anne was still mourning the death of her parents.

Archie had never known this side of Anne when they dated—one ridden with fear and anxiety, trying to please everyone above herself. Despite Anne's realization that the completion of her history book was a form of self-love and self-care, she was struggling with all it entailed.

Most recently, Archie had been asked to take on some projects, and the council had instructed him that he needed to prepare Anne for a time when he would be unavailable to her— something he wasn't looking forward to. She was fragile, more than even she knew. Throughout her life, Anne had become very skilled at hiding her vulnerability, which often manifested as anxiety. He had hoped she would have finished her history book by the end of March, but that deadline had come and gone, and this, he knew, further upset Anne. In life, Archie had been good at deadlines, so he thought giving Anne a date would prove helpful. He knew the history was important to her. She saw it as the completion of her academic cycle.

But now Archie just wanted the book done. It was blocking Anne and Archie from finishing the very last piece of their contract, the book they had promised to write—after which Anne was free to go and they could be together.

CHAPTER 16

Straddling Two Worlds: Their Room and Sky-House

Archie: I love the poem you read tonight—"Everything That Was Broken" by Mary Oliver.

Anne: Me too. When we connect on the other side, do we have a special place?

Archie: Yes and no. Sorry to be vague. There is a place where we spent much time together before we incarnated. We will often be there. It is a sacred space that no one knows about.

—Anne Jeffrey, *Anne & Archie's Journal,* Vol. 4
(March 8, 2019).

Anne was sitting at her desk, as usual. Staring at the computer screen displaying a page from her chapter on the feminization of obituaries, she was having trouble focusing on the material at hand. And so, in way of distraction—in way of prepping for the novel, she was contemplating "setting"—deemed a key component in the telling of any story as it established the mood, revealed characters and conflicts, and gave clues as to the story's themes.

Over the years, as a student of history, Anne had become quite skilled in the art of straddling two worlds, past and present. She knew the importance of setting: time, place, and environment, physical, social and cultural. She prided herself on her ability to place historical characters and events in the context of time and place, to gain a greater understanding, a broader perspective, of not only the past, but her present world as well.

As a child, she had been intrigued by the concept of time-travel. And early on, she had learned that books were a bridge, a portal through which she could be transported to other worlds, real or fantastical. And truly, in doing history, she felt that she *was* living her dream. On their last wedding anniversary, Anne, so engrossed in eighteenth-century newspapers, had unconsciously dated her card to Jack, 1718.

At present, Anne was aware that she moved between worlds — the physical and spiritual realms—but she had few, if any, conscious memories of her time spent with Archie on the other side of the veil.

She decided to begin with the world she knew. She practically lived in her study/bedroom, especially when she was writing. Since she spent most of her time there, and it was the place where she and Archie journaled at night, Anne knew she had to provide an apt description of this room. The challenge was that Anne spent so much time staring at the computer screen, she had grown somewhat oblivious to her surroundings.

What was she doing? She had promised herself that she would finish her history before embarking on this second project. But since her brain was thinking about the novel anyway, Anne realized she might as well do so intentionally. Maybe it was okay to let herself dream about the novel as motivation for completing her book on obits.

As Anne surveyed her room—her and Archie's room— she realized it was in stark contrast to the neat, clean, sparsely furnished apartment that had been Archie's home when they'd dated. Multiple boxes of research were stacked in one corner by the window. Not one, but two desks occupied another corner of the room. While she tried to keep the one with the computer and printer relatively clutter-free as a workspace, the other desk's surface was rarely visible—piled high with books, files, journals, and papers.

Messy. Whereas some might think it was disordered mess, it was not. Anne knew exactly where everything was, and could retrieve whatever information she required at a moment's notice. So perhaps "organized mess" might be a better descriptor.

Anne recalled the movie *The Odd Couple.* Was she Oscar and Archie Felix, the neat-freak? Is that how they would have been as a couple?

That night she asked Archie that very question. "I have been thinking about our book and settings, the home bases we have on both sides of the veil. I feel this room is in stark contrast to the neat, minimalist surroundings of your old apartment. It recalled to me the movie *The Odd Couple.* I feel like I'm Walter Matthau, the slob, and you, Archie, are Jack Lemmon, the neat freak."

Archie laughed. "Anne, sweetheart, I cleaned up because I knew you were coming to my home. I was trying to impress you."

"You did? Somehow I think you're just trying to make me feel better."

"This room, our room, is not just where you sleep, it's your workspace and it evolves as your projects do. All the books, files, and papers—it was a side of you that I never got to know when we dated. Though I did catch a glimpse of *that* you at the university coffee shop. In reviewing our past lives, yours and mine, I learned you spent lives as a librarian, a writer, a copier of ancient texts/scripts, and as a gypsy who communicated your ancestral history through song and dance. So, really, it's no surprise that you have drifted to studies based on your past skills and talents."

Since Archie clearly had a higher perspective of Anne and her life, she asked him how he would describe her office, the main setting on Earth where they interacted. She sincerely wanted to hear his take on it.

"To be honest, Anne, at first I didn't pay attention to the room. I only had eyes for you. Over time, though, I have come to love it. Rather than simply being a room in a house, it's a house within a room. All things are here. It is a room of chosen privacy.

The energy here is different than all the rest of the house. It is so very peaceful. The room is bright, filled with light. It is *our* home when we are here together."

Anne could not have said it better. And indeed, she had come to think of it as just that—*their* home when they were there together. The room held everything needed for work, sleep, and pleasure: her desk, computer and printer, CD player for her music, photos of her children, her books, her papers and files she was working on at any given moment. And a bed tucked away within a nook, underneath a vaulted ceiling. Beside the bed stood an antique dresser in which Anne kept the treasured wooden heart and her journal. The room had two dormer windows with different facings, so there was plenty of natural light. Whereas Anne had taken ten years to frame her PhD, Jack had ensured it had pride of place, hanging high on a wall above her desk, in full view for all to see. Archie had shared with Anne how very proud he was of that degree, as was she.

According to Archie, Anne's spirit was very adept at leaving her body and crossing the veil. Until now, her amnesia about time spent with Archie over there had not concerned her. Helen had said it served to protect her, and she'd been fine with that. But now, she worried: how was she going to write their story, if half of it was missing?

When she questioned Archie about where they met on the other side, he wasn't really helpful at all. She guessed it was considered privileged information. And so, Anne realized she had to go to the "higher powers that be" to get the information: the council.

And then, one night Anne had a dream of going to meet with Council.

I found myself standing on an upper level overlooking what appeared to be a generic city or town streetscape. I really had no idea where I was or why. I then heard a voice say, "Just a hop, skip, and a jump."

I immediately found myself in a large white space (with no walls, ceiling, or floor). Standing a short distance in front of me was a woman whom I recognized as my guide—a middle-aged woman with dark hair pinned in a bun at the back of her head. She bowed her head slightly by way of greeting, and I bowed mine in return. My guide then pointed me in the direction of another open space that felt like a corridor.

From there, I needed no prompting. I moved—more like glided—confidently to a door and knocked. A face I knew to be Archie's guide's face came into view. No words were spoken, but within seconds, Archie's face appeared. He was grinning with delight upon seeing me. And then the two of us, with our guides following, began walking, heading in a direction where I knew we would be meeting the council of our guides.

That was it. Anne woke up, but somehow she knew the dream had been real. That she and Archie had gone to see the council—about what, she had no memory.

One night shortly thereafter, Anne dreamed of what she would come to know as her and Archie's sky-house, their abode on the other side of the veil. In her dream, she and Archie seemed to be on the top of a mountain overlooking water, a lake, or a fast-flowing river. Archie was pointing out what appeared to be a stone and wooden structure, very rustic and architectural. It had walls, but was open to the sky.

"That's for us, to be in when we write our book."

"Wow!" It felt beautiful and sacred.

"Yes, it's ready and waiting for us to begin." Archie noted that, in Anne's diligent efforts to record their conversations, she was constructing what would be a very moving time in their relationship, when they would write their love story. He was excited, and shared with Anne his personal thoughts.

"We, our 'characters,' act with grace, integrity, and respect for each other. The quietness and unconditional love in action is a linchpin, a very important point in the love story. You were so quiet and accepting. You never made a scene or challenged me when I broke up with you. Knowing you're a very emotional woman who feels things intensely, I was amazed and even disappointed that you never put up a fight. It crossed my mind that you had never cared for me, as I did you. It was only on the other side that I appreciated your gentle acceptance of my decision. The simplicity with which you tell your side will be very potent."

Anne wanted to talk more about the dream. "After being on the mountain, it seemed we were among people and there was a baby. I heard 'Frank' mentioned. Was that the name of the baby?"

"They were talking about our book. 'Frank' means open and honest, which will characterize Anne and Archie."

"Who were the people?"

"Not to intimidate you Anne, but there is a tidal wave of curiosity on the other side about our book. While there have been other stories such as ours, ours is unique. The consciousness of how we approach it is intriguing to entities on the other side. We are opening a door to unexplored possibilities. Until our book is launched, though, I'm not able to discuss it with anyone over here, with the exception of the council and my guides. And, I must admit, this has been hard for me."

In a later session with Jane, Archie asked if Anne wanted to know more about the architectural structure in her dream.

"It's our retreat, a sacred place just for the two of us to be. When together on the other side, we attract a lot of attention, and this structure blends into the landscape. It has walls that enclose us, but no roof, so it's open to divine wisdom. It acts as an invisibility cloak, like in *Harry Potter*."

Anne was curious why they would attract attention on the other side. "Does it have to do with the fact that I'm still in-body?"

Archie conceded that that was part of it. When Anne's soul left her body and crossed over at night, her energy vibration was lower, and Archie toned his down when they were together. Also, souls were used to seeing Archie alone, so when he and Anne came together, they were interested to see the two of them.

There was more, but at the moment he didn't want to overwhelm her. He laughed. "When you cross, all will be revealed, Anne. Remember, I took great offence when you called us ordinary."

That was true. Anne had never considered herself or Archie as anything but ordinary. But this last year, with Archie's revelations and his energetic presence in her life, she had begun to revise this impression, at least when it came to Archie.

"I realize no soul is. I do remember you saying that spirits and friends know us as a couple over there."

"True."

"When alone, do you use the retreat space?"

"Not as much, but sometimes. When you come, this is where we usually are for intimacy and privacy, and to commune with divine wisdom."

Anne liked to think Archie was sending her dreams, much as a man would send his girl love letters. "I would like to talk about last night. I was dreaming, and at one point I was skating. Lots of people were around, and then all of a sudden, a man skated up beside me. He put his arms around me and started kissing me. We skated to the edge of the rink and continued kissing each other, passionately. Was that you?"

"Yes! Remember our first date? We went skating at City Hall."

"You definitely have a way of making me pay attention."

"That was my plan. Last night I was feeling a lot of love for you and wanted you to feel it."

"You were with me pretty much the whole night."

"There is no time here, but yes, I think that would be correct."

"I felt very connected to you," Anne said.

"Yes, me too with you—it's like we've never been apart."

"I felt a lot of physical passion in our kissing."

"Yes, it was something I imagined about us while we were dating. Still beautiful and I loved being close to you."

Anne was a bit puzzled. "But I thought spirit really didn't bother with that."

"When it comes to you, Anne, there's still a part of me that's moved by your being, your nearness, your physicality. Yet ultimately, it's your soul."

"I *loved* our kissing in the dream."

Archie laughed, "More of that to follow."

"So, what's up for tonight, more of the same?"

"Perhaps, one never knows." At the beginning, Archie found the easiest way to communicate with Anne was through dreams. And even now, though they conversed very well through spontaneous writing, Archie often liked to give Anne dreams, to remind her of the love and joy they shared and continued to share.

"Is it important to know why we had the soul contract to be apart?" Anne asked.

Archie paused before he answered, "In time, but not now, not really."

~~~~~

Later, Anne dreamt again of their sky-house, and documented it in her journal.

Anne: Last night, I had this dream. It felt like you and I were in a speeding car; it was unclear who was driving. Maybe there was no car and we were energy. It felt like we were moving through darkness, possibly a thick woods or deep forest. It was dark, so much so that I couldn't discern anything up ahead. And suddenly, rising out of the blackness, a massive ancient stone wall was just there. And I saw what looked
~~~~~

to be a gate. The next moment, I found myself in a large room with a big desk or table in the middle of it. I walked across the room and sat down on a chair placed in front of the desk, facing my guide, who was seated behind it. She asked me questions and was recording my answers. In the dream, I did hear the first question, but upon waking I couldn't remember it. And I don't know where you went.

Archie: I was there. Do you know where you were?

Anne: No.

Archie: It was our sky-house.

Anne: Really! Well, I find that astonishing. That's certainly not how I envisioned it in my other dream.

Archie: For the most part, everyone on the other side has a structure. Ours is the sky-house, and it has different aspects to it. Last night, you dreamed of another aspect of our structure. And you were realigning your soul. I was there with you.

Anne: It's interesting. The structure looked like an ancient castle, but there were no turrets or towers, just walls.

Archie: Exactly! There is no roof.

Anne: The gate in the wall—was that the gate you said we would be going through together?

Archie: Yes. When I crossed the veil, I knew we had a place somewhere. But it's ours. Thus, it was only after we connected, and you committed to stay for the book, that we entered through the gate together. Without you, I couldn't access it. You opened the door for me.

Anne: I love that, Archie—that we entered our home together. This part of the sky-house also seemed to be well camouflaged by the surrounding landscape. We must be a very private couple over there.

Archie: When we choose to be. We have a large group of souls with whom we commune. To my amazement, you have twice had dreams of the two of us socializing. They are real, Anne.

—Anne Jeffrey, *Anne & Archie's Journal*, Vol. 21
(Sept.19 and Sept. 24, 2020)

CHAPTER 17

Self-Care Revisited: Yoga Retreat

Anne was feeling overwhelmed with completing her history manuscript and proposal, and sending it off. And this didn't even speak to her across-the-veil relationship with her twin flame, as she continued to negotiate her own earthly life as wife, mother, and grandmother. Anne was stressed to the max. She had no idea how she was going to manage all that was expected of her—all she expected of herself.

When Jane shared that one of the ways she exercised self-love and -care was taking mini-sabbaticals, Anne had wondered what opportunity might manifest for her. In late March, Jennifer telephoned to let her know of a weekend yoga retreat at Collingwood that was happening early April. Was Anne interested? It was very limited in terms of space, so if she was, she needed to act immediately.

Anne thought it was perfect. Although she was still in the midst of writing (when was she not?), she appreciated the need to get away.

The night before she departed, Archie said, "This weekend is about you, fun, and self-care. I love to see you full of joy and laughter. That's how I remember you. Whenever I thought of you over the years, it's how I envisioned you—having an idyllic life with your family. I don't think you realize what a bright light you are when you're being you—your authentic self."

Anne thought that funny, considering that was how she'd thought of him, so full of love and laughter. Not long ago, Anne had met a son-in-law of a friend. He was a steamfitter, a salt-of-the-earth kind of man, a loving husband and hands-on dad. "It's how I imagined you to be, and I think you were."

Archie confirmed that he had been.

Anne informed him that when she returned from the retreat, she was going to line up a movie fest of sorts for the two of them—the first movie being *The Lake House,* about a couple separated by time and space. She was eager for them to view some contemporary films that depicted the challenges of love relationships that were extraordinary—and mystical, maybe. Her hope was that the movies might lend some insight into how to approach the telling of their own love story.

Anne drew her signature little heart, something she did to mark the end of each of their journal conversations. Initially, Archie had teased Anne about the hearts—but the truth was, they had surprised him. It had been a side of Anne he had never fully realized, and the sweetness of her hearts touched him. She confessed that if they had stayed together, he would have received lots of hand-drawn hearts on cards and letters she would have sent him. "Think of each heart as one of our kisses."

In life, Archie would have loved to receive even one card from Anne. Still, he loved them now—her letters, her hearts, and more.

"Oh, I almost forgot—our journals!" Since Archie's return, Anne had filled almost five journals and she was anxious about going away for three days; she feared Jack might discover them. For the time being, Archie advised her to place them in one of her research boxes; he would ensure their safety. Anne had raised an important point though, and the issue of the journals was something they would need to address.

Friday noon, Anne hit the road with her CD music playing the old classics she loved. Jack wasn't happy about her going. She knew he didn't like being alone. But today, he'd surprised her.

As she stowed her suitcase into the car, Jack had shared, "I don't like it when you're away. At night, I feel like spirits of dead people are hovering over me. See what you've done! All your talk about spirits has finally got me spooked."

All she could think of was to assure him that if indeed ghosts were around, they were likely deceased family members who had loved him in life. "They're watching over you, protecting you while I'm away."

Long ago, Jack had confided that, as a teenager, he had once seen the faces of his dad's late parents smiling at him from his bedroom door. According to Jack's mother, in life they had both adored Jack, their only grandson. Maybe Anne being open with Jack about her spiritual path was a good thing after all. She'd always suspected he was more intuitive than he cared to admit.

Upon arrival at the retreat, there was much ice and snow, minimizing the designated area for parking. Anne was asked to park her car alongside a very luxurious SUV. As she maneuvered her car in beside the other vehicle, her tires lost their grip. Anne could feel her car slipping sideways.

"Stop! Stop!" yelled Susan, one of the yoga instructors, who was directing Anne's parking. Looking in the rear-view mirror, Anne could see Susan frantically waving her arms. Anne was a nervous driver at best, and for a second her brain froze. Then Anne slammed her foot on the brake—the car stopped, missing the other by an inch. She looked back and saw Susan exhale. And then, without thinking, Anne steered her car into the parking spot, no sweat.

She was astounded. Jack would never have believed it, even if he had seen it with his own eyes. Anne was sure some divine being had stepped in, possibly Archie. And Susan—well, she was jumping up and down, clapping her hands, and for the rest of the weekend, referred to Anne as a rock star.

The yoga retreat was held on a large property. The main lodge was one huge room with a large kitchen, a long island functioning as a kind of room divider that separated the food prep area from the lounging and dining spaces. Outer buildings scattered in close proximity to the main house were guest accommodations, with shared sleeping quarters. Anne's bed was one of five situated on the second floor above the yoga studio—and at night, the energy in that bedroom was so very tranquil. Anne slept like a baby.

The food was entirely vegan, prepared lovingly and joyfully by three fabulous women who sang and danced while they cooked. Anne loved to sit at the island and watch them. And the food was delicious. If and when she ever had time, she would love to start eating that way. After three days on the diet, Anne felt so much healthier and happier.

At the close of a morning yoga session when everyone was in shavasana, resting on their backs, the instructor had read a poem, "She Let Go" by Safire Rose. It was the most exquisite poem Anne had heard in a long time, and it registered with her physically, emotionally, and spiritually.

The three women who facilitated the retreat were uplifting and joyful, as were the women who attended. They had yoga classes morning and night, with art classes and nature walks spread throughout the day. Everyone was so full of love and light—at least that was how Anne felt them to be. When it came time to leave, Anne felt she'd been gifted, graced by the experience, very much like she'd felt when in Ireland with the goddesses.

Sometimes, Anne was in awe of the life that was hers, and this weekend had been just such a moment. Everything about the place and people was magical.

~~~~~

Upon returning home, Anne was brimming with excitement, wanting to share the experience of her weekend with Archie.

Archie: You do lead a graced life. And come on, you loved that Susan called you a rock star.
~~~~~

Anne: I did. I was so moved when she gave me a rock that she'd hand-painted with the words "Rock Star." I have the feeling it was divine intervention that helped me move my car without a scratch.

Archie: As far as I could see, you were the only one driving the car, Rock Star.

Anne: Okay, no more imposter syndrome. Just don't ask me to sing. Nevertheless, it was remarkable that I could move the car and park it, while it was slipping downhill on the ice about to hit a fancy SUV. It astonished me, never mind Susan. But I had no time whatsoever to journal or write.

Archie: You needed to take the whole weekend for yourself.

Anne: My body is so sore from all the yoga, but what a way to live, even for a couple of days. Doing yoga, art, connecting with like-minded women, and eating vegan food prepared lovingly by three women takes a lot of energy. I'm so tired. Need to sleep, Archie.

—Anne Jeffrey, Anne & Archie's Journal, Vol. 5
(Sunday, April 7, 2019)

~~~~~
~~~~~

At home, Anne looked up the poem "She Let Go" by Reverend Safire Rose on the web. She wanted a printed copy to fully contemplate the words. It was so powerful, especially for Anne, a chronic people-pleaser. *She* in the poem simply let go. She released the expectations, the fear, the judgements, the anxiety and emotions that held her back. And Anne felt her freedom, her joy. In letting go, *she'd* created space for herself to be, to breathe. Anne thought someone at the retreat mentioned that the poet had written it after a love relationship had ended. And Anne recalled her friend's comment about how great it would be to love yourself first, and then fall in love.

Anne wished she'd had this poem and wisdom when she was younger. But it had come to her now, and for that she was grateful. She realized that, in writing her history book, she'd have to have confidence in her work, finish it, and then let it go, without worry, without expectation.

That evening, she shared the poem with Archie. "You said once that you had been very controlling with yourself in life. I think I have been too. Maybe one of our lessons in life is about letting go and allowing ourselves space to be, and to honour our authentic selves."

"Anne, you and I are a lot alike. And this poem, if I had ever paid attention to it (not sure I would have), would have given me some very wise direction. That being said, I must say, I love experiencing the wisdom through and with you. You are a marvel, as I always knew. How's the writing coming?"

Anne replied that it was going slow and steady, and when it was ready she would let it go, as simple as that.

"I sense a new calmness in you tonight."

"Are you sure it's not fatigue?"

"Well, there is that, but no. There's a peace within you. It's there, though you may not know it yet."

Anne hoped that was true, but, deep within, she thought this letting go business was going to be a journey unto itself.

CHAPTER 18

Missed Exit, Spring 2019

It was spring and Anne could feel the sun's rays getting stronger, smell the freshness of the air as she walked in the forest behind her house. She especially loved the return of the birds and their chirping songs—heralding the promise of new life, new beginnings. She was never sure if she suffered from seasonal affective disorder, but the coming of spring always lifted her spirits. Last April, her mother had died, so this year Anne was especially appreciative of the natural world stirring into life, into colour. Since the yoga retreat, Anne had been taking daily walks along the river trails in late afternoon—part of her new self-care regimen. While her initial intention behind the walks had been to alleviate stress, Anne found a sense of peace, clarity, and joy as she moved through the trees.

Almost from that first day, Archie accompanied her on her walks. She felt him, his energy, as if he had his hand pressed on her back, underneath her coat. And sometimes, when she sat by the river, she felt his energy around her head, like he was sprinkling fairy love dust upon her. While at first caught off guard by his presence, Anne had come to love their communing together in the woods. Their communication was often telepathic in that she immediately heard his words, and then silently responded in her thoughts. While the writing made Anne slow down and pay attention, in conversing, Archie said their minds had a kind of shorthand with each other.

A couple of weeks earlier, Anne had wondered if she was hearing Archie correctly. And so she asked, "Are we really having this conversation about my breasts?" And immediately she heard him answer "yes," and she felt him smile. "Jack's right. They are beautiful."

She laughed and said, "Thank you. Moving on, then." Nevertheless, Anne was slightly taken aback by Archie's comment. When they had dated, he had never said anything about her physical appearance whatsoever, at least that she could remember. Nor had she about him, come to think of it. Again, it seemed to speak to their spiritual bond that transcended the physical. While it went without saying, Anne had loved how Archie's blue eyes sparkled, softened, and conveyed such depth of feeling when he looked at her, only recently had she shared with him how she had loved his hands——that his hands had somehow embodied the very essence of who he was: solid, capable, sensitive and tender-hearted.

It was on their walks in the woods that Anne began to formulate the storyline for their novel. It would be two entwined stories: one being Anne's and Archie's relationship in 1975, and the second, their present relationship. The inciting incident?—Archie's return to Anne. For the most part, she felt Archie listened attentively, but occasionally she would hear him quip, give one of his witticisms, designed to make her laugh, have fun, and not take life so seriously. He lightened her—he always had. And it was these moments that reminded Anne of how intimately he knew her, and how much she wished he had a body she could embrace—a hand to hold, his.

In life, Archie had always loved being in nature, and across the veil, since he and Anne had connected, they loved going for walks. It was part of how they experienced being together on the other side. Thus, he was thrilled when Anne finally incorporated the practice into her everyday life. Needless to say, he cherished this time when she let her spirit soar free, and was more herself, her sacred self. Anne did her best thinking among the trees, and he was impressed as she outlined possibilities imagined in the telling of their story. When especially excited or upset about something, Anne spoke to Archie in her *out-loud* voice, all the while using her hands to convey more fully what she was feeling.

Oblivious to passersby, Anne's laser focus on their conversation recalled to him how they had been as a couple. How he had loved to listen to her talk passionately about something as they walked, often aimlessly with no specific destination. He teased Anne about talking aloud to him, but truthfully he loved to hear her voice, to hear her laugh. Then she somehow forgot he was energy, and that he was Archie, her Archie.

When he died, Archie had been done with his earthly life. But for him, this relationship, his relationship with Anne, was not done. And so now he was exploring what their love and relationship would have been like if they had stayed together—the reality being far better than anything he could have imagined. Finally, he got to do and say all those things he never could when they had dated. It moved him deeply to know she felt what he felt, what he'd always felt.

A few months after the breakup and letter, Archie had wanted to contact Anne, but his guide, the voice, had said he would hurt her if he did. And Archie had never wanted to hurt Anne. Nonetheless, when he'd finally returned to her, he saw Anne's despair. Two years later, though, while he knew she had few memories of their time on the other side, it filled him with joy to see her laughing more, so committed to their relationship, their love and time together, and now the writing of their story. He was so proud of her. With each passing day, he felt their profound connection deepen.

Anne let Archie know that she had an appointment with Jane and asked if he would be present—she had some matters to discuss with him. As a historian, Anne had a keen eye for inconsistencies and readily identified discrepancies in stories as points of interest and study—and her historical acumen for detail uncovered clear inconsistencies in Archie's version of things. Furthermore, she felt a pressing need to understand the soul contract that had asked that they meet, fall in love, and separate. It made no sense. All her life, she'd heard about individuals finding their soul mates and living happily ever after. Obviously, with Anne and Archie as twin flames, this had not been the case. Anne was giving serious consideration to calling their story the anti–fairy tale.

Two months had passed since Anne had initiated spontaneous writing with Archie. Every night after climbing into bed, she would take out journal and pen, and they would converse. She really had no idea what she was doing or how it worked, other than that she seemed to hear or know Archie's words and write them down.

She had so many mixed emotions. Part of her was amazed by their conversations. She felt they were truly a couple. That they had just seamlessly picked up their relationship from where they had left off, before the breakup. But for some reason, Anne felt it to be a deeper, more intimate connection than in 1975.

Recently, she'd visited her friend Helen, who also did spontaneous writing with her deceased husband, as well as with her angels. To have someone to talk to about all of this meant the world. That afternoon when they were out for lunch, Anne expressed her fear that, if someone came upon her journals, they might think she'd gone stark raving mad and have her committed to a loony bin. Possibly, this fear reflected her own worry that she was making these conversations up in her head. That she *had* actually lost it.

Helen laughed. She said Anne was in good company then, as many on the spiritual path did this writing as common practice to tap into many sources of wisdom from the other side. And with that, Anne laughed too.

Two days later, at Jane's, Anne had no sooner settled into her chair when Jane informed her that Archie had been to see her ten minutes earlier.

Dumbfounded, Anne asked, "Why? What did he want?"

"Archie's concerned for you. He said, 'Anne thinks she's making this up—what she's writing in her journals. I want you to tell her that she's writing down the conversations as they happen.'"

A little overwhelmed, Anne sighed and shared with Jane how moved she was that Archie would do this for her. It was something she wasn't used to—Anne was fairly independent, so she was usually the one taking care of others.

Anne pulled out a list of things that she wanted to address with Jane's help. First, she hadn't met the end-of-March deadline for completing her obituary book, suggested by Archie. She confessed that she had some anxiety about putting herself out there—because she hadn't pursued academia as a career, she had a sense that her book wasn't good enough. Nonetheless, she'd found a publisher to whom she thought she would send a proposal.

Jane was pleased that Anne was making progress. She knew what a relief it would be for her to have the work done so she could move forward.

"Archie's here. He wants to talk about when he first came back to you at 'the Gathering' over a year ago now. He says his biggest fear was that you had forgotten him completely."

"I didn't forget. But I was definitely confused, and there was a lot of energy moving around the room. By the time I came home and was fixing dinner, I had thought of you, Archie. I felt your energy as I was clearing up the kitchen. However, that would mean you were dead—something I didn't want to acknowledge. Nevertheless, I feel I recognized, at some level, that our soul contract was completed. We had been successful." Anne paused and reflected that the overflowing of tears after learning of Archie's death had, perhaps, been both grief and relief on her part. "While I grieved his death, my soul understood that the contract was done and we didn't have to be separated anymore."

Jane said Archie was nodding in agreement. Anne asked why they had a soul contract to be apart in this life.

Archie's response was that he was still learning about their contract. Be that as it may, he wanted Anne to know that a contract was bigger than one lifetime.

Hearing this, Anne said, "It breaks my heart to think we are doing this 'being apart' over a number of lifetimes. I'm not sure I could do it again."

"Archie says that after his death, when he found out about the contract and that you were his twin flame, he yelled at his guides. He learned you were his twin flame and that, now dead, he couldn't be with you."

Alarmed, Anne looked to Jane, who quickly assured her, "They can handle it."

Through Jane, Archie explained, "For the longest time, I felt I had heard wrong and made a mistake letting you go. And I worried about you, that I had hurt you. Thus, when I found out this was a contract, I lost it. I wanted to go and tell you right away. Of course, they wouldn't let me until I had reviewed all of our past lives. Their rationale was, 'You don't even know yet what you have to tell her.' It was a few of your months before I could contact you. I wanted you to know the truth."

Jane continued, "Anne, Archie is standing beside you. Do you feel his energy? It's quite big."

Oh, yes. Anne could feel his loving energy pouring into and around her.

"Archie wants you to know that this life was the final piece of your contract. With his death, the contract has been completed. Other past lives involved you being siblings, looking after aging parents. Two lives, you were married—one life, you died early and Archie was left alone, and in another life, Archie died first. He says you're both very old souls, but still have another life on Earth. This one will be spent together as a couple.

"Archie says he is just waiting for you to cross, a time when you can be together on the other side. He sees it as an oasis for the two of you."

Yes, Anne thought. Looking down at her list, she wanted to address something that had been troubling her, something Archie had talked about in a past session. When he had first come to Jane's to explain all, he said he had known about her son and that she'd moved to Guelph, though she had been alone in the grocery store when she'd run into him and had yet to move to Guelph; she still lived in Toronto at the time of their meeting.

"I thought your son was with you at the store," Jane said.

"No. I was alone." Anne said, "One night about a month ago, I asked Archie this very question. And I had an image of Archie driving past my parents' house. That was when he saw me with Alex. Archie confessed then that he had followed me in his car to find out where I lived. At the time, he had no idea he would be driving to Guelph."

Jane looked to Archie, standing behind Anne. "Archie is grinning like the Cheshire Cat in *Alice in Wonderland.*" He was definitely a charmer. "Do you have anything you wish to share with Anne?"

"Archie says you caught him. After you rushed past him in the grocery store, he was understandably very upset. He had seen your wedding band and knew you were married, yet it didn't sit well with him. The way you had snubbed him, he wondered if you were okay. He started driving past your parents' house, and one morning he saw you outside with your little boy. He never missed a day of work, but that day he did. It was worth it. He followed you that day and home to Guelph. He saw you had moved on. You had a son, a husband, and a home. You had made a life for yourself, and he felt relieved to know you were in a good place. Knowing that, he realized he too had to move forward with his life. And he did, all thanks to you, Anne."

"It would have broken my heart to think you hadn't moved on." She turned to Jane and said, "Archie was well loved by family and friends. That makes me happy."

Jane reported that Archie was nodding in agreement, and saying: "While we were both on the other side, we had to consider how we were going to manage being apart for the duration of our lives. One of our thoughts was that we could be friends. But, as we quickly discovered, once we started dating, our love—well, it was a thing of wonder. Being friends would have blocked our ability to move forward and have independent lives."

Anne asked, "Is it my imagination or do we laugh a lot when we're together?"

"Yes, we do. There's so much joy, on both of our parts, being together again. One night when I was drinking with my guy friends, the topic of conversation turned to 'the one who got away.' All I could think of was you, and that I had sent you away. It wasn't a great evening, very awkward."

"So what did you say?"

"Archie is smiling and says, 'Nothing. I was a master of changing the conversation.'"

Anne had felt Archie try to do that sort of thing in their journal conversations. She would ask him a question and he would talk of something else. In the future, she would have to keep a closer eye on him.

Anne wanted to learn Archie's answer to her next question, and she didn't trust the spontaneous writing with it. "You said that when you first came back, our relationship was tenuous, but then we really connected."

Archie explained that when he first came to her through the medium, the relationship was definitely shaky. "After all, you were married. It troubled me how this whole thing would play out. However, within a month we really connected. Since then, we have been together."

Jane asked, "Archie wants to know when the connection happened for you, Anne."

Her first thought was Valentine's Day, a couple of months after his ghostly return. In a way, she felt Valentine's Day was their anniversary, marking the day of their first date and kiss. And of course, she'd chosen to write him a letter. Yet, the memory of Archie spooning her in bed, comforting her, that night her mother died, still brought tears to Anne's eyes.

"I think Valentine's Day, but the night my mother died was moving beyond words."

"Archie is nodding and smiling. He says that Valentine's Day was your day, and even though he was dead, he had put so much effort into making it special for you. Though he agrees that your mother's death was a big turning point in further deepening your bond."

Anne nodded. Noting the session was nearing its end, Anne asked if Jane would balance her energy.

Jane was smiling as she replied, "Your energy is all tangled up with Archie's right now. Should I leave it?"

Anne sighed. "Yes." She so loved when their energy commingled.

"Archie and you are both protective and respectful of each other's wishes and needs. The love you share is very precious, and you treat it as such. It's a beautiful thing to witness, Anne."

On her way home, Anne stopped at a T-intersection. Preoccupied with thoughts of Archie, she took her foot off the brake and started to make a left turn, just as a car whizzed by in the very lane into which she was about to turn. It had been going so fast she was unable to make out the colour of the car, let alone the make. *Whew! That was a close call.*

CHAPTER 19

June 2019

Jane had come down to her office to do some paperwork and ready the room for Anne's appointment. She was surprised to find Archie already there.

"You know Anne's not due for another hour."

"I know. Is it okay if I wait here?"

Jane didn't mind. She truly liked Archie. He was funny and gently kind, and he was good for Anne. She had known Anne a long time, and with Archie she just seemed lighter, happier, at least when they were together at the appointments. Lately, Archie had started coming and remaining for Anne's entire sessions. Jane was the only person who saw and knew them as a couple, and Anne had commented on more than one occasion, that this meant the world to her and to Archie. Jane felt that, over the past year, she'd gained Archie's trust. And this, she knew, helped support Anne and all she was going through.

When Anne arrived, Jane let her know that Archie had come early. He was waiting for her. Anne smiled. She loved that. He continued to surprise her with acts of his care and thoughtfulness. He made her feel special. Yet at the same time, it was so easy being with him; he soothed her soul. She sometimes fretted that, being in-body, she couldn't reciprocate in kind.

Despite feeling stressed about her manuscript, Anne said she didn't want to talk about it. For the past two months, Anne had been striving to get her book finished and the proposal done. She figured that in a week or two it would be ready for submission to the publisher. She'd been feeling so anxious of late.

"I thought old souls like me would be better at life."

Today, Archie wanted to talk about their soul contract, to let Anne know what a big deal it was. Through Jane, he said, "You remember that I mentioned how closely our guides worked with us before we incarnated? They wanted to make sure that we understood exactly how big an undertaking this life's soul contract would be, so that we could make an informed decision." Archie wanted Anne to know that their guides had been genuinely concerned for them both.

"Perhaps we should have listened," Anne interjected.

"Maybe. But I do feel differently about the challenges we have faced in this life, now that I understand that they were simply a reflection of the magnitude of our soul contract. Big soul contracts often require big challenges."

This was a lot for Anne to absorb. Throughout her life, she had felt this deep loneliness. When Archie ended their relationship, she had rushed into marriage a year later. Is this why she always felt anxious—challenged by even the slightest thing? Interestingly, when she was with Archie, in 1975, but more so now, he was the one person in her life with whom she felt calm, safe. That she could be herself and she was enough. Sighing, Anne looked to her list of questions.

"When did you start hearing the voices that told you we couldn't continue?"

"Archie says it was only two weeks before your breakup. But after the breakup, he thought he had heard wrong and made a mistake. He says, 'The stories we tell ourselves.' As a woman, he would have had friends to talk to, but as a guy, he really had no one. However, once on the other side, he saw that he had been honouring the contract."

Archie said that they had each taken separate paths as to how they dealt with a life apart. "You married an anti-Archie!"

Anne was slightly taken aback by Archie's depiction of Jack as the antithesis of himself. In a way, he wasn't wrong. In the early years of their marriage, Jack did have a temper, and Anne had struggled with that. Nevertheless, her husband was a good man with a generous heart. Anne knew that. It was why she'd fallen in love with him. Why she loved him to this day.

"Did you marry an anti-Anne?"

Jane seemed to watch him as he paused, then answered, "No. She was like you, Anne. She was a very good friend. She was older than I was, and together, we had a son. It was a good, loving relationship and I grieved deeply when she died. After her death, I was done. And the next time the voice said I could go, I took it. No hesitation." Archie said he had lost a lot in his life. He couldn't bear to lose his mother too.

"I think his mother is still living. She must be well into her nineties," Anne said.

Because of their contract to be apart, Anne had asked Archie a few months ago if it was okay that they were together now. Archie's response then had been that as far as he knew, with his death, their contract had been completed, and they could be together. But since Anne had asked, Archie had sought council's approval. Today, he finally informed her they had received official confirmation for their relationship.

Prior to this, Archie had not really felt the need to clarify, in part because he thought Anne would decide to go. Instead, she'd chosen to stay to write their book, and things had shifted to support her in the endeavour. And part of that support was the gift of their relationship. Even though their guides and the council well knew that Archie and Anne had been connecting almost every night since Archie had made his presence known to her—nevertheless, the official recognition was something Anne had requested.

And now Archie teased her, "What Anne wants, Anne gets. However, I will not call you Princess."

Anne countered, "But Jack calls me that."

"Good for Jack."

Anne laughed. Archie was so funny. She loved his lightness, his humour, his authenticity. There had never been any pretence with Archie, a rare and endearing quality.

"Archie wants you to know that he came back and visited you before December 2017."

Anne's eyes widened. "Were you the one who held my hand? Remember, Jane, I told you about the time when I woke up one morning to feel someone holding my hand? My first thought was that it was my spirit guide, but then I had the feeling that it was someone who had known me in life."

Jane said Archie was nodding his head.

Anne was also thinking about late summer 2017, when she'd been out for an evening walk and had told spirit that she was done. Afterward, sitting on her bed, she'd felt two hands placed firmly on top of her head, and Anne had felt this amazing energy pour into her head and through her body. "Was that you, Archie?"

"Archie is saying it was him. He had been very worried about you."

Anne then spoke about the incident that had happened as she was leaving her last appointment two months ago. She joked that it would have been somewhat ironic if she'd been killed just as she was leaving the office of her life coach.

"Was that my exit to go?"

"Archie's laughing, and says that it was." Jane, however, did register some concern on hearing Anne's story. Then she continued, "Before you leave, Archie wants you to know that he has a couple of things coming up, and at that time he will be unavailable to you. He says he will let you know when."

Jane saw Anne's eyes fill with tears as she received this news. "It's hard, isn't it?"

Anne could only nod. How would she manage? She had come to love and trust their being together. Soon, she would be sending off her manuscript proposal. She anticipated beginning their book sometime this summer. *What have I got myself into?* There was no way she could write the book without Archie. He was integral.

Anne looked forward to the time when she didn't have to be in-body. Before Archie's return, she'd never given much thought to a life beyond the one she was living. But now everything had shifted. Anne confided to Jane, "When I'm finished with our book, I will go."

"Archie is telling me, 'You have better places to be.'"

Anne smiled. After settling her account with Jane, she rose to leave. Jane gave her a big hug. As she did so, Anne could see Jane looking past her to Archie, whom she felt to be standing behind her.

"So, Archie, do you know how Anne will die?"

There was a moment of silence, during which Anne imagined Archie to be considering his answer, his head tilted to one side as he did so. And then, Jane reported that he said, "You know I can't tell you that."

Anne shrugged and laughed as she grabbed her bag. "Frankly, I don't care how I die, as long as it's fast and I don't have to do it myself."

Jane nodded. "That makes sense. As an old soul, you've probably experienced every kind of death possible. So, from that perspective, I can see why it really doesn't matter to you how you die."

Anne had never feared death, perhaps because she'd nursed patients dying of cancer. But she thought it was more than that—her old-soul worldview, in which death meant a joyful return Home. Jane, in her role as a spiritual life coach, often accompanied family and clients to the other side, at their request, and she shared a similar attitude to death. Both Jane and Olivia, facilitators of the spiritual workshops Anne attended, had shared stories of feeling overwhelming sadness and a sense of homesickness—Jane called it "being Home-lonely." Jane conceded that she often felt quite weepy the day after accompanying individuals to the other side.

As Anne walked to her car, she felt the stirrings of apprehension. Archie was going away for a while. That night she struggled to sleep, without success.

~~~~~
~~~~~

The following evening, Anne attended a meditation at Soul Store, the local spirit shop, given annually by Angelica, who channelled a healing collective on the other side. Last year, she and Archie had gone together, and she'd found it to be a very powerful experience. Because of Archie's upcoming commitments, Anne had chosen not to bother him, and to go alone.

It was an incredibly hot evening and there was no air-conditioning. The back door and a window had been propped open for more air flow, to little effect. Nonetheless, Anne felt very calm and centered among the circle of women present.

The guided meditation led Anne on a journey that took her to a huge willow tree, which had a heart cut through the base of its trunk. As she moved through the open-heart space, she could feel all the light and love travel up the tree trunk, out into its branches, and down into its roots.

As she made her way to the other side, Archie was there. He came forward and pulled her into his arms. Anne realized she'd crossed the veil and they were together. The thoughts or words spoken were:

Our separation is an illusion that will soon pass. You and I are together, and that is real; and there is no time here on the other side. When you feel lonely, just be in the present. Do not overwhelm yourself. That is how you and I dealt with our three-month relationship. We decided to simply be and enjoy the present moment. And so when you miss me, think of a time we were together and be present in that moment. You are tender with your grandbabies. Be tender with yourself.

And as Anne and Archie came together in the heart-shaped space, Anne was overcome with the love and joy she felt.

When Anne went to thank Angelica for the evening, Angelica informed her that the healing collective wanted her to know that she'd received a major download, one she would be processing for the next week or so.

Driving home, Anne felt as if she were flying. She turned on her music to hear Rod Stewart crooning selections from *The Old American Songbook*. Singing along with Rod, she opened the window to get some breeze.

Immediately, she felt a woman's presence and heard "Thank you." An image came into Anne's mind—of Archie when he had taken the day off work to follow Anne, the day he saw her with her son and realized she'd moved on with her life. And then another image followed—of Archie coming home to this woman and saying, "Let's get married and have a baby." The woman was taken by surprise, quickly followed by joy and delight as she wrapped her arms around Archie. Anne felt the joy and gratitude emanating from the female spirit, who then disappeared as suddenly as she'd appeared.

~~~~

Later the same evening, Anne was still feeling emotional about the possibility that Archie's wife had come to thank her.

"I have to tell you something. I'm not even sure, as I don't know your wife, other than what you shared with me yesterday at Jane's." Anne went on to relate what had occurred. "When she expressed her gratitude, tears started coming and I was incredibly moved. It meant so much to me. You have no idea. Archie, was that your wife tonight?"

"Yes, Anne, that was her. I said she was like you. My wife knows you've been having a very difficult time lately, and she wanted to let you know how appreciative she was of your great gift to her, to us and our family. She is aware of the struggles you encountered, and still do, on the life path you have chosen. She also knows that you respected her relationship with me by honouring her privacy and that of her family—when your spirit guide informed you in the grocery store parking lot that I was with someone, you honoured her by not going back into the store to see me. She simply wished to return the love and respect you have shown her."

"That was so kind. Thank her for me, will you?"
~~~~

"When you cross, she wants to meet you and give you a hug. So, all in all, you had a great evening. I'm glad, because I have to tell you, Anne, I don't like to see you cry as you did last night. I'm so glad I never saw that when we dated because, honestly, I would never have been able to break up with you. I'm continually astonished by how emotional you are. Of course, that is what I loved about you, your big heart and sensitive soul."

"So, did you really come home one day and say, 'Let's get married and have a baby'?"

"Yes. I quite swept her off her feet. I think she was convinced it was never going to happen. She was crying and laughing all at the same time. We were married and had our son within a year."

"Beautiful. I love that. I'm very thankful for her loving presence in your life, that you had her, and your son. I couldn't bear to think of you alone. You were so wonderful, Archie, and had such a big heart."

"It took a lot of courage to do what you did and continue to do. Olivia, Jane's friend, said the first time she met you, 'You are very brave.' And you are. Whether you know it or not, you have made a difference in people's lives—and you will continue to inspire others, deservedly so, Anne."

<h1 style="text-align:center">CHAPTER 20</h1>

Grief Anew

Over the next couple of weeks, with mounting anxiety over Archie's imminent withdrawal of energy, Anne found herself sinking into a depression. Nevertheless, she pressed on to get her book finished and the manuscript proposal sent off to the publisher.

On a Thursday, Anne was in Toronto at the graduate library. Not for the first time, she had the feeling that she didn't belong in the ivory tower of academia anymore.

When she finally arrived home, Jack thought she looked pale and suggested they go to their favourite Indian restaurant for dinner. The family who ran it knew the couple as regulars. As they finished up, the waitress came over and noticed Anne had barely touched her meal. She asked if Anne was feeling okay.

Anne thought she felt fine, but later that night she was overcome with a sudden onset of stomach flu. The last time she'd been this ill was many years ago when she and Jack had been in Prague on a tour. Within a day, however, Anne was back at her desk, putting the final touches on her submission. Every night she worried whether Archie was going to show up, but except for the night she'd been ill, he came without fail. Anne was perplexed, but let it go. Archie had said that he would let her know when he would be unavailable to her. And so, she had to trust that.

She sent off the manuscript proposal to the publisher. She had thought that with that off her plate, she would feel better.

Instead, she continued to feel very down, so much so that some family and friends noted her sadness.

One night, as Anne was waking up, she heard herself telling Archie, "Take all the time you need." She intuitively knew that one of the things Archie had to take care of was his mother, who was dying. Anne knew how important his mother had been to him, throughout his entire life. She had once asked Archie what had pleased him in life. His immediate response was, "My parents, my mom. I loved her. She was an awesome mom, and I left before she died because I couldn't have coped with losing her."

Anne found it fascinating that since Archie's return, she felt she had a whole team on the other side caring for her. She had known for quite some time that this was the case, but now she was more aware of them than ever before.

One early July evening, Anne received an unexpected phone call from Jennifer, a friend whom she occasionally saw for reiki energy work. Jen said she'd had a space open up the next day and wondered if Anne was interested.

"Yes. Actually, I was thinking of calling you. It's been six months since my last appointment. What time?"

In anticipation of beginning to write their love story, Anne was eager to ensure her wellness. Presently, she seemed to be struggling with grief and exhaustion. She thought it was connected to her realization that her exit point had closed. Anne found it significant that Jennifer had called her out of the blue, something she'd never done before.

When Anne arrived, Jen was finishing her lunch outside her office, so Anne sat down and they chatted a bit. Anne shared that she'd been feeling *very* tired of late.

As Jen began the appointment, she asked Anne to state her intent. Anne's response was to be centered and grounded, and she asked if her guide could be there to support Jen's own team of healers.

During the session, Anne was so exhausted that she drifted off to sleep for a bit. Afterward, as was her practice, Jen checked in with Anne and asked how she was feeling.

"Still weary. I fell asleep for part of it. Was my guide here?"

"Yes. I sensed your guy, your twin flame, was present as well."

Anne nodded, but said nothing. She'd known Jen for well over twenty years, and had come to trust her not just as a reiki healer, but a friend. Shortly after Archie had returned, at one of her reiki sessions, Anne had confided in Jennifer about her twin flame. As expected, Jen had been cool about it.

Jennifer then grew quite serious as she expressed her concern. "When I started, your energy was so low, it was almost nonexistent." In all the many years she'd known Anne, she'd never felt her to be so drained of energy. She felt Anne was holding a lot of grief.

"I filled a whole bowl with grief, at a spiritual level. You should be feeling somewhat lighter. I would like to see you in a month, if that works for you." Anne set up another appointment mid-August and then headed home.

Later that night, as she and Archie were journaling, Anne said that Jennifer had sensed Archie's presence. "Were you there?"

"Yes." Archie revealed that he and the council had been anxious for Anne and had organized the emergency session with Jennifer. "Actually, we are still worried."

Emergency session? For me? Anne had worked so long on her history book, her baby—and now, having given birth to it, so to speak, she wondered if she was suffering from postpartum depression.

Archie was deeply concerned—all her guides were. Anne had no idea how close she was to dying, to her heart ceasing to beat. Her life force was waning, and both he and her guides acknowledged the very real possibility that Anne could die before the book was completed. Still, the last thing he wanted to do was alarm her by telling her this. "Anne, I care about you, sweetheart. I know you don't want to hear it, but maybe you shouldn't come to me every night."

Anne told him, in no uncertain terms, that this wasn't an option. As it was, she was dreading the time when they wouldn't be able to be together because of Archie's upcoming commitments.

"Okay, I just thought it might help your energy."

"You help my energy. Your love has done much to heal my heart. I would not be here now, if not for you. So, please, don't bring it up again. It upsets me."

Archie knew better than to argue with her. It wasn't in Anne's spirit to give anything less than 100 percent. Besides, he loved their time together. "You know how I feel. So, we will honour our time together and I will say no more on the subject. Still—be kind to yourself. It distresses me to see you so weary as you move through your day."

"I'm not sure there's a cure for that. You see, I find myself missing you during my waking hours, so I try to keep busy. I'm sure you can relate. Jennifer said that I have a lot of grief."

Archie had not communicated to Anne that his mother had passed. When Anne heard nothing, she decided to look up his mom's obituary. She was shocked to learn that she'd died the very night Anne had inexplicably become ill.

Straightaway, she wrote Archie a letter, conveying her condolences and love to him. She knew how integral his mother had been for Archie. In their journal conversations, Archie had often talked of his mother with great love. She was the one who had encouraged him to move on with his life and marry. And after his wife's death, his mom had been his mainstay of support.

When Anne asked if Archie would tell his mother about the two of them, he said, "Eventually, after she transitions. I think she will be distressed to learn how much I suffered and never talked about it. But the problem was me. I could have talked with her, and it would have brought us even closer. I could have trusted her. She would not have failed me. And I have come to understand that it might have helped to know I could talk to someone about it.

However, in the end, Anne, the truth is you and I couldn't have avoided the pain and grief we felt at not being together."

A couple days later, Anne revealed to Archie that his mother's obituary had listed the cemetery where she was buried. Anne had looked it up and found that Archie had been interred in the same plot. Thinking she might drive there, she google-mapped where the grave was situated. She hoped Archie wouldn't be upset with her.

"Anne, I'm not upset, but you know I'm not there. Aww, honey, please don't go. I won't tell you not to, but really, I would rather you not. I think it would be too distressing, and you're more fragile than you know."

Anne was still feeling incredibly depleted, so she promised him that, for now, she would leave it. That didn't mean she wouldn't go at a later date.

"Fair enough—you're a funny little one, Anne, very sweet. I mean, I always knew it, but not to the extent that I see now. Even when you're so down, you put yourself out there for others, maybe too much. You need to take care of you."

Anne thought that was what she had been doing. Nevertheless, she was extremely fatigued, and struggling. Her body was so very worn out.

Anne apologized for being a pain. "I know you have your mom, and you need to be with her as she transitions. I feel like I should be able to push through all this, get the books done, and then be Home, no sweat. Unfortunately, I feel my soul and heart are having none of it."

"Jen was correct in her assessment that all of this is hard on you. I know you're trying to push through the grief, but you need to step back. Maybe stay in bed for the day and just sleep."

"Did you do that when you were grieving your wife?"

"No. I was like you. I fought it. Not saying it was the right thing to do."

Even though Anne was feeling unwell, when Archie was present, she experienced an enhanced sense of well-being. She felt energized. When he was gone, however, the emptiness that accompanied his absence was profound. She honestly didn't know how she was going to get through the next month, let alone the next year or so. One day at a time.

CHAPTER 21

Seeing Red

It was strange, but except for the night when Archie's mother had died, Archie was present every evening to journal with Anne before she went to bed. She kept waiting for him to let her know when he would be gone, but it never came. Anne let it go. She trusted Archie—that he wouldn't just disappear without telling her.

Three days following her reiki session with Jennifer, Anne woke at four a.m. and went out for a thirty-minute walk. Bizarre, she knew. But she couldn't sleep and was feeling agitated and angry. Anyone who knew Anne knew she didn't play games. She felt this contract was a kind of game, a reality show. But how could one be angry with ghosts? No faces, no nothing, no answers back. She was annoyed at Archie, herself, and their guides. No one had yet seen fit to let Anne know about the full extent of their soul contract, and this too infuriated her, given she'd consented to stay and write a book about it. For her, at this very moment, the contract was a mess, executed without consideration of compassion for all involved. There were no words. Nonetheless, she ranted at whoever was listening.

"And I apologize for my anger, my grief. What disturbs me the most is I feel am speaking to empty spaces here on Earth. This is a complete muddle. And if you think I'm coming back here, well, that may not be happening. No wonder the world is in disarray and there's so much pain—a clumsy operation!"

Later that morning, Anne wrote Archie a letter to let him know she was fine. If he sensed her anger, he should know it was

190

"her stuff" that she had to work through. Anne was fully aware that anger was one of the five stages of grief, so perhaps she was making progress. She regretted that she'd vented her anger aloud to God knew who: Source, high self, her guides, Archie—any or all of the above. However, she hoped that later she and Archie could discuss it. In the storyline she was structuring for their book, Anne envisioned it as a chapter entitled "Seeing Red."

In the letter, Anne continued: "Perhaps you can relate to my feelings, Archie. I recall you saying that after the breakup, you were ticked off at me for not giving you a hard time when you broke up with me, for not caring." This is what Anne meant about the contract being clumsily executed. *They programmed everything for success, but paid no heed to our feelings, our emotions. We did make it from A to B, but in the process, devastated both of our hearts.* She was unsure, when she finally came Home, how she would score the success of the journey.

That evening during their time, Archie was sending Anne loving energy and Anne was bitching. "Whatever this contract was that you and I had—it was cruel and unkind. I'm disillusioned with a spirit realm that would support such things. I thought God was about love. What kind of love is this, I'd like to know? Anyway, this is how I feel. I have anger."

"Anne, I was furious when I crossed. I learned you were my twin flame and being dead, I couldn't be with you. And both you and I know what a wondrous love and life we could have shared."

"I think that is what breaks my heart anew every day. My daughter-in-law has noticed I have been down lately. Time seems to drag. Each day I sit at my computer, but it's hard, especially when I feel empty and exhausted. And on top of that, I realize this is trivial compared to what you and your family are suffering on account of your mom's death. And so, I apologize for all of this."

"Listen Anne, you're experiencing deep grief, just as my family is. Don't apologize."

"Is it too late to go, to exit?"

"Yes. You have committed to stay and write our story."

She had been thinking how caring and supportive Archie had been when her own mother died. He was so tender and loving. He knew how to care for people in pain. Anne was thinking of Archie's son and brothers, sending love to their high selves, gently and easily for their highest and best good. She also sent love to his mother's soul as she transitioned Home. "And as always, I send all my love to you, dear Archie. You are a great light."

A couple of days later, Anne told Archie that she felt her anger had dissipated. "I think it came because it had something to say to me." Interestingly, the day before she'd come across an article entitled "What Is Anger Saying to You?" Synchronicity!

"What do you think your anger was saying to you?" Archie reflected back to Anne.

"The article said that our cultural mores judge anger to be a not-okay emotion. Even in the spiritual world, it's downplayed. But Elisabeth Kübler-Ross identified anger as one of the five stages of grief. For a long time, particularly lately, I have been very sad and depressed about our situation. Anger is definitely an energizing emotion, and perhaps I needed this kick in the butt to wake up and get motivated."

After Jennifer had drained a bowlful of grief, it was then that Anne's anger had come forth. And certainly today, Anne had felt energized. She'd had her kids and granddaughters over for a swim and barbecue. She loved her family, and these times when they were all together were so special. Joy, pure joy!

Still, it was a lot of work. Anne was often so busy getting everything organized, she had little time to sit and enjoy her family's company. Nevertheless, today she had joined the girls in a water-fight. Erika, the eldest of her granddaughters, was blasting water at her younger sister who had yet to master the art of using a water gun. Anne grabbed the water gun from Violet, not yet four, and blasted Erika, who then suggested that they direct their efforts to getting Jack.

Anne agreed, and immediately, with glee, soaked Jack who had been quietly minding his own business, lounging by the pool.

The girls shrieked as Jack sprang to his feet. "Okay, both of you are getting dunked!" Jack was heading toward Anne, prepared to follow through.

"Don't! Please! I still have my watch on," Anne pleaded, as she held up her wrist to show him. Surprisingly, Jack backed off.

"Next time, I *will* dunk you, watch or no watch. Let this be a warning to you too, Erika."

Erika sobered, taking time to consider, then turned and blasted Anne, a safer opponent.

Eventually, Anne went inside to prepare the food and set up the deck for outdoor dining. Beside the picnic table for the adults, she had placed a little table for her three grand-girls, who were close in age and loved to be on their own.

Anne had just cleared the dishes and was in the kitchen getting dessert ready when Violet came in from outside. "Wow, Nana, you do everything!"

Anne stopped what she was doing and looked down at the fair-haired, wide-eyed little pixie—Lizzie's wild child. Violet was staring up at her in seeming awe. Anne was astonished, rendered speechless. This was definitely a first, and how interesting that it had been Violet who had seen her. "Well, thank you for noticing."

And with that, her granddaughter nodded and cheerfully grabbed two dishes of ice cream and dashed back out to the deck. Anne smiled. *I will definitely have to keep my eye on that one.*

Later, after everyone had left, Anne shared with Archie the pleasures of the day. "Alex stayed late to talk with Jack, in such a loving, patient, and compassionate manner. It was a beautiful thing to watch. He is so wise. I just keep thinking what a wonderful man he has become."

"You have great kids, Anne. Both Alex and Lizzie are quite remarkable. And Violet, she's definitely a charmer."

Anne agreed. She had been blessed with a beautiful family, and every day she felt gratitude for their presence in her life.

"Oh, and by the way, Anne, I would have thrown you in the pool, watch and all."

She smiled. "Oh, of that I have no doubt."

Archie thanked her for receiving another of her letters. He had not been expecting it, and it had been such a sweet surprise. Anne explained that she'd written it because she'd thought he might not come tonight. When Anne had learned that Archie would be withdrawing his energy at some future date, she'd made the decision that if they couldn't be together, she would write him letters so they could keep in touch.

Laughing, Archie said, "Well, if it means you'll write me letters, I'll keep you guessing. I could get used to your love notes. Not something I really ever did. Writing wasn't my forte in this life."

"Well, the letter you did write me was moving in its simplicity and sincerity. Thank you. I wish I could have kept it."

"I'm so glad the message registered with your soul. I must admit I had hoped you would call me, and I was hurt and angry when you didn't. When I think about all the pain I suffered, I do see your point. When you come Home, this is something we need to talk about with our guides. What more could we or they have done that would have supported us spiritually and emotionally?"

Perhaps her life review would help Anne sort it all out. Archie's letter was so dissonant from the cold way he had broken up with her. "I wish, in some way, you had called to explain, because your letter again indicated that you didn't want to interact with me in person. And yes, I'm annoyed with my guide and what she said to me at the grocery store. I wish she'd said, 'He is with someone, but you need to go back in and talk with him.' It would have helped resolve so much of the hurt and confusion for us. I'm aware that our spirit guides were in fear of us physically connecting, and again, it was all about the end game. You told me that was a very bad day for you, and I'm deeply regretful of that."

"I know. Since coming together, I have come to the realization that the one and only person I could have talked to about the voice was you, Anne. I know now that you and I could have talked about it, and you, being you, would have been kind and understanding. Hurt, yes—but because of the unconditional love we held for each other, we would have ended our relationship in a better place."

"We'll never know. Would you like me to write more notes to you during the day?"

"Yes, I would love it. You know, you have such a way of making people feel loved and special. I had forgotten how kind and joyful you were. I have to say, our relationship is more than I hoped for. What we have is quite unique and special, groundbreaking really."

"I always knew that. That's why it's so difficult some days. I can be driving, and a wave of love hits me."

Nevertheless, Anne was very aware of the gift of Archie's presence in her life. That at this late stage of her life, she'd been given this grace, this precious opportunity to truly know, to experience a loving relationship with him was beyond her wildest dreams. Magic!

But with that appreciation, Anne came to the full realization of the joy, the love, the beauty they had missed in this lifetime, what could have been. And that broke Anne's heart.

CHAPTER 22

Anne Loses It

Near the end of July, Anne booked a numerology reading with Margo, who, along with her partner, owned Soul Store, the local spiritual shop situated at the north end of town. In addition to selling high quality products such as crystals, singing bowls, various tarot decks and spiritual books, the store hosted the annual Gathering, where, in December 2017, Archie had first come through to Anne. Since Anne had sent out her manuscript and was in the midst of writing the storyline for the love story—novel—of Archie and herself, she was looking forward to her reading, hoping to hear some positive news for the upcoming year. Margo was an intriguing woman who had been on her own healing spiritual journey for some time. Anne truly liked her, and had found her to be highly intuitive and accurate in a previous reading.

Anne was a number five, the Hierophant.

When Margo read Archie's numbers and Anne's, she said that she didn't think they were twin flames, and that, in fact, Archie hadn't cared for Anne, had not loved her.

"After he broke up with you, did he call you to see how you were doing? If he loved you as he says, he would have ensured you were okay."

"No, he never did," Anne said softly.

"What kind of a person does that to someone they profess to love?"

Anne looked down at her hands folded in her lap and thought perhaps she did see Archie through rose-coloured glasses. Jack often accused her of being too kind, too generous, giving

196

people the benefit of the doubt when they didn't deserve it. Anne began to cry, and once she started, she couldn't stop.

Margo instantly came around the table, took Anne into her arms, and held her as she sobbed. Eventually, Anne was able to regain some semblance of control and sit back into the chair. She felt exhausted, drained, wiped out. She had never broken down like that before. The truth of Margo's words, however, hit Anne at the very core of her being. And she broke wide open, her fragility apparent.

Margo had not seen Anne in over a year and was shocked by her appearance. "I'm very worried about you, Anne. You are white as a sheet. For someone who has just completed a manuscript that you have been working on for a long time, you should be beaming with a sense of accomplishment. Instead, you're pale and haggard. This is a number eight year for you, the year of justice, the year one reaps rewards for their labours."

"In the last couple of years, both my parents have died," Anne said, by way of explanation.

"How many people have you lost in the last two or three years? I want you to write their names down on this piece of paper."

Anne started from present day and worked back: Jack's mother, both her parents, Archie, three academic mentors. Fiona, a longstanding friend and mentor, suffered a serious illness. She had not died, but Anne mourned the loss of her all the same. She returned the paper to Margo.

Margo examined Anne's list and counted. "There are eight people on this list. That's a lot of loss to endure! And they seem to have been important pillars of support for you. What are you doing to support yourself, to care for yourself? Here is the number for my energy healing practice. I want you to come see me and we can work on this together. You really can't continue as you are, Anne. There's grief and sorrow in your heart, and it's clearly affecting your well-being."

As Anne was leaving, Margo congratulated her on her book. "It's a huge accomplishment. Celebrate yourself."

Anne thanked her, but once in the safety of her car, she simply sat, feeling numb. Eight people. How had she missed that? How was she still walking around?

Arriving home, Anne scrutinized her reflection in the hall mirror. Was she that pale? Granted, she'd been working many hours at her desk and had recently been ill. Maybe with her greying hair, she needed to amp up her makeup. Anne shrugged and went upstairs to her room to dump her purse. Jack and Alex were in Toronto to see the Blue Jays game, so she didn't have to do dinner. She thought she might lie down for a bit and have a sandwich later.

As she sat on her bed, she thought about Archie saying that if she ever needed him, all she had to say was, "I need you, Archie." She was feeling unbelievably stupid and hurt, vulnerable—very vulnerable.

She started to cry again. She told Archie she had some things to say to him and he needed to listen, with no idea if he was there or not. Still, she trusted he would get the message.

"Archie, I'm very upset at the moment. Margo, an acquaintance really, told me a hard truth today, one I needed to hear. I was only twenty-one when you broke up with me—how could you have done that to me? It was not so much the what—the breaking up—but the how. When you came back, you said you had always loved me, and that when you broke up with me you had been devastated. Sorry, I don't believe it. You were twenty-eight. You knew you were my first serious boyfriend. And you broke up with me on the phone—ON THE PHONE!!! I had no warning, no comprehension of what happened. For many years, I blamed myself and thought I had not been enough, not good enough for you. I thought I had done something wrong. Although for the life of me, I could never figure out what.

"On our last date, we were getting very up close and personal. We were both feeling the love, and then suddenly you told me I needed to get out of the car. And when you drove away, you didn't even look at me or say goodbye. The next day, you broke up with me on the phone. And then, when you said we could meet and talk about it, you neither showed nor bothered to call to say you weren't coming—all indicative of your total lack of regard and care for me. Bewildered and hurt, I shut that part of my heart down, locked it up, and threw away the key. And I carried on. I did. It was what my mother did when her father died. She just kept making dinner. No tears. And this is what I did. I just kept waking up, doing the best I could. No tears.

"Remember when you first came back and said you loved me and had been so worried about me? You kept telling your spirit guide that you needed to know I was okay. You said your worst fear was that I was alone and miserable. When I was explaining this to Margo today, she asked—rightly so—'Did he ever check himself to see if you were okay? Call you to just check in?' I had to answer no. Knowing there was nothing I could possibly say in your defence, I broke down. I cried in Margo's arms. I cried for my twenty-one-year-old self. It felt so good to be held and comforted while I cried my heart out. Nobody has ever done that for me, I don't think ever.

"And if this was all part of our soul contract, then you can tell the guides for me personally, 'It was very clumsily executed and I'm not impressed.' To hear Margo's words hurt because I recognized their truth. She said that I was a very complicated person, very bright, but thinks I'm emotionally stunted, closed. You tell me I'm very shy, but other people have described me as closed. Perhaps I've been shut down for a very long time."

Wiping her tears away, Anne went down to the kitchen and made herself some dinner she barely touched. Tired, she returned to her bedroom, lay down, and slept. She dreamt a fish had jumped out of the tank and she couldn't put it back in. It kept slipping out of her fingers. She knew it was going to die if she didn't hurry up. She kept calling her mom to help her, but she never came, and the fish died.

Anne woke up and reached for her watch. It was nine p.m. She could feel Archie's energy. "Did you hear my rant?"

"Yes, I was here with you."

"Thank you. You wouldn't talk to me all those years ago. I need your words, Archie."

Archie had indeed heard Anne's tirade and, in some ways, he was relieved to hear her anger—he deserved it. Not his finest moment for sure. If his mom had ever known how the breakup had all gone down, she would have given him what for. Possibly that was one of the reasons he had never talked about it with her. But he'd been back almost a year and a half. He thought all of that had been addressed, and thus was slightly shocked by Anne's outburst. His guide had warned him that Anne was still in-body, and this emotional outpouring revealed her vulnerability, which she usually hid quite well. Not today.

"Anne, this is still so hard all these years later—even though we are together now, loving each other. You have to know I was so crazy in love, and being anywhere near you I couldn't have broken up with you. Margo is right to have asked if I had bothered to check in to see if you were okay. I absolutely should have. I thought the letter would be good. I could control what I said without having to see you. To be honest, I thought you would phone or write me back. In fact, I was hurt, ticked off when you didn't."

Anne interrupted, "You—you were ticked off at me?! Did you even read the letter? It was very fulsome in your praises, but that was it. You never said you missed me, or to call you. After much perusal of the letter, I could never figure out why you wrote it."

"Looking back, I realize now it raised more questions than answers, for both of us. But anyway, Anne, you're correct when you say it was a total mess and caused too much unnecessary pain. I do think our guides were very nervous about us getting together and talking at any time after the breakup, because again, it was their job to support us in our contract to be apart. 'What Not to Do When Breaking Up with your Twin Flame' would be a good title for one of the chapters."

"You can see why I thought you never loved me, never cared for me."

"Yes. I was careless of your heart, and you deserved better. If you made a list of the bad things I did in my life, this would be right up there at the top." And over the years, whenever Archie thought of Anne, he had always felt bad.

Anne said she didn't want to talk about the book right now. "I'm just too sad. Truthfully, I think I made a mistake. I should have gone when I had the chance. I'm not sure I even want to write our story."

"It breaks my heart to learn that Margo was the first person to hold you while you cried. My God, Anne, that's unbelievable! You see Jane mid-August. I will be there, hon, for the whole appointment, in whatever capacity you need me. Okay?"

Anne calmed down. She reminded herself that she and Archie were together, and all of that was in the past. But she still was furious with their spirit guides, the council. They'd known of the deep emotional abandonment she'd experienced as a child. She had trusted they were wise elders who knew what they were doing. When she got Home, she was going to give them a piece of her mind. Yes, the contract had been successfully completed, but at what cost?

"They can handle it, Anne. When I first crossed and they told me you were my twin flame, I shouted at them a good long while. I was fuming as to how it had all played out."

Anne exhaled. Somehow, her rant had eased her anxiety. And typical Anne, people-pleaser extraordinaire, apologized. "I know the timing of this is probably not the best. Your mother has recently died, and you have projects to work on."

"Anne, this is important. And if, after all of this, you want to go, perhaps we could ask council to reconsider. But knowing you as I do, I think you will stay to write our story. People are coming into your life to support you in this. You won't be alone. I mean, you aren't alone now. I'm with you and, as I have assured you, I'm not going anywhere. I'm holding your hand and not letting go. I let go once, now I'm not letting go until you're back Home with me."

"Thank you. I'm just feeling so overwhelmed."

Anne had read Brené Brown's *Rising Strong,* in which she stressed the importance of having boundaries. She argued that it's more than a matter of self-care—it's a matter of integrity and generosity. It's important to stand in one's own truth and let people know how you want to be treated. Anne needed to be up-front about this to the people in her life.

She sighed. "I'm cognizant that I need to tell people what is okay and what is not okay. Maybe I should have given you 'what for' in our last phone conversation. I guess lately, I'm letting it all hang out. First our spirit guides and now you, Archie. Should people be very afraid?"

Archie laughed, but then got serious. "Somehow, I think you will continue being nice, though I'm not sure it's working for you. I do love this new side, and I think it may be the beginning of a new and improved you, setting boundaries and standing up to certain people in your life who drain you. If we had stayed together, I would have got that people-pleasing thing out of you, except when it came to pleasing me."

~~~~~

The next morning, Sunday, Anne was alone having her morning coffee in her happy place on her back deck, her "treehouse" set high amidst a forest of trees. Anne rarely went to church anymore and this had become her sacred space, in which she could just be and commune with nature and spirit. As she reflected on all that had occurred yesterday, she felt Archie's energy come gently behind her.

"Anne, there was nothing, absolutely nothing, either of us could have said or done that would have eased the hurt we both experienced after our breakup. I know this is not easy to hear right now when you're in such pain. But the truth is, our love for each other was so profound, and being apart—well, it was devastating for both of us."

Anne replied, "I do feel gratitude and joy that we are reunited. I love what we share now. And in the meditation led by Angelica, where I met you within the open heart of a tree, you stressed the necessity for me to be present. I'm fully aware that this relationship we have is a gift of divine grace. Nonetheless, I'm still in-body, and my mind drifts back to our season of love in 1975. We had so little time. Sunday mornings, such as today, I grieve the loss of the simple things we never had the opportunity to share—lazy
~~~~~

weekend mornings in bed…making love and cuddling…sharing morning coffee together…taking walks out in nature…going away for a weekend, just the two of us."

"I know. I regret that too. I do try to do what I can."

Anne nodded. On weekend mornings, she often felt his energy at her back and she would rest into it. With her eyes closed, she felt his weight, as if he were spooning her. It touched her that he did this for her. She wished she could reciprocate, but always felt at a loss.

As beautiful as their relationship was in 1975, Anne was surprised to admit to herself that she wouldn't trade what they shared now. With each passing day, she felt her love for Archie deepening.

CHAPTER 23

It's Complicated

Anne was sprawled on the leather couch as she watched a movie she'd seen multiple times—the Nancy Meyers flick *It's Complicated,* starring Meryl Streep. She and Jack had hosted what had become an annual summer barbecue for Jack's office staff. When Jack had first started his practice, it had been a family affair—they all had children and it was a daylong event with swimming and burgers. Now, with their children grown, it was just staff and their spouses. Everyone had left, and the mess from the party was yet to be cleaned up. But Anne, exhausted, decided to take a moment and watch the movie. It was about a mature woman with grown children who was having a fling with her married ex-husband. For so many reasons, Anne loved it. As she watched, she felt Archie's energy come beside her.

"They think *that's* complicated!"

Anne started giggling. "They have no idea!"

Archie was so funny—he could always make her laugh. He stayed, watching the rest of the movie with her, which she loved. For some reason, whenever he was present, he brought such joy, calm, and peace to her. With him, she felt truly herself. That it was okay to be Anne.

She had recently confessed that she was a better person with him in her life. His love did that. There was no question Anne missed Archie's body—she would have so loved to hold him, to feel his arms around her, his lips kissing hers, and more. However, everything else that was Archie—his humour, his kindness, his care and consideration, and his love for her—were present in abundance. When they conversed at night and at Jane's office, Anne made every effort to be respectful of Archie's privacy. She had never asked about his wife—with the exception of the night her spirit had come to thank Anne. Neither had she asked him about the vivid dreams he'd had of her in his mid-fifties. Her feeling was that if he wanted to talk with her about any of that, she trusted he would. Otherwise, Anne respected his boundaries—even though Archie said that on the other side, there was nothing they hadn't shared with each other.

Slowly, over the last year, Anne had come to realize that she was traversing a very intricate landscape, one that crossed the veil. This was especially challenging, given that Anne, in-body, wasn't conscious of or privy to what was going on when, at night, her spirit crossed the veil to be with Archie. It disturbed Anne, more than she ever let on to Archie. For some reason, she worried about him, for him. As more and more details of his life were disclosed, Anne became aware of all the pain and challenges he had encountered as a result of their separation. She surmised that much of this was due to the fact that he was the one who heard the voice that told him he had to break up with her. As his suffering distressed her deeply, she was grateful for their nightly time spent together.

~~~~~

Of all the intricate challenges Anne had to face, one of the most difficult had to do with the journals that she and Archie had been compiling. Very soon after the two of them had started conversing through spontaneous writing, Anne became aware that they were going through a journal per month. In the few months, Anne had filled almost five journals.

When Anne expressed fear that her husband might come upon the journals, Archie said that once their story was published, she could destroy them. Their purpose was to help her make quick work of writing their novel, and once it was done they would hold no further use. Neither of them wanted to hurt anyone and, if discovered, the journals would indeed do that. Prior to this life, one
~~~~~

of the stipulations she and Archie had insisted upon was that they would do no harm. That in writing their story as fiction, they wouldn't hurt anyone, especially those family and friends they loved.

Anne knew it was the wise thing to do. Still, the journals were beautiful to her. Their conversations were so full of *them,* the love, joy, and humour they shared. Whenever Anne felt especially lonely and was missing Archie, she would read a selection from their journals. It soothed her. The books were the only tangible evidence of their love for each other; that their relationship was real and profound could be found on every page. It broke her heart to think one day she would have to destroy them. She wasn't sure she would be able to survive without them.

Talking with Jane about this, Anne said, "It's too bad we can't put the journals in a time capsule, to be opened at a future date when all the people who could be hurt would be dead." Margery Kempe's book that was written in the early fifteenth century had not been discovered until 1934. All those centuries, it had been "lost" and protected in a private library until the time came when the world had been ready to accept it—or at the very least, not destroy it.

Knowing the beauty contained in the journals, Anne pondered, "Perhaps there's some way the same thing could be done for our journals." Nonetheless, Anne would never wish to hurt Jack and her family. And there was Archie's family to consider. Eradication of the journals might prove the most loving thing to do.

One July evening as they were conversing, Archie said, "Our journals are being studied as we speak. So, when we begin writing our story, there will be help from the other side. A couple of our guides are in awe of our conversations. How much we have to say to each other. And by the way, they are very impressed with your spontaneous writing. Your third eye has completely opened now, so don't be surprised by your knowing things." *Ah, the journals are not just for me, but for the council as well, to support me when I write our story.* "Seven volumes and counting, they have a lot of material to go through."

The next day, Archie came upon Anne crying.

"What's wrong, hon?"

She had sent out her book proposal to the London publisher and last night, Archie had said that he had planned a surprise for her in way of celebration. But when Anne woke the next morning she had no memory of it, except that she was missing Archie.

"What was the surprise?"

"It was just the two of us, very romantic. It was a road trip of sorts. I thought you and I needed that, just time together."

Archie didn't share with her that he and the council had had words. In the last session with Jane, the council had said he needed to prepare Anne for the time coming up when he wouldn't be available to her, given he now had projects that would keep him busy. When he told Anne at Jane's that day, he had seen her tears, and since then Anne had been on edge, anticipating the time when it would happen.

The council had underestimated both of them and their love. Archie found he could handle both. In so many ways, their love and relationship was groundbreaking. And he was so proud of Anne. He had great admiration for her dedication to her husband and family, and to him and their book. They were proving to the council that their relationship could straddle both worlds.

Perturbed, Anne said, "I want to go Home to you. Wouldn't the journals be sufficient?"

"No. They would hurt the ones we love most, and neither of us want that."

"Is our story that important?"

"Yes. You know it is. Our guides are presently scouring our journals. Archie and Anne will go down in history as one of the world's great love stories."

Anne found this astonishing, given that their earthly relationship had lasted a mere three months.

For Archie, it had taken some time to open up to Anne as she recorded their conversations. Initially, he had been very nervous about revealing too much. Anne had been respectful of his privacy, but one evening she'd asked him to talk about his family and marriage. The next morning, Archie had asked her to destroy the pages. Anne heard him and immediately cut out said pages and shredded them. Over time though, Archie revelled in their ability to converse with each other on a daily basis, to share their most private and intimate thoughts. He marvelled at her and at them as a couple.

"It has taken me some time to get used to opening up. As I have said, in life I was very controlling of myself. On the subject of you, I was extremely closed after our breakup. Nevertheless, now that we have this relationship, I treasure our time and conversations. With my mother's death, there's freedom with our book."

"Do you really think she would have known the story was about us?"

"Yes. Since she has crossed and learned of us, she has shared with me that she knew how much I loved you. I had never been demonstrative with other girls, when in her presence. But with you I was openly affectionate. She saw the love on both our parts. She had been both surprised and saddened when our relationship ended. And she witnessed firsthand the deep grief I suffered after our breakup. Oh yes, she would have known."

Archie assured Anne that she need not worry. The council would ensure that her work and journals were protected for the time she needed them. Knowing that, and with Archie's mother gone, Anne began inscribing Archie's name next to hers on the frontispiece of the journals, to honour his official status as her coauthor—her ghost-writer.

As summer was drawing to a close, from across the veil came news of a shifting view regarding the status of their journals. Anne's spirit guide came to check in with her about the possibility of securing the volumes in a time capsule.

At Jane's, Archie addressed the matter as well.

"After reading our journals, the council of guides has come to a consensus: our journals are important and need to be preserved.

Their information has been deemed *precious,* and as such, a discussion has been initiated around the question 'How do we treat them as precious?' They have decided they must be stored and locked away, and released *only* when they can be accepted. Just think—if the Dead Sea Scrolls had been discovered too early, they might have been destroyed."

Jane could see the comparison had gone right over Anne's head. "Anne, did you hear that? Your journals are being compared to the Dead Sea Scrolls."

This was too much for Anne to grasp. She was speechless.

"Don't worry, Anne," Archie said through Jane. "I promise you—the journals will not come to light while any of our loved ones are still living."

"Thank you." And this was all Anne had to say about the subject.

Prepping for the Book— Boundaries, Summer 2019

Archie: When I came back, I feared you wouldn't want to speak to me. When you walked away in the grocery store, I thought you were angry at me for breaking up with you. And when you didn't recognize me at the coffee shop, it broke my heart a little. So, when I came through to you at the psychic with my spirit guide there, you were clearly numb with shock. I understand that now. When you're feeling overwhelmed or stressed, you can act out. But more often than not, you shut down. And at that time, you were shutting down big-time. You have since expressed to me that you had given up.

Anne: I realized it was you as soon as I left the psychic. But I didn't understand. You said we were soul mates, but you had broken up with me. It made no earthly sense, as you can appreciate.

Archie: I stayed with you over the next couple of days. Did you know that?

Anne: I think I felt your energy after Kat and Charlie left and I was cleaning up from dinner.

Archie: It still amazes me how alone and lonely a person you are. We are two of a kind. When I see you with your girlfriends or your granddaughters, however, you're the girl I remember. So, Anne, I have a question for you.

Anne: Are you asking me to run away with you? Because the answer is yes!

Archie: Whew! It's a good thing I'm dead. No, seriously—do you want to start writing our book, say mid-August? We can do that, you know. What do you think?

Anne: I have been working on the storyline, though it's still a work in progress. Yes, let's do it. You know what thrills me? You are taking charge, planning for our future. It was something we never did in this life when we dated.

Archie: I thought our being focused on the present had to do with being in love, and this was what love looked like. So head over heels *with each other, I thought we both knew we were going to be together, and we would take things as they came. After all, it was early days for us. Little did I know that was one of the things we set in place for the contract—to be fully present in the time we were together, and we did that.*

—Anne Jeffrey, *Anne & Archie's Journal,* Vol. 8
(June 26, 2019)

Since Archie and Anne had planned to begin writing their book mid-August, Anne had organized a couple more appointments to ensure her wellness, including another reiki appointment with Jennifer.

Jen always talked with Anne first, to assess how she was doing since her last appointment. And Anne, being Anne, may have overshared about Archie, what she'd been going through the last month, and her overwhelming feelings of grief and depression. After Anne lay on the table, she set her intention "to release any and all remaining grief."

With that, Anne closed her eyes and let Jennifer do her magic, beginning with laying the appropriate stones on her chakra centers. After Jen moved away from her head, Anne felt an exquisite energy surround her crown chakra, energy she'd come to know as Archie's signature. Anne felt Archie talking with her, like they were having a whole conversation. At one point, Anne asked, "Are you keeping my brain busy while this other healing is taking place?"

"Maybe."

Anne couldn't remember the specifics of their conversation, only that it felt intimate. Archie assured her that it was, and that this was how they were as a couple, how it felt when they were together on the other side. He told Anne that Jennifer would soon leave the room, after which she felt transported to her first date with Archie: skating, parking, and their first kiss. Tears dripped down the sides of her cheeks. It was so exquisite. She heard Archie singing lyrics from Faith Hill's "This Kiss."

"Believe me when I say, Anne, you ouched me like no one ever has or will. I learned that, in my life as Archie. We are each other's heart and home. It just is."

When Jennifer returned, Anne had risen from the table and was seated in the chair by the desk.

"I lost you there for a bit."

Since sometimes Anne could fall asleep during the sessions, she assured Jennifer that she hadn't been asleep, but had been connecting with Archie.

"That's what I meant." Jennifer explained that at each session, she invited Anne's guides to work with her own guides. "Your guides were telling me to put more quartz on your power centres and a shaman stone on your heart chakra. There was a moment when I became aware of Archie's presence. When that happened, Archie basically told me to back off. His words were: 'Anne and I communicate perfectly and don't need a mediator. What passes between Anne and me is not your business.'"

Anne was astonished at the revelation of Archie's forthright manner and his protectiveness of them as a couple. He had once said that if they had stayed together, he would have wanted to take care of her.

In the last thirty years, she'd led a pretty independent life. Nonetheless, at times, she'd felt a deep loneliness, never fully appreciating the source of it. She kind of loved the fact that Archie had told Jennifer that there were boundaries, and that what they shared wasn't Jen's business. She loved he had been so clear, all the while conversing with her. Talk about multitasking.

However, this also served as a reminder to Anne. When it came to their relationship, she'd need to exercise more vigilance about boundaries.

Later that evening, Archie stressed the importance of boundaries as they moved forward with their book. Anne agreed, but the challenge for her was that she was straddling two worlds and in love with someone who wasn't in-body.

"It's definitely complicated. No question. But together, Anne, we can do this."

"I loved you surprising me today with your presence."

"As I said before, I'm not going to pass up any opportunity when we can be together."

"I loved your presence, our conversation, and our sharing of love and affection. It's incredibly real to me, and oh, so beautiful."

"It is real."

Anne broached a subject that had been worrying her. "So, considering your words to Jennifer, I'm wondering about our session with Jane in a couple of days."

Archie immediately put her mind at ease. "Our sessions with Jane are different. First, you have said that you like me there, if only to support you. At present, we have things to discuss about our book, and Jane is perfect for this. She's *our* life coach, selected and suited to us and our journey. So don't worry about the appointment."

"Okay. I just had to ask."

"Anne, I will tell you if I have issues or concerns. You will know. We tell each other everything. There are no secrets between us. As you have learned, I don't hold back."

Anne appreciated that. He made her feel safe. Jennifer had said that most of the heaviness and grief Anne had released was at the spiritual level. Her emotional and physical bodies were pretty clear.

But the next day, Anne felt physically drained again, and was feeling down. She truly wished she knew what was going on with her.

Anne asked Archie if, when they met with Jane, she could talk about her sudden onset of flu symptoms the night his mother died. "Or would you prefer me not to?"

Archie said he was fine with it. "Our situation is definitely hard on you. That's why boundaries are essential at this time. You need to be aware of them, what they are, and what they mean."

With mid-August fast approaching, the second appointment Anne had scheduled in support of prepping herself for the book was with Jane. Upon arrival, she was disappointed that Archie wasn't there, and felt this didn't bode well. Although Anne did have a lot to talk about with Jane, and perhaps Archie was simply honouring her privacy.

Anne spoke of how very low she'd been feeling the past month or so. How she was experiencing waves of pain and grief and didn't know what to do with it all. She then shared her recent dream of an old building that was collapsing due to the crumbling of the pillars that supported it. Anne felt like she was that building.

"Your energy is extremely closed and narrow to your body, more so than I have ever seen," Jane observed.

Since Archie had given Anne permission to talk about his mother's death, she disclosed how she'd suffered flu symptoms the night his mother had passed. "I only met his mother once, when Archie's parents took us to the theater. I liked her. But frankly, it shocks me that I would become physically ill when she died."

"You were upset because Archie was very upset."

Anne thought about it. She felt there was a piece missing, but left it for now; maybe it was just another indication of the profound twin flame connection she and Archie shared. She then spoke of how, on reading Archie's mother's obituary, she'd learned where Archie was buried. She had also learned that her PhD supervisor was buried in the same cemetery, not far from Archie's grave.

Jane smiled and said, "Someone is saying 'We made it easy for you.' Now that you know where he's buried, will you go visit?"

"I'm not sure. At the moment, I'm feeling very worn-out and physically not up to it." And as she and Jane both knew, Archie wasn't in some burial plot.

For some reason, Anne began to talk about Archie's yellow car. Lately, she'd been thinking about the car, a space where they had done much of their interacting and kissing. She had been talking to her friend Helen about it, who asked, "Why are you obsessing about his car?"

Anne shook her head and said she really didn't know why.

Helen was silent for a moment, and then said, "Oh, it was your home—your and Archie's home."

Her words had resonated with Anne emotionally. So much so, she'd had to ask for a tissue.

Since then, Anne had given it further consideration. "When I think about our last date, I think about Archie and me kissing in his car. I love to think about it, as truly it was the most loving and intimate moment we ever shared. Each time I do, however, it always ends with Archie telling me I need to get out of the car, and driving off without looking at me. And that was the last time I ever saw him. It's a moment so very compelling to me for its beauty. Nonetheless, it's always juxtaposed with that very painful memory."

"Archie's here. He wants to know when we are going to talk about the book."

Anne sighed. She looked down at the list of topics she'd jotted down for the session. "Our book is next on the list."

Jane smiled, "Thank you, Archie, for keeping us on track."

Archie spoke of his concern for Anne's low energy. He explained that Anne needed to know this feeling within her, this knowing that she deserved better.

"What gives you joy, Anne?" Jane asked.

"He does. Archie gives me joy."

Jane looked to Archie. "He knows that. He wants to know why you're focussing on his car. Archie says you could have created a home anywhere. You were happy just being together." Though Archie conceded that when he told Anne to get out of the car, his words were harsh.

"About the book, Archie says there's freedom now that his mother is gone. But he's concerned for your safety. He says you have his permission to change the setting. Maybe you could set it in London. After all, it will be published as fiction."

Anne took a moment to contemplate this. She did know London, past and present—but no. "I won't do that. I have to write what I know. If I write our story, I'm going to tell it as it happened, period." Anne was very clear on that point.

And with that, Archie started to review what he saw as important points for Anne to know as she undertook a fictional telling of their story. He said their book would help people enormously.

"When we dated in 1975, I heard this voice that told me, 'You and Anne cannot continue.' It was a persistent thought in my head. I kept asking 'Why? Why am I having this thought?' My first thought was that you were too good for me. I just kept hearing, 'You and Anne cannot continue.' The voice never answered my question why. I hoped that the voice was wrong, and we would get back together at some later date."

Jane continued, "That's partly why, that summer, Archie says he felt driven to write you a letter. He hoped that upon receiving it, *you* would get in touch with *him*. He realizes now, however, that he had given you nothing. Seven years later, Archie says his worst fear was that you were alone and miserable. When he ran into you at the grocery store, he had two images as you walked past him: your wedding ring and a little boy. He knew then that you were a wife and mother. After he tailed you to Guelph and saw you were in a good place, he was able to move on with his life and family. Archie is saying that the letter, the grocery store, and the university coffee shop had been built-in tests for you, with regard to your contract. In each and every case, you both demonstrated a great deal of integrity. The coffee shop had been a gift for him, not you. But it was a test as well."

Archie said, "You know that if we had had sex, we would have stayed together and put aside our contract. Our love was so very intense."

Anne nodded—it was sad, but true. It grieved her. Perhaps it always would.

"Regarding the book, Archie says that when he came back to you, none of this was set. However, since you have been doing spontaneous writing for the past seven months, the book is now a go. It's a rather unique setup. He has been given special dispensation and has his own guides—and there's a council directing the book. The council has three members, one for each function: wisdom, support, and questions. He says that you already know that your relationship is a gift for the two of you; your book will be a gift to others.

"Archie says he lived his life with great integrity. All he had was his character. He says that while he will cowrite the book, you will hold the story, which details your growing awareness. Archie is telling you that it's important to honour your part in the story."

Jane laughed then. "Archie wants to know what you're going to give him for helping write the book."

Anne took his question seriously, but Archie was laughing. "Anne, I'm joking." Jane continued, "He wants you to know the book bodes well for your future."

Anne smiled, and said, "I have the feeling that Archie's mother blamed me for the breakup and breaking Archie's heart."

And then unexpectedly, Jane said Archie's mother was there, saying she just wanted her son to be happy.

Jane said Archie was shrugging. "He says he knew his mother blamed you and that, well, he may have let her think that, and did nothing to correct that impression."

Anne shook her head. Sometimes he could be so annoying. Anne had been up-front with her own mother about what had happened—that Archie had broken up with her.

"Are we close on the other side?" Anne asked.

Jane said Archie was using his hands. He put his palms flat together, leaving no space between them, to demonstrate just how close they were.

Anne sighed. She knew this to be true. As twin flames, they were two halves of one soul, a profound spiritual bond that only seemed to deepen with time. When he was near, she felt his presence, and most often knew, rather than heard, what he was thinking or saying. Although, sometimes, when between sleep and waking, Anne did actually hear Archie's voice, his words, particularly if it was a message he deemed essential for Anne to know.

It was then that Anne acknowledged what she knew to be the reason why Archie didn't go when he was fifty-nine. "Archie's wife had been driving the car and Archie wouldn't have gone, knowing his wife was with him. Considering his wife died shortly thereafter, I guess the accident would have been a possible exit whereby they could have gone together. Though, at the time, Archie couldn't have known that."

Jane said, "Archie is putting his hand to his heart and saying—that you would know this about him moves him greatly."

Anne said that, after hearing his wife had died soon after, she put the pieces together. Archie would never have intentionally hurt his wife so he could go. He took care of the people he loved. That was who he was.

Later that evening, Anne was reading a book on how to create a compelling protagonist. As a historian, she had never had to worry about the people she wrote about. They had been real people, and her mission had been to make them credible, using the sources at hand. But writing a novel about herself and Archie? What was she doing?! Days like this, she truly worried about herself.

She felt Archie's energy and pulled out her journal. After sessions with Jane, the two of them liked to do a personal recap of all that had been discussed.

"You touched me today, Anne, when you acknowledged that I didn't exit at age fifty-nine because my wife was driving the car—that you knew this about me."

"You always put others above yourself, Archie. You have a good heart, always did. Even after you broke up with me, seven years later you were living with your significant other, whom you loved. You stalled her wish to get married and have a baby until you knew I was in a good place—even though she was older and time was running out for it to happen. That was kindness. You were and are absolutely wonderful in every way, and I love you more with each day that passes. I know our relationship is a gift, and I will honour you and our book to the best of my ability. And I hear you about my need to be more discerning."

Anne had confessed to Jane today that she felt both Jack and her sister, Laura, were draining her energy. This was nothing new. But since her mother's death, Anne had been feeling more vulnerable. She knew the answer to this was boundaries. And as she began the writing of their book, she knew she'd have to be especially wary. Writing about all of this was going to be tough enough as she revisited her relationship with Archie.

That night, Anne slept fitfully. It seemed after every session with Jane, she always felt a bit of a letdown. She knew some of her feeling had to do with the fact that at Jane's, she and Archie interacted as a couple. When they were with Jane, it felt so real, maybe because Jane validated Archie's presence, shared his expressions. After spending such a concentrated amount of time together, the next day Anne felt lonely. She missed him, despite knowing they were together every night.

ACT III:
WRITING THE LOVE

CHAPTER 25

Writing the Book

Anne: I like looking at your obituary photo.

Archie: If I had known this would be the photo you hold dear, I would have tried harder to look happy.

Anne: It's your eyes mostly that hold me, and they are you—windows to your soul. Did you have a photo of me?

Archie: No. Quite frankly, I never needed one. You were always with me.

Anne: Archie, that's so beautiful. I had forgotten how tender and sweet you were, always, and are still.

—Anne Jeffrey, *Anne & Archie's Journal*, Vol. 4
(March 10, 2019)

The next morning, Anne, sitting at her desk, was perusing their journals. She'd finally started working on their book, and was giving serious thought as to how she might use their conversations to allow readers glimpses of the immense unconditional love of twin flames who find themselves in an across-the-veil relationship. What would that kind of love and relationship look like? The possibilities—the magic—were evidenced throughout the journals. Anne just needed to figure out *how* to use them.

She heard Archie say, "Maybe, just maybe, my yearbook photo will not be an improvement over my obit photo."

A couple of months ago, Anne learned that Archie and Jack had attended the same high school. And so, she'd initially hoped that she could find a yearbook photo of Archie's younger self. Unfortunately, Archie, being so much older, was long gone by the time Jack and his buddies were there.

She laughed. "Seriously, Archie, I'm so far from getting your yearbook photo, I don't think you need to worry about it."

Last night, Anne had been pondering the notion of body language as subtext in the art of crafting dialogue. This might prove challenging given Archie didn't have a body, at least one she could see.

"Well, we will just have to think outside the box. We're good at that."

Anne sighed. She kept forgetting their twin flame connection and that he knew almost everything she was thinking. Archie clearly wanted to chat; she could feel him beside her. She leaned back in her chair and waited.

Anne had always been very self-conscious of her writing and disliked anyone looking over her shoulder when she was doing it. Jack would often deliberately do this. He knew she hated it. His justification was that she needed to rid herself of what he considered to be a bad habit.

She had no idea if Archie did the same thing. She knew he read her writing—he told her he did. When? She had no idea.

After a minute, Archie said, "This book is about your growing awareness. So, up to now, what is the hardest thing you have had to deal with as you reflect on our relationship?"

Anne considered this. *Her growing awareness of what?* First, to discover that Archie had always loved her—had never stopped—and that his life had been hard without her in it. That had been devastating to learn. She knew this had distressed Archie as well, to discover that she'd gone forty-three years thinking he had never loved her, never cared for her.

After a moment or so, Anne replied, "The toughest thing, at this very moment, is my realization of the depression you suffered on account of me, starting with our breakup and continuing at various periods throughout your life. Though it's the emotional pain you suffered after our breakup and our grocery store encounter that disturbs me the most. Perhaps because those were the times I could have chosen a different response and could possibly have helped you—to check if you were okay."

Anne concluded that the hardest time she continued to grapple with was the time she ran into him in 1982. She could never forget Archie's eager smile, his face beaming with joy, his blue eyes looking at her with such love. When he'd stepped forward to embrace her, Anne remembered feeling panic—fear maybe. Archie was welcoming her into his arms, his heart, his life, and Anne had turned away—from great love, from Archie.

Of course, knowing what she knew now about their contract, she understood completely. Or did she? At the time, however, she'd never quite understood her reaction. It was not like her—not in her nature to be rude. Anne was generally polite and friendly. Even those times when she didn't recognize individuals who clearly seemed to know her, she would stop and say hello. So naturally, once she'd reached her car, seen Archie's truck, her first instinct had indeed been to go back and find him. But she hadn't.

If Anne had known, in any way, the deep emotional pain she'd caused Archie that day, and how he had been struggling to move on with his life because of her, she would have gone to him immediately. And perhaps they would have had coffee and had a chance to talk through all this. For that, she held some resentment, maybe anger at her guide. Nowhere, at any time after their breakup, had their guides allowed Anne and Archie a moment to connect and talk. As a result, there had been so much hurt, especially for him.

A couple of years after Anne had moved to Guelph, she'd once again had a desperate desire to get in touch with Archie. She'd had no idea why—she had just felt a deep urgent need to talk to him, to hear his voice. Anne, always diligent in recording phone numbers and addresses of everyone she knew, had failed to keep Archie's address, information he himself had written down for Anne on the envelope of the letter he'd sent her—again, very out of character for Anne.

One day when in Toronto, she'd looked him up in the phone book. There had been so many people listed under his name. She cold-called some, but couldn't find him. *Just as well.* As she now knew, Archie had moved on and had a family. After the grocery store, he had finally been able to let her go.

This truly had been a tough lifetime for both of them. Nevertheless, they had managed, each in their own way, to live a full life, to love and be well-loved in return. They had managed it with the help of their guides. Archie had said they had done everything to fulfil their soul contract. Hence, Anne should feel relief—not grief. But the pain and grief continued to come, like ocean waves ebbing and flowing, for the loss of what could have been. Their relationship had been so profound, so full of love, and held such promise. And lately, as Anne reflected upon her life, she was becoming increasingly aware of her own struggles to find a meaningful path, beyond being a mother and wife.

Over the last couple of decades, Anne realized she had had so many dreams in which she found herself moving through long convoluted hallways, endless stairwells, trying to find the room where she lived, to no avail. Upon Archie's return, she dreamed that he had met her, taken her hand, and led her into the elevator. He pressed the eighth-floor button, and once the doors opened, they walked down a hallway to a door to which he held the key. All the while, he never let go of her hand—assuring her he wasn't going to let go. That was it, but in so many ways it made Anne acutely aware of how lost she, her soul, had felt in Archie's absence.

Archie assured her, "I'm good now, Anne. Once I crossed, I felt only love for you. You need to let go of the pain and sorrow. This book tells the story of our love, in the past and the one that continues. Just because we parted, it was never over. Our deep love and relationship remain. That was the point of our soul contract. Could we hold our immense and unconditional love through incredible challenges, through separation and hurt, through other loves and lack of understanding? We know the answer to that now —the answer is yes! Our love is greater than all of the challenges. Our book will tell that story."

CHAPTER 26

Tenderness

Dear Archie,

I woke up to the word "tenderness." It's more than a word, though. It's a feeling that, in many ways, defined how we were, how we still are together.

You say I married an anti-Archie. But upon reflection, the way you broke up with me made me not trust tenderness. Jack is a lot of things, and our relationship works. It's loving and supportive, but I wouldn't characterize it as tender.

Truly, until today, I had not thought about that aspect of our relationship, Archie. However, now I'm remembering our first kiss, so sweet and tender, and also the gentle way you parted us in the car. You were smiling, and I guess I was too.

Anyway, I woke up and felt driven to write this down, because it's a feature of our love and needs to be shared. I don't think we can write the love without addressing the tenderness *that's ours. We can talk about this tonight, if you wish.*

Love,
Anne

At 11:30, during their special evening time, Anne read Archie the note she'd written earlier.

Archie: Tenderness—yes, Anne. We were, and are tender with each other. Kindness too! We have a beautiful relationship—it began that way, and remains that way to this day.

I wasn't happy at all with how I ended it with you. I had planned to do it in the car when I dropped you off on our last date. But, well, all I can say is that whenever I was in proximity with you—I loved you so much—I couldn't find the courage or desire. You have no idea how turned-on I was by our last kiss. So, that was the only way I could do it.

And after, I suffered tremendously. I felt like such a shit. And I did worry about you. You were true to your word and our contract. You made no attempt to get in touch with me. But at the time, neither of us knew about a contract. After coming home and seeing how you struggled, I felt your hurt and pain. It has been hard on both of us. I know too how difficult it has been for you to stay. You are heartbroken again. Everyone here is cognizant of how challenging it has been for you.

Anne: I was never angry when you broke up with me, just confused and sad. I think I turned it all back on me. That it had been my fault, that I wasn't good enough for you. So how are we doing, hon?

Archie: Anne, over here, everything is great. I'm not bragging. But I'm in awe of our love. It's a thing of wonder.

—Anne Jeffrey, *Anne & Archie's Journal,* Vol. 9
(July 20, 2019)

A year later, as Anne contemplated the remaining chapters of their story, she realized something was missing, something she needed to address. Archie had said to write the feelings; that facts don't matter. However, she couldn't write the feelings without talking about the tenderness that was theirs. In so doing, however, Anne had reached an emotional impasse.

"I hit a wall this afternoon, Archie. I hit a wall."

Archie knew. He was the one who had told Anne to turn off the computer and put the journals away. Yesterday, at Jane's, he'd been reluctant to answer Anne's question as to when the feeling of tenderness had been first felt by him, after his return. He knew with his answer, Anne would turn to their journals *again.* And he worried that this would lead to more stress for Anne—that in revisiting the journals, she might start to question what she had already written.

Nevertheless, against his better judgement Archie had answered Anne's question—about when, after his return, had he first felt tenderness for her. He'd told her that it had been early on, a month or so after they had begun journalling together. He had asked Anne to shred some pages from the journal. Anne had heard him and destroyed the pages. He knew then that he could trust her. This lifetime had left both Archie and Anne with trust issues, and so this was a big deal for Archie. Shortly thereafter, Archie was explaining something that was distressing to him, and Anne's eyes filled with tears. At that moment, he'd felt heard and understood by Anne.

Anne was aware of the moment Archie had been talking about. One night, he disclosed to her that after she'd snubbed him in the grocery store, he had slipped into an emotional breakdown. That he didn't even know how he finished out the day at work. How devastated and hurt he had been. How much he had suffered in the days and weeks following. He said he couldn't stop obsessing about her, and that he knew how stalkers felt. That was when he began to drive by Anne's parents' house.

To hear his revelation had been heart-wrenching for Anne. How could she have been so cold?! But truthfully, if she'd known any of this, she *would* have gone back into the store and taken him into her arms.

Going through the journals again, re-reading that passage had done Anne in. It was like she was reliving it all over again, feeling Archie's pain and feeling helpless, fully aware she could change none of it. There had been so much tenderness, then and now. And not for the first time, Anne felt she was missing a piece of the puzzle, but had no idea what. As a historian, this was when she would head to the library and do more research. For their novel however, she had no idea how to proceed.

~~~~~

Late October, a couple of days before her birthday, Anne made the decision to visit Archie's grave. They had never said goodbye. And so today, Anne was bound and determined—it was something she
~~~~~

had to do for herself, and for Archie. She felt driven to see where his body rested and to say goodbye.

Anne had a scheduled appointment in Toronto, a couple of blocks from the cemetery where Archie was buried. The night before, she'd googled the grave's location and had printed a map.

The next day was stunningly beautiful. It was cool, but the sun was shining, not a cloud in the sky. Anne turned right and drove through the gate of the old cemetery. It was larger than she'd imagined, covering many city blocks.

Parking her car near the office, she chose to walk. She loved autumn, and as a historian of death, she loved cemeteries. Even as a child, she'd loved going with her grandmother to visit family graves. She found the markers and the people buried there a source of endless fascination.

As Anne meandered along the paths in and around the stones, she felt happy. There were so many tall, stately trees, clad now in their autumn garb of yellows, oranges, and reds. Some of the stones were works of art. To the side of one was a life-size statue of an angel whose one hand rested on the tombstone, her head bowed as if in prayer. It was breathtaking, and Anne took a moment to gaze upon it, to note the names of the individuals the angel was mourning.

As Anne continued her search, she ran into a groundskeeper and showed him her map, asking if he knew where the plot was.

He laughed, patted her on the shoulder, and said, "Just keep walking in the direction you're heading."

After a few minutes, she finally came upon the gravestone of Archie's parents. The name MCALLISTER was etched in large letters across the top. Some months ago, Archie had said that if she went to the cemetery, she wouldn't find anything she didn't already know. As she looked at the inscription, she noted the dates had yet to be filled in for his mother.

Anne walked around to the other side of the gravestone. She looked down and saw a flat stone commemorating someone in the tomb erected behind that of Archie's parents. Anne walked back around and looked down to the ground stretching in front of the McAllister stone. And there he was.

Archie *did* have a stone to mark where he was buried. The flat, rectangular black granite marker bore Archie's full name, birthdate, and date of death. Someone had cared! *His mother,* Anne thought. She crouched down and gently touched his name. As she did so, a black squirrel hopped up to her.

"Hi, how are you? Are you gathering nuts for the winter?" The squirrel stopped, stood on its hind legs, and looked at her. His eyes were quite large, luminous, and looked so empathetic, as if he knew Anne loved the man buried here. When he moved around to the back of the stone, Anne thought he'd gone. But no, the squirrel came back. For some reason, Anne then thought, maybe Archie's spirit was with her at the grave and the squirrel had sensed him.

"Is Archie here?"

The squirrel observed her and moved closer. Anne gazed into his eyes and felt the squirrel asking if she wanted him to come into her lap. He started to move ever so slowly toward her.

Anne, get a grip. This is a squirrel! Anne eyes widened, and the squirrel picked up on her body language instantly. She swore the animal had shrugged his little shoulders, before he hopped away.

Anne looked down at Archie's marker and placed a kiss on it with her hand. She thought she'd held it together pretty well, until she started to walk away.

Suddenly she was overcome with emotion. It hit her that she'd said goodbye to Archie. Somehow, she knew she wouldn't return. She remembered she'd brought a tiny quartz heart, one she'd purchased a couple of years earlier, when up in the Austrian hills. At the last minute before leaving home, Anne had decided to bring it with her today, not really sure why.

Anne went back to Archie's marker and knelt. With her finger, she dug a crevice next to the stone and tenderly placed the heart in, and then covered it with dirt. A heart for a heart. She noted the squirrel had disappeared. And with that, Anne walked back to her car.

As Anne drove home, she wondered if Archie had manifested as the squirrel. With Archie she just never knew. He was continually surprising her.

"So, did you have fun today?"

Archie laughed, "So much! Did you?"

"Let me just say that when I first saw your marker, I laughed, because you were wrong. You said that if I visited your grave, I wouldn't learn anything more than I already knew. Today, I discovered the actual dates of your birth and death, which I had mistaken. Numerically, you're a ten, the Wheel of Fortune!"

"I could have told you I was a ten."

"Very funny! Well, if you were there, then you would have seen and understood my connection with this amazing black squirrel."

Archie laughed, and revealed to Anne that he *was* the squirrel. "Anne, seriously, you're so easy. You have such a childlike innocence. You had no idea."

No. She'd fully believed that the squirrel, living in a cemetery, would have learned empathy, that he had a special talent for offering compassion to those people grieving the loss of loved ones.

"You were so cute, Anne. I would have come into your lap."

"I felt the squirrel asking me if I wanted a hug. I had no idea it was you. Although, come to think of it, just last week at Jane's, you said that, as energy, you could be anything you wanted to be. Are the guides and council having a good laugh?"

"Actually, it says so much about you, who you are, and why you're so special. Why I love you!"

"Just to be clear, Archie, when I asked if you would physically manifest to me, do I have to be more specific, give you more direction?"

"Aw, sweetie, today was so perfect. I was there with you, and it was really lovely." Archie had not foreseen how special it would be, how joyous it was with Anne there. He had been concerned how Anne would be, but she was great. And the heart—days like today reminded him of how much and why he so loved Anne. "Thank you. I loved today."

"Thank *you,* Archie. I'm so used to not seeing you, it never occurred to me that you were the squirrel.

At the next meeting with Jane, as Anne shared the cemetery story, Archie corrected her. He said that he had not physically manifested as a squirrel—rather, he had asked the squirrel ahead of time if he could use the squirrel's body. And the squirrel had readily agreed. "Anne, the eyes you remarked on *were* the squirrel's eyes."

"Well, he was a cemetery squirrel. It probably wasn't the first time he had done this sort of thing."

Archie laughed. Anne was right. He most likely had not been the squirrel's first. Archie had felt strongly that the squirrel was teaching him. "As soon as I entered the squirrel's body, it was strange. I was hopping, and thought, *I don't hop!* But there I was, hopping."

That Archie had requested the squirrel's permission to use his body, and that the squirrel would be so gracious to do this for her, a stranger—it was humbling. "I'm glad you enjoyed the experience as much as I did."

"As I have said, I never liked cemeteries. Whenever I went, people were always crying and in pain. But you were so happy to be there, and how you engaged with the squirrel! Both you and the squirrel were teaching me."

~~~~~

Archie recognized that Anne was coping with a lot of stress on the home front. In addition to finishing their book and addressing some computer snags, there was the COVID-19 pandemic, and all of the ramifications that came with it. She had been incredibly anxious of late, affecting her quality of sleep.

One night, as he accompanied Anne's soul back to her body, he'd felt Anne was about to jump out of her skin and had tried something new.
~~~~~

As Anne felt her soul return to her body, she couldn't be still. Lying on her stomach, she felt a physical weight press firmly down on her back.

Archie. Each time she moved, she felt Archie's energy press gently and firmly down, as if he was lying on top of her, holding her. Feeling him, his physical weight, soothed and calmed Anne, and soon after she fell asleep. When she woke, Archie was still with her. He had stayed the entire night.

At Jane's, Anne spoke with Archie about the new physical manifestation of his energy.

Jane said, "Archie says that night, he felt as if you were going to jump out of your skin, and he wanted to let you know that he was there with you, and to remind you, 'Be here now.'"

"I loved feeling him. It soothed me, and I fell asleep in his energy."

The next morning, Anne had written a note, expressing how wonderful it had been to feel him, to feel his loving presence throughout the night. And since that day, whenever Anne was jittery, she felt Archie's physical weight and support, letting her know he was there for her. That he had her back.

"I'm still learning, Anne." Tenderness!

CHAPTER 27

The Soul Contract of Anne and Archie

I seemed to be an observer standing on a riverbank. It felt to be a sacred river in India, the Ganges perhaps. A man and a woman were on a boat, and it seemed like they were getting married. For certain, they were a union (wedded maybe, but definitely a couple). Hand in hand, they jumped into the water, and then continued to circle together, in and out of the river. Their love for each other and the joy they felt being together was palpable. In my mind, I wondered if the river was polluted, but the couple didn't seem to care. They just kept joyously jumping and cycling from under the water to up in the air, their bodies forming a circle. I could feel their love and joy. It was celebratory.

—Anne Jeffrey, *Anne &Archie's Journal,* Vol. 3
(November 14, 2018)

Anne woke at five a.m. and almost instantly felt Archie's energy. She recalled the joy she felt when they kissed and held each other. She felt more than heard his words that imparted the message that he would be with her for the duration of her life here. He wasn't going anywhere. Anne became quite emotional and thanked him. Somehow, she knew the couple in the dream to be Archie and herself.

I was in a huge stadium on the upper tier, looking down. The whole place seemed empty. I turned around. Four or five rows up, at the very back of the stadium wall, sat a man who looked like Archie, although he seemed older than I remembered. He had a fairly big dog sitting beside him. The dog looked like a mixed-breed, but mostly a golden lab. It appeared to be very old. I walked back to ask the man if that was his dog. He said yes. I asked the dog's name and he replied "Casey—he likes chasing balls." Then I noticed a young man; he looked to be about sixteen, maybe older. He was standing in the same row near the dog, but was respectful in giving Archie and me space.

—Anne Jeffrey, *Anne &Archie's Journal,* Vol. 3
(November 17, 2018)

A year or so later, at Jane's, Anne asked Archie who had met him when he crossed the veil. He answered that it had been his father and his dog, Casey, with whom he had developed a very special bond in life. Anne was amazed as she remembered the dream Archie had communicated to her.

"Archie is asking if you know what the stadium represents," Jane said.

Anne thought for a minute but had no idea.

"The enormous stadium reflects the size of our relationship," Archie explained.

~~~~~~

"We are writing the story of our love through the ages, as experienced in this lifetime." This was Archie's answer whenever Anne asked why staying to write their book was so important. A little daunting to say the least, considering he had yet to reveal the specifics of their soul contract. For some reason, Archie wasn't being very forthcoming. She had no idea why.

It had been almost two years since his return, and now that Anne was actively engaged in writing their story, she was feeling anxious about being kept in the dark. Her need to more fully understand their soul contract was growing every day.

To be honest, Archie was stalling.

Before Anne had started doing the spontaneous writing, Archie had tried to impart the enormity of their contract to Anne through dreams. The first dream represented the joyous, loving relationship that he and Anne had shared, both in the water (on Earth) and in the air (in spirit). It also sought to depict the many lives they had spent together, cycling from one plane to another, over and over again. The second dream, of the stadium, spoke to the vastness and depth of their relationship and love.

It was early November and, with another Christmas season advancing, Anne's grief seemed to be slowly lifting. The council was pleased about how both she and Archie were handling this last part of the contract. But with the writing of the book, the emotional triggers being set off for Anne caused Archie to suggest that, for the foreseeable future, she should see Jane every month. It was at these sessions where Archie would finally stop stalling and at last release the details of their contract.
~~~~~~

~~~~~

When Anne arrived, Jane let her know that for the last couple of months, Archie had been coming early to her appointments.

"What does he do?"

"He just likes to hang out. He is very respectful. Sometimes we chat."

"Should I worry?"

Jane laughed, knowing neither Anne nor Archie had experienced jealousy of the other. Their love was unconditional. As such, they had honoured the respective partners of the other and those bonds.

As Anne settled into her chair, she pulled out a rather lengthy list of questions. "I'm trying to pull all the loose ends together and finish *our* book in earnest now, and I have questions that need answers."

Before she could start, Jane said, "Did you know Archie came to the spiritual workshop this past Saturday? I saw him come in and welcomed him. Archie's so funny. He said, 'They let me out and Olivia let me in!'"

Anne had wondered if he'd been there. In a discussion about soul contracts, Anne had spoken about Archie and his not knowing what his soul contract had been until he had crossed the veil. The dichotomy of his life had been that what he thought had been a major mistake in his life had turned out to be the honouring of his contract. As she was speaking that day, she'd felt Archie's energy beside her.

"Archie's present, but quiet and subdued," Jane said.

This raised a red flag for Anne, but she said nothing. Instead, she asked Archie about their contract.

"Archie wants you to know that soul contracts span more than one lifetime, and for both of you this has been a huge learning lifetime, and you have both grown in self-knowledge. Your contract was about eternal relationships."

Archie began to talk through and pull together the pieces of the soul contract that they had assembled over time, through the writing of the journals. Through Jane, Archie explained, "The
~~~~~

contract was a test of an eternal relationship—an experiment, if you will. The guides called us in to ask if we would be willing to do this, in order to test an eternal relationship—to be apart and still loving of each other. We both agreed immediately and then turned to each other and thought, *How will we do this?*

"It was really a very clever plan. This life was the last piece of the contract, which spanned hundreds of lifetimes. This lifetime asked if we could be together, feel the depth and intensity of our love, and then spend the rest of our lives apart, while still holding each other in love. While as twin flames we learned aspects of unconditional love and eternal relationships as we spent time *together* in past lifetimes, a much tougher test is to see if we could hold that knowing while being apart. And harder yet, when we were allowed to have firsthand knowledge of the incredible love we shared, and then be asked to continue to live it while being apart. It was an incredible test of our bond. No wonder our guides were concerned for us.

"You remember me telling you that just before we incarnated, we had a big meeting with all our guides—yours, mine, and the ones we share? They wanted us to be fully aware that this was a big thing we were doing. That it was going to be very difficult. They asked if we still wished to proceed. While our major guides felt we were ready, other minor guides revealed all the various pitfalls we could possibly confront. We knew this last piece had to be done and we were anxious to complete the contract, so we agreed to move forward with it. There's great comfort knowing that, in each lifetime, the council asked if we were willing to go ahead. At any time, we could have chosen not to continue.

"I know I have said this before, but it bears repeating. This lifetime truly was an incredible test of our bond, our relationship. There was no time limit as to when we would break up. The timing of our breakup was dependent on the intensity level, with our remembering the intensity and depth of our love and relationship. The remembering of how much our love mattered was integral. If we didn't feel the intensity, knowing how much our love mattered, then being apart wouldn't have had the impact it did.

"It really was a very clever plan we set up. While we participated in the broad strokes of its orchestration, we didn't know all the pieces. It was our guides who filled in the missing pieces. They wanted to make it hard for us without pushing us over the edge. The real backstory of this lifetime was how spirit has been active in life, nudging the two of us along to this point in time. Our contract had not specified the length of time we would be together. There was no discussion about sex in the contract. We were free to engage in it, if required. The key stipulation was that we *each* had to remember the intensity of our love. That was essential. Otherwise, the second part of the contract would have had little significance."

Jane said, "Archie says that your first kiss was the beginning of your remembering. He told you that he felt the kiss before your lips touched."

Anne nodded. She had felt the remembering. But since Archie had been her first boyfriend, how could she have possibly known the intensity of that love, until she had had something to compare it to? When Jack had first kissed Anne, she'd thought that he simply couldn't kiss—didn't yet know how. So she'd never fully comprehended the depth of her feelings for Archie—until she'd called him on the phone—twice—in the early months of her marriage. And for that, she'd been both confused and quite angry with herself—*what was she doing?* Archie had broken up with her; he had made it clear he never wanted to see or hear from her again. That first year of marriage though had been a struggle for Anne. *No wonder!*

The Tests

After the breakup, there were built-in tests or challenges. These tests were the missing pieces set in place by the guides. In terms of the breakup, Archie had been deemed responsible for that part of it. In point of fact, the breakup itself was the first test for Anne and Archie. It asked them to separate, all the while knowing how profoundly they loved each other. Of Archie, the voice asked— would he listen? And even though he had not understood, he did listen. Of Anne, the breakup asked if she loved Archie unconditionally and would honour and respect his decision to end their relationship. And she had.

The second test was the letter. After two months of missing her, Archie had felt compelled to write a letter. He wanted her to know how much he thought of her. If Archie was totally honest, he had hoped that his letter would open the door between them, and Anne would contact him, and was angry when she didn't. Of course, now he understood that her lack of response maintained their soul contract, and he saw it very differently.

Archie said, "One of our thoughts of how we could manage being apart and still hold each other in love was to become friends after a certain period of separation had passed."

The grocery store was a test originally designed to ask if Anne and Archie could be friends after a seven-year separation. In their plan, it was hoped that both of them would have moved on in terms of marriage and family, and this might be a viable possibility. While Anne had moved on, this had had not happened for Archie. After seven years, Archie was in a relationship but had been unwilling to fully commit—he was holding back. In part, he worried about Anne. He kept telling the voice he just needed to see her.

"Archie says at the grocery store, the guides were stepping in through you, Anne, to let him know you had moved on, and that he needed to let you go and move forward with his own life. That was a very hard day for him. Up to that time, Archie had always held the hope that the two of you would get back together. He says your soul connection was so strong, he knew you were there at the store before he saw you."

After that meeting, Archie, with a clear mind and heart, was able to let Anne go and marry his girlfriend. The next twenty years or so, Anne and Archie were both kept very occupied and preoccupied with their lives, their growing families, and neither of them really thought about the other—they had finally passed that test.

The third test was for Archie. Anne's tough time would come later. In his mid-fifties, Archie began dreaming of Anne, and this caused him to start *seriously* questioning if he had heard wrong and made a mistake letting her go. He had always questioned it, but the dreams brought the question back to him strongly. When they had dated, Archie had always found Anne enchanting, and with the dreams of Anne the enchantment returned, as did the voice. Archie began to wonder—what if they had stayed together?

"Archie concedes that this could have been a danger point for him. And ultimately it led to your meeting at the university coffee shop. This meeting had not been in the plan, but the guides realized it needed to be allowed. Because Archie got the messages through the voice, he needed confirmation that he had done the right thing all those years ago. Seeing you again, knowing you were okay and living a life of purpose, kept Archie going for a long time. He came away having a sense that this was right. He had made the correct decision. You were doing okay, and knowing that helped him enormously. All of a sudden, Archie says he was fine and could go on."

The last test was Anne's. Would she go after Archie's death, or stay to complete the last piece of the contract? Did she have the courage to stay, all the while knowing this would be her most challenging time? Anne realized that this test was still ongoing—a part of every day of her life—and although she still had bad days, she was proud that she'd made the choice to stay.

The Exit Points

Archie said that, given the very difficult aspect of their contract, exit points (those times in a life when a situation arises that would allow a person to leave this world and go Home to the other side) were set in place for each of them at various times in their lives. At this point, Anne acknowledged that in an earlier session, Archie had revealed that one of his exit points had been in his mid-forties, circa 1993.

"Archie is nodding. He had a very high fever with pneumonia. At the time, he felt okay about going. But then the guides stepped in and took away the fever, making it harder for him. He wants you to know that this was an example of your guides not making it easy for you. And he says you know about the exit point when he was fifty-nine and a semi missed his car by an inch."

As Archie spoke of exit points, Jane had a thought. "You know, Anne, for your novel, it might prove interesting for you to chart your exit points. It would be a way to chronicle the intricacies and cleverness of the plan, skillfully designed and executed."

Anne thought that an excellent idea. She too was curious to discover how their exit points coincided with each other's life. Knowing Archie's, Anne gave serious consideration as to when and where exit points had come up for her.

After 1982, Archie said he shut the voice down and for twenty years didn't think about Anne. In letting Anne go, he had finally moved forward with his life. It was then that Anne was given an opportunity to exit.

In 1983, Anne and Alex had spent the day out with Anne's mother. It was afternoon rush-hour and her mom was driving Anne's car on the highway. A transport truck hit the side of their car and sent them spinning, heading full speed straight into oncoming traffic—into another car. At the time, Anne was pregnant with Lizzie. She remembered turning to look at three-year-old Alex strapped in his car seat. Not wanting anything to happen to Alex and her unborn child, she'd chosen to stay. And just like that, her car had stopped an inch away from a head-on collision. She recalled how deeply upset her mom had been after the accident, how apologetic she was to Jack.

Five years later, in 1988, another opportunity presented itself in the form of an ovarian tumour. Again, Anne chose to continue.

In 1993, when Archie had pneumonia and an opportunity to exit, Anne was doing her masters' degree in history and was beginning to make her mark in academia, garnering attention from her professors. As she now knew, she was actively engaged in acquiring the skills she would need to write the love story of Anne and Archie, the book she was born to write. If she'd gone in 1988, Anne wondered if perhaps Archie would have chosen to go in 1993.

Archie's next exit was in 2006, when he was fifty-nine. This was three or four years after he had seen Anne at the coffee shop, so he knew she was doing well. Anne was curious and asked whether, if Archie had gone then, they would have done the book earlier. He said no. It would have been too early to go to her about the book. He would have had to wait on the other side until 2017, a year before another exit possibility opened up for Anne, as per their soul contract.

Anne's last exit had been selected at about the same time as Archie's death. If she'd been unprepared to write the book, she'd organized an exit close to his, whereby they would be together after living full lives apart. Now that the contract was completed, free will entered into the domain. Though they had promised each other that, if the contract had been successfully completed, they would write a book, there was no obligation.

It was fascinating to see the interweaving of these exit points, and their timing.

Through Jane, Archie said, "It speaks well of us, Anne, that we both moved on to live full lives independent of each other." Jane continued, "Archie thinks sometimes you give him more credit than he deserves, that you see him through rose-coloured glasses."

Anne listened, but remained quiet. All of this was a lot for her to take in.

At the end of the session, Anne expressed a fear that Archie was withdrawing his energy. Some nights, she could barely feel him.

"What's going on, Archie?" Jane asked.

"Things have shifted, and we're not planning our next life. Anne, kids are still on the table. If you like, we could import your kids (Alex and Lizzie) to be *our* children in our next incarnation together. At present though, my job is to be supportive of you."

Archie explained that he had the power to connect with Anne on such a deep level, he could create in her such an intense longing for him that it would make it unbearably hard for her to stay. And that was a no-no, considering she had a book to write.

Again, Anne wasn't happy, but chose to let it go for the moment. "What are we doing on the other side, Archie?"

"We are not doing, Anne. We are being. We are enjoying being together."

Later that evening, Anne and Archie talked privately about all that had been revealed about their soul contract, as it related to this lifetime. Truthfully, Anne was feeling a bit shell-shocked, and so it was Archie who began the conversation.

"I want you to know, Anne, that with the completion of our book we will have successfully completed our enormous contract. That's no mean feat. I know you believe that I had a harder time of it. Nevertheless, I'm fully cognizant of how very difficult it has been for you. You must honour the challenges you have confronted and overcome. And don't underestimate your accomplishments. That was all you. Once you moved past the hurt and grief felt at our separation, you forged forward, ever determined to finish the contract and be ready to write our book upon my return. In your high school yearbook, a friend of yours wrote 'You're a real wiz!' And you are. Even Merlin acknowledged your being and your light. Yes, Anne, I know your soul, your heart, and what it has taken to get yourself here—to get us here, where we are now. And I couldn't be more proud."

Overwhelmed by Archie's praises, Anne quickly changed the subject. She had been thinking about their contract, specifically as it related to sex. Archie had said the contract had made no stipulation regarding sex.

"Had we fully expected to have an affair before we parted?"

Archie confirmed that had been the plan. But neither they nor their guides had foreseen the power of their connection. They had underestimated them and their love. It was the guides' decision to end the relationship before they had sex. Certainly, Anne and Archie had been on the verge of it when they parted ways.

"So, Archie, I guess you could say our love is of epic proportion. How lovely if we could be remembered for that, for our love of each other."

CHAPTER 28

Anne and Archie Challenge the Council

Anne: Are you here? I'm having trouble feeling your energy tonight.

Archie: I'm here. I have learned the art of subtlety.

Anne: Really. Well, for now, could you amp it up just a touch more? Otherwise, I feel like my crazy is showing.

Archie: (Laughter)

—Anne Jeffrey, *Anne & Archie's Journal,* Vol. 16
(November 2019)

It was mid-November and as the days grew shorter and darker, Anne felt a growing dissonance that something was amiss. It was almost two years since Archie's re-entry into her life, and she was beginning to feel a shift in terms of his presence and energy. At their last session, Jane too had noted that Archie was quiet and subdued, which was so not him.

Anne was concerned. Just a month ago, Archie had been brimming with excitement, actively engaged in planning their next life together. He kept interrupting Jane and Anne with questions like, "Genders—should we switch? Or the same gender?"; "Kids?"; "Ireland?" His exuberance was infectious and Anne found herself being drawn in, regardless of the fact that she'd yet to finish her current life. Reflecting back, Anne had always loved Archie's enthusiasm and passion for life, for her. After knowing all that had gone on with their contract, it filled her heart with joy to feel his delight and anticipation of their being together in a next life.

Anne had first sensed a shift in Archie's energy in the evening when they were journaling. Some nights, she wondered if he was even there. This was an emotional trigger for Anne. Archie's withdrawal of energy reminded her of the time shortly before their breakup when he would periodically become quiet, withdrawn, and sad—the preface to his breaking up with her. Anne couldn't help but think that Archie was preparing to leave her, now that she'd agreed to stay and do their book. Given that she was still in the midst of writing, Anne felt she was being abandoned.

When Anne voiced her worry, Archie explained that once on the other side, souls like theirs — "they want us to take on projects." At the moment, in addition to supporting Anne and their book, Archie had been asked to take on a couple of assignments. What Archie didn't share with Anne in-body (different from Anne in-spirit) was that he was feeling overloaded. Now that she'd expressed her growing unhappiness, Archie replied, "I'm not thrilled about the situation either."

That day at Jane's when Archie said that he had the power to connect with Anne at such a deep level that he could make her go before she finished their book, she'd been slightly taken aback. She had always considered herself to be fairly strong and independent. She had trouble believing anyone could make her do anything she didn't want to do. After forty years of marriage, Jack would vouch for that.

The inconsistency of Archie's energy was beginning to unnerve Anne. She was suffering from insomnia, having frequent spats with Jack, and was still complaining to Archie that she should have gone when she'd had the chance. Nevertheless, the council of guides didn't seem to clue in to Anne's rising stress levels, even though they were fully aware that this lifetime had severely tested Archie's and Anne's bond, and there were still underlying trust issues where Anne was concerned.

There was, however, a perfectly good reason for their neglect of all these signals. In all of their experience, the council conceded that they had never known anyone who could move in and out of body and back and forth across the veil with as much ease as Anne did. Anne in-body had no idea how truly remarkable her soul was in its innate ability to bridge the two worlds. As such, they had come to view her as one of them and thus, impervious to the ego-related vicissitudes of love and life on Earth.

One evening as Anne and Archie were conversing, Archie again sought to clarify exactly why he was toning down his energy. "Anne, I keep forgetting how deeply connected we are."

"I know, and I love feeling your energy. But I'm strong, Archie. I can handle it. And if you need to tone it down, I will let you know." She continued, "This is *our* relationship. I trust you. It took a bit, but I have come to rely on you to get me through this time and the writing of our book. Does that work for you?"

Archie promised he would crank up his energy to "normal." "Will that make you happy?"

"Ecstatic! Otherwise everything just gets too heavy. Now, you said something else in the session that I would like to address." Last time at Jane's, Archie had mentioned that he thought Anne gave him too much credit. That she saw him through rose-coloured glasses. At the time, Anne had chosen not to respond.

"I'm talking to you as the woman who loves you. And because I love you, I do see you through rose-coloured glasses, lenses of love. And you also said I give you too much credit. Perhaps you don't give yourself enough credit for all that you are and have been. As your twin flame, I'm your mirror, Archie. I'm merely reflecting back to you who you are. This is who I see. You ground me in love, joy, and gratitude. Not an easy feat, but you do that. I like to think we are mirrors of each other's magnificence, you for me and me for you.

"So that's it. I think I'm done. Are you mad at me?"

Anne always brought out a deep feeling in Archie that he needed to protect her. If they had stayed together, he would have wanted to take care of her. Knowing the woman she'd become, he was pretty sure she would have challenged him on this, as she was doing now. When it came to her love for him and for them as a couple, Anne could be fierce.

"Never. Okay, do we feel better now? Note I said 'we.'"

"Do we?"

"Yes, we're great, hon."

"Great. And if the council has an issue with what I've said, then they should speak with me. I know you said you have the power to connect with me so intensely that you could make me go before I finish the book. But you have always exercised good judgement. Still, you have gone too far the other way now." And with that, Anne put her pen down and turned out the light. As was their practice, Archie stayed with her until she slept and her spirit left with his to go to their sky-home. Somehow though, he knew this wasn't the end of the matter.

Despite Archie's assurances that all was well, he did have serious reservations. Recently, the council had assigned him two projects, over and above his supporting Anne and their book. To be honest, it was more than he could handle. When he said something to that effect, the council told him the work would help him manage his connection with Anne.

Archie had tried to explain the matter to Anne in their last session with Jane. But in true Anne fashion, she was buying none of it, and told him as much when they were together at night in their sky-house.

Anne had a foot in both worlds, and Archie was so proud of her. However, he also appreciated the wisdom of what the council was saying. Anne wasn't sleeping, often waking two or three times during the night. She had said on more than one occasion that she was exhausted. Archie expressed his fear that she was burning the candle at both ends, and something was going to break. He just hoped it wasn't Anne herself. But when he suggested she cut down their time together on the other side, Anne told him it wasn't an option. And since Archie felt the same, he wasn't going to fight her on that.

When Anne finally blew up—lost it—neither Archie nor the council should have been surprised. Be that as it may, they were.

It was past midnight when Jack and Anne arrived home. They had been up north for dinner with nursing friends Anne had known most of her life. She loved them dearly, as well as their husbands, and had always taken great pleasure in their get-togethers. Tonight, however, she'd felt somewhat detached. She had tried to enjoy herself, but a deep disquiet was simmering within. Jack hadn't seemed to notice, so perhaps the others hadn't either.

Arriving home late, Anne was utterly spent when she finally crawled into bed. As she pulled out her journal, Archie immediately picked up on her mood.

"What's wrong, Anne?"

"Honestly, I don't know. Except that when you talk of things shifting over there with regard to me, it makes me nervous."

Archie assured her that nothing had shifted.

"Well, on Tuesday you said things had shifted, that we were not planning our next life, and now your job was to be supportive of me. At the same time, however, you have been told to manage our connection by toning down your energy."

Archie was abundantly clear that Anne wasn't happy. Even so, he had to convince her of the wisdom behind the shift. "Oh, that. Well, you said you were feeling deluged with decisions about our next life, while still living your present one and writing our story.

Being together in spirit at night, I forget sometimes. For me, Anne, you're a kind of super-woman—a goddess, if you will (going back to your goddess circle days). And I did mention that kids are still on the table."

Anne was yawning and said she had to go to sleep. They would have to continue this conversation later.

Despite her fatigue from lack of sleep, Anne woke up at two in the morning and, after an hour and a half of tossing and turning, she got out her journal to talk.

"I feel you're here with me. Not sure I can do this. I need your help, Archie—I'm so tired. Sitting at the dining room table with all my dearest friends, I tried to feel engaged, but a part of me was coming up empty. I feel there's a disconnect happening within me. What is with me getting up in the middle of the night, feeling anxious?"

Archie knew he had to answer Anne. The truth was that council feared Anne would die before the book was completed. Her soul had been ready to go Home even before Archie had returned to her. She had stayed to write their book, but lately Anne was failing—her exhaustion profound. And so, Archie was taking no chances. Some nights in their sky-house, Archie would just sit with her. Often, he would accompany Anne back to her body very shortly after she crossed the veil. But then Anne would wake up anxious, because she didn't understand what was going on. And so, Archie reassured her as best as he could.

"Anne, what you are doing in your life, what you are writing about—our love and relationship—well, it's revolutionary. And the soul contract has been physically, emotionally, and spiritually hard on you. Once the book is complete, you'll feel better. I promise."

The next night had started out well enough. As per their routine, Anne closed the door, signalling to Archie it was their time. Anne crawled into bed and read a Mary Oliver poem.

"I loved that."

"I'm converting you, am I?"

"Yes, in large part because Oliver's poetry has become something special we share together." Archie admitted that in life, he had never been a fan of poetry. However, when Anne read a poem to him, he loved the intimacy of it.

Archie then got serious. "I'm worried. I feel you're stretching yourself too thin, Anne."

"It's been a challenging day, and I've had a lot to think about."

"I know you're in a lot of pain. But you weren't ready to go, just as I wasn't ready when I had the chance at fifty-nine years old. I grieved as you grieve now."

Despite all reassurances by Archie that everything was fine, Anne's intuition told her it wasn't. Archie's energy had toned down to the point where some nights it felt nonexistent. And this wasn't Archie, at least not the one who had returned to her almost two years ago. At the time, he'd said he couldn't be apart from her for any length of time. Archie was attributing her mood to grief, but she'd told him, in no uncertain terms, that she wasn't happy with the new arrangement.

A couple of nights later, Anne tossed and turned in bed for over an hour, *again.* Exasperated, she threw back the covers, got up and sitting on the edge of the bed, spoke directly and firmly to the council and Archie.

"Okay, I've had it! I am not happy with this arrangement. I have committed to stay and write this book, and the withdrawal of Archie's energy wasn't part of the deal. I'm fulfilling my end, but you, on the other hand, are not. And it's *not* fair, and *not* acceptable!"

And with that, Anne left the room, closed the door behind her, and went downstairs to the basement couch. She had intended to turn the television on, but quickly fell into a sound sleep with the light still on.

Much later—she had no idea what time it was—Anne was wakened by Archie. She had been sleeping on her stomach when she felt his energy merge with hers from behind.

There was no mistake. Archie was mustering all his energy to make nice. It was working. There were just no words.

Anne was never sure what happened that night. Nevertheless, it would seem the situation had been resolved, and things quickly returned to normal. Although Anne was pretty sure that none of this could ever be construed as normal.

~~~~~

Only at the next appointment with Jane did Anne learn what had truly transpired that night when, in her own words, she kind of lost it and told the council off. It was a month before Christmas at what now had become a monthly meeting. Anne spoke of her experience, part of which related to the last session when Jane herself had remarked on Archie being quiet and subdued.

"After my spouting off, I guess I won't be dying any time soon. The council probably sees me as a troublemaker."

Jane laughed. She observed Archie was back to being Archie.

Anne recounted how disgruntled she'd been with the council—how she'd expressed, in no uncertain terms, that they were not holding up their end of things, whereas she was.

Jane nodded. She had definitely noted that Archie had not been the usual outgoing, funny man she'd come to know and love.

By way of explanation, Archie said that he'd been instructed to manage his energy and connection with Anne.

"What does 'manage your connection' mean exactly?" Jane asked.

Archie went on to say that the council had said he needed to get very clear about the fact that their connection was very intense, and that this might make things much more difficult for Anne, who still had soul work to do on Earth. When Anne confronted the council, she gave them all a reality check.

Archie had told them that he felt they were asking more of him than he could give. Anne reminded the council that she couldn't complete the book without Archie's full support. Archie would tell
~~~~~

anyone who cared to listen that few people knew the spiritual warrior Anne was. It was enough to say that when Anne went before the council, she didn't mince her words. Both she and Archie were seeking clarity as they moved forward.

And at the end, the council admitted that they were not perfect, and in this matter had erred, and that this episode was a good reminder of Anne's vulnerability. As such, she required the full support of Archie. The book had to be *their* book.

By the end of the night, Archie loved the fact that all had been resolved. He knew with clarity that his main focus was to help Anne finish the book. And Anne was happy too.

CHAPTER 29

Self-Love and Self-Care

Anne: Would you like to start, Archie?

Archie: Is this practice for our book?

Anne: If you like. Although at this late date, I'm not sure any amount of practising is going to help. You said this story is about my growing awareness. That I hold the story. Oh, my nails are a mess. Don't even know what I was doing that I would get them this dirty.

Archie: (Laughing) I feel like we're married, now that you bring up your dirty nails. I guess you have stopped trying to impress me.

Anne: Archie, you're in-spirit, and this is the authentic me. It's easy for you—I can't see you. For all I know, your fingernails could be dirty, but I assume there's no dirt on the other side.

Archie: You are absolutely correct. I have an unfair advantage. I apologize. And I love that about you. In many ways, you're pretty real, in a cute, funny way!

—Anne Jeffrey, *Anne & Archie's Journal,* Vol. 10
(September 8, 2019)

With one foot in each world, Anne fully conceded that she didn't always exemplify grace and gratitude. As she contemplated Christmas and the approaching New Year and decade, she was ambivalent. Unlike a year ago when Anne had wavered in her decision to stay, a year later she was mindful of the task set before her, before both Archie and herself. They were in the midst of writing their story.

Still, she hesitated. She had no idea why. Archie had assured her that he and the council were supporting her in the endeavour. This morning, however, she felt she'd come to a complete standstill.

Anne found it somewhat ironic that, at the very moment her twin flame returned to profess his love for her, her grief had initiated a growing consciousness about self-love and self-care. Maybe it was the twin flame thing where one is supposed to surrender to self, go within, and do soul work. And this was hers. Even Archie was advising her to take care of herself. He often joked, "We still need your body, Anne." She contemplated whether her life without Archie was about learning and actualizing self-love, self-mastery. In loving herself unconditionally, she could then be wholly present in her wisdom, her authenticity, and her relationships.

As Anne continued to write and ponder what *was* her growing awareness, she was once again experiencing a shift in focus to self-love and self-care. In *Your Soul's Gift,* Anne had read that, as one experiences courage, one experiences self-love. Had her brave decision to stay caused a redirection of attention and energy? Feeling the need for clarity, Anne meditated, asking her spirit guide for some guidance about self-love. Her guide was smiling as she related the following to Anne.

Since you were a small child, aged four or five, you have always sacrificed what you need for the sake of others. In doing this, you have been kind, generous, and in that time, it was necessary. But now—and truly you have been ready for this in the last ten years— it's time for you to separate your identity from those you have pulled along and tended to for so long. This doesn't mean you can't love them, be in a relationship with them, or be in communication with them. But you cannot surrender yourself any longer because of their need.

As you love yourself more, know that to be a model for what's next, for what's possible—a model of happiness and ease— which is really quite natural for you. But because you have been carrying so many, pulling them along in your knapsack, you haven't had a chance to model these things. And so, right now, the best way to love yourself is to model for yourself and others the ease of self- care and self-love. Happiness and joy are what is needed.

And yes, there will be pushback, but just carrying on and being committed to yourself is the best way of loving others. It's showing them another way, another door for themselves. It's time, Anne, well past time—please walk through that door for yourself.

~~~~~

"I wish you could see yourself as I see you." That was one of the first things Anne heard Archie say to her upon his return. And she wished she could too.

As her twin flame, Archie, more than any other, could reflect her authentic soul to her. For Anne, this past year, she felt her love for Archie ever deepen, something she marvelled at. How could it be? But it was.

She lived in two worlds. At night, she was with Archie, and during the day she was a loving wife, mother, nana, and writer.
~~~~~

She knew she needed to look at self-love. And now was the time. She still had no idea what self-love looked like, but as always, when one stated an intention, the universe provided opportunity and space for it to manifest.

As Christmas neared, Anne initiated some conscious changes. Every year, when putting up their Christmas tree, she and Jack ended up in an argument. Last year had pretty much done her in. Archie had recently confided that, in life, he had always envisioned Anne and her family having idyllic Christmases. That first Christmas back, though, Archie had witnessed the fighting, quickly dispelling any illusions he had held.

And so it was that Anne decided not to put up the big Christmas tree. Jack was thrilled. Instead, Anne set up a small Christmas tree in their room—Archie's and Anne's. Strung with white fairy lights, it sat on the desk by the window, and every night as they journaled, Anne switched the tree lights on.

Archie was happy and, indeed, had supported Anne in her decision about the big Christmas tree. "We have Christmas in our room, and that's what matters."

Anne agreed. She secretly loved that the two of them had their very own Christmas tree.

Another decision Anne came to was that she would no longer host the big extended-family Christmas gathering, even though it was her turn this year. She informed her brothers that she and Jack had been hosting dinners since they had first married more than forty years ago, and they could do it no longer. She would happily hold a Christmas celebration for her children and granddaughters, but wouldn't do the big extended-family dinner. In letting go of that responsibility, she allowed whatever was to be, to be. Interestingly enough, her brother Max and his wife said they would happily host the family Christmas dinner, and Anne was grateful to them both. She knew just how much time and energy it required.

The predicted pushback did come when, on Christmas day, her sister asked Anne to promise that she would always be there for her. At the time, Anne had been sitting at the children's table, enjoying dinner with her three young granddaughters. With her entire family around, she instantly assured Laura that she would be.

However, later that night as they were driving home, Jack asked Anne what that promise had meant. What did her sister mean by "being there for her"? What would that entail?

Anne replied that frankly she had no idea, but it was weighing heavily on her mind. As much as Anne loved her sister, Laura had always been a drain on her energy. And she did worry that she'd made a promise that was counter to her new intention and focus on self-love.

A couple of nights afterward, Anne asked Archie if, when alive, he had ever thought about self-love and self-care. And if so, what that had looked like for him.

"Anne, self-love never ever came on my radar. I think if it did, I would have associated it with being selfish. I came from a very loving, very kind family, and it was all about making sure your family and friends were okay, that you were there for them. Consequently, when I fell into a deep depression, I didn't seek help as my brother suggested. Once I crossed, it was shown to me that even if I didn't want to talk to anyone, there were plenty of self-help books I could have accessed at the library. But I chose not to. What you're focusing on and writing about is very important, Anne. You have no idea how important."

Was letting go part of self-love and self-care? Somehow Anne felt that it was. Lately, she'd let go of her history book which had been rejected by the publisher. She had spent way too much time and energy on it already.

In contrast, writing their story, with Archie's love and support, gave her a sense of purpose. Archie said she was writing the book she'd been born to write. And so, Anne had let the history book go. Of course, Jack had been very disappointed with her decision. He knew how much effort Anne had put into it, and couldn't comprehend why she wouldn't just send it to another publisher. How could she explain to him? But good on Jack! Even though he had vehemently disagreed with Anne, he supported her on the new venture of writing what she described as a spiritual novel. And for that she was so very grateful.

It would seem that in letting go of the things and people that drained her, Anne would have to create boundaries. After all, just this past April, she'd had an opportunity to go, and a part of her was still annoyed with herself for staying. Had she remained because she'd not been ready to let go and detach? With the writing of their book, Archie had stressed that boundaries were especially necessary for Anne.

Shortly thereafter, Anne had a dream in which she was walking up Queen's Drive, a long steep street, at the top of which stood her grandparents' house. Ahead of her was a small girl riding a red tricycle. As she pedalled, she seemed to be struggling. Anne came up behind her and said, "I can help you." Turning her head, the little girl smiled at Anne. "Thank you," she said. She wore a red dress and her dark hair was cut in a short bob. Anne was astounded. The little girl was Anne herself.

At the next monthly spirit group meeting, Anne shared her dream. She asked if they thought the dream was an affirmation of her new focus. Was her inner child showing Anne that her whole life, she'd been striving to get up the hill? And when Anne offered her help, the little girl had expressed gratitude. As Archie had once said, Anne knew she deserved more. And perhaps the only way that was going to happen was if Anne let go of those individuals who had been sucking her dry. She had to start looking after herself, loving herself.

The next day, Helen emailed Anne to say that her loving image of pushing her five-year-old self on her tricycle up the hill was so touching and beyond beautiful, it had stayed with her for the entire day. She felt Anne's dream was definitely about her new shift of consciousness.

For Anne, the dream had touched her very soul. To be sure, it was an image that would stay with her—a reminder that she needed to support this wee one. While often Anne had little empathy and compassion for herself, she needed to be ever mindful of her inner child who still grappled with her uphill climb.

~~~~~

At her next appointment with Jane, Anne shared the rest of her dream. When, at last, the little girl reached her grandparents' house, there was a round table set up under the trees, in what would have been the driveway. Around the table family members were gathered, looking as they would have when Anne was five. It was a celebration of sorts. Food was on the table, and all seemed happy to see Anne. Their welcome was joyous. And while the house had been situated on a street that intersected with another, the other street had been blocked off, so Grandma's house was literally at the top. One could go no further.

"Sounds like a most beautiful dream, Anne. Do you think that the family celebration is what is forthcoming when you reach the top of the hill? That after going the distance, this is what awaits you, your homecoming?"

"Maybe." Anne confided that she was dealing with pushback as she made a commitment to herself regarding self-love and -care. "I'm just not sure how to deal with it."

Jane broached the subject of boundaries as a form of self-love. "Boundaries are not for keeping people out, but rather for giving you space to be. As such, boundaries are a part of self-love. I have many quotes about boundaries, but one of my favourites is: 'Boundaries are the distance at which I can love you and me simultaneously.'"

Archie was present and Anne again asked his thoughts about self-love and self-care.

"It wasn't something I ever really thought about. I would never have considered it a matter of self-preservation. But now on this side of the veil, I see how much you give to others, and it's not returned in kind. And this kind of action is not helpful to either party. Sometimes, helping others and doing things for them prevents them from learning to be self-sufficient and solve their own problems."

Anne said that, with regard to her sister, she knew she needed to talk to her. Nevertheless, Anne had no idea how to even begin to have this conversation.
~~~~~

Jane advised Anne to talk to her, or to send an email in which she communicated her love for her sister, but at the same time advised her of Anne's needs for space and time to write her novel. "We have often discussed how your mother-in-law taught you a lot about boundaries. Perhaps it's your turn to define your boundaries and limits to your sister."

As Anne listened, she knew what Jane was saying was wise and something she ought to do. Even so, she also knew her sister would give her grief about it. She had been through this once before many years ago, and the two had become somewhat estranged. And when Anne tried to talk to her sister on the phone, her sister said in no uncertain terms that she didn't want to have the conversation.

And so, in the end, this time Anne wrote a letter to her stating her need for space. As expected, her sister took it personally. For some reason however, the image of Anne's five-year-old self stayed with her. And she did remember what Archie had said about unconditional love—there were two parts: love for the other; and love for oneself. So perhaps it was no accident that since his return, the universe had been sending Anne little reminders about self-love.

CHAPTER 30

Boundaries, Again

Anne was still not sleeping well, and one night at 3:45 a.m. she was wakened by a voice saying, "You need to stay another twenty years." Needless to say, Anne was so upset she turned on the light and got out her journal. She felt Archie with her.

Anne: Who was that? It was a female voice.

Archie: Not sure. Just say no. Be firm and clear.

Anne did as Archie directed, then asked: Did you hear it?

Archie: Yes. Again, just be clear—and you have been. Done! Now come back to bed, Anne.

—Anne Jeffrey, *Anne & Archie's Journal,* Vol. 13
(November 14, 2019)

Shortly thereafter, Anne was sitting in Jane's office with much to discuss. Archie was there, waiting for her as had become his habit. She liked that he was prompt as he had always been in life. Anne brought up the question of the voice and how much it had perturbed her. She explained that in the last few months, as she was coming to consciousness in the morning, she would sometimes hear Archie ask or say something to her, but never had she heard this voice.

"Twenty years. I completely understand your distress, Anne." Jane asked if she had any sense of who it was.

"It was a female voice. Her tone and words—saying 'I needed to'—were such that I have since concluded it wasn't a guide or angelic presence."

Jane looked to Archie, who shook his head.

Hesitant, Anne thought of Jack's mother who had died over a year ago. It would be like her. In life, Anne had found her to be challenging, difficult. "My intuition is telling me…"

Jane and Archie both leaned in to hear Anne's thoughts. "Yes?"

"I was thinking it might be my mother-in-law."

"Yes, Archie is affirming this."

And just like that, Anne's mother-in-law barged into the session.

Calmly, Jane said, "Your mother-in-law is here. She's all huffy and puffy. She's a baby soul. She's saying that she loves her son, and that you need to stay and look after him."

Anne was shocked, although upon reflection she shouldn't have been. In life, her mother-in-law had never understood or respected boundaries, so why should it be any different now that she was dead? Nonetheless, Anne was shaken by the intrusion.

Silence—it seemed everyone was waiting for her to respond. Her thoughts drifted to a story a friend had recently shared with her, about an encounter she'd had with the guardian angels of her then very ill daughter. Hearing the guardian angels were present with her daughter, her friend had thought, *Some guardian angels you are!* The angels' response had been, "We love your daughter, but this is her journey."

Anne repeated the story aloud and then said, "And so I'm saying to you, I love Jack, but this is his journey."

Anne's answer had been respectful, loving, and clear. Jane followed up, saying that Archie had been absolutely correct in telling Anne to be firm and say no in response to her mother-in-law's demand that night. Anne's mother-in-law had indeed taught her much about boundaries, so much so that as she lay dying, Anne had expressed her deep gratitude.

Anne looked to Jane, who addressed her mother-in-law's spirit very firmly: "You have your answer. You can go now." And thankfully, she did.

Anne then shared that in writing their book, she was having trouble remembering details of the time she and Archie had dated. Being an introvert, Anne was often oblivious to her surroundings, and perhaps that was the reason her memory of things was challenged.

"Archie says that he was always very aware of his surroundings. He was good at that. And that's why when you and he were kissing while watching an Elvis movie, he could make funny comments about it."

Anne remembered Archie telling her to write the feelings, and that the facts don't matter. So maybe remembering the details of their dates wasn't as important as she'd originally thought, and she could let that go and continue with her writing.

Jane spoke to Anne now about grace, and moments of grace when Anne had been protected. "At the university coffee shop, your High Self set a veil in place so you wouldn't be conscious of Archie's identity."

"There were moments when Archie and I made eye contact, I felt there were glimmers, an awareness that led me to wonder—do I know him? But the awareness was foggy." In the grocery store, Anne recalled the feeling she had when she saw Archie—panic, sheer panic at a soul level. Her conscious awareness came only after she reached her car.

"Archie thinks I'm not giving him enough credit," Jane said.

Seriously?! Astounded, Anne turned to face him, holding up her hand to stop him from going any further.

"Hold the phone! Just hold the phone! What do you want, Archie? Just a while ago, you told me you thought I gave you too much credit and saw you through rose-coloured glasses. And now today, you tell Jane you don't think she gives you enough credit. Which is it?!"

At first, Jane was startled by Anne's forthrightness, but then she started to laugh.

"I wish you could see Archie. He's laughing so hard, he's bent over. He's trying to respond. He keeps putting his hand up, struggling to speak, but then he starts laughing again."

Anne smiled. She loved being reminded of the joy and laughter the two of them had shared all those years ago, and continued to do so now.

"Archie is asking again if you want to spend your next life in Ireland. He says that whatever soul contract you create for your next life, it will be big if you're coming together."

"Well, if it's anything like how we came together in this life, we will no doubt attract attention. Our love for each other was apparent to all who knew us." Anne then shared with Jane a recent dream in which her mother came to her and said she knew about her love for Archie—and that that was why, at first, she'd thought Anne was making a mistake getting married so quickly. Nevertheless, her mother had honoured Anne's wishes.

"Did our mothers know about our contract?"

"Archie says no, but that you both chose mothers with integrity."

Anne nodded. After Anne married, her mother had been her ally and advocate, as well as an awesome grandmother. And she'd come to love Jack dearly.

As Anne was leaving, she gave Jane a Christmas gift of a journal. At the last spiritual workshop, she'd noted that Jane had almost filled her journal and was in need of a new one. "This gift is from Archie and me. We are both so incredibly grateful for you. Your friendship and support mean the world to us."

Later that evening, Anne said, "I loved today. You were back to being Archie, my articulate, witty, sweet, and funny love. You give me such joy and delight. Thank you."

CHAPTER 31

The Voice

For some time, Anne had been curious about the voice Archie heard, but had resisted asking. The burning question was: Why would Archie listen to a voice telling him to break up with her, especially if he had cared for her as he professed? Since she was writing their story, she needed to understand. If she had trouble grasping it, so would readers. So today, with Jane present, Anne asked, "When did you first hear the voice?"

Archie had long anticipated Anne's question. In life, he had never shared this with another living soul. His reasoning was that, in his experience, only crazy people heard voices, and he had not wanted to be nuts. Also, Archie had never had the language to talk about it.

For the first time, with Jane's help, Archie put into words his experience of hearing voices; in actuality, it was one voice. In the planning of this lifetime, no one had foreseen the power of Anne's and Archie's connection, their love. Six weeks after their first date, the council of guides realized Anne and Archie were remembering the intensity of their love and relationship far more quickly than anyone had anticipated. Something had to be done before it was too late. It was decided that one guide would step in and make a connection with Archie.

"Six weeks into the relationship, end of March, I was alone at my parents' house and I heard a voice asking, 'Can you hear me?'

The council had chosen one voice to communicate with me. It was a calm and steady male voice."

Jane said, "Archie wants you to know that it was the tone that made it compelling. He knew he needed to listen to it, and that it cared about him. The moment he heard that voice, his life forever changed. The voice worried him, but also soothed him, and over time he learned to trust it."

Archie continued, "On our last date, when we were getting hot and heavy in the car, the voice said, 'You need to tell her to get out of the car.' At the time, I was thinking how awesome loving you was—how good it felt—and then the voice came. After I crossed, my guide (the voice) explained that, in saying those words, he was both honouring the contract and acknowledging that I was in a young male body. It was always a give and take. The council wanted us to fully understand the intensity of our love and connection. However, that night in the car, the guides knew they had to step in. They were well aware that if we had sex, it would have been amazing for our physical connection, but game over for our soul contract."

"What caused you to initially trust the voice and what it was telling you?" Anne asked.

"Archie says that at first, the voice told him very practical things. Archie is blushing. He says, at the beginning, he was purposely obstinate. He tested it. He had no language or experience with being guided by voices from unseen sources, and would say, 'Just let me muddle through on my own.' For example, when he was driving, the voice would tell him to turn onto a particular street, and Archie refused. As a result, he ended up stuck in a traffic jam for two hours. Another time, the voice would tell him to go to a specific store to get a part, and Archie intentionally went to another, which wouldn't have what he wanted. The voice was always steady, kind, and persistent. Archie was initially stunned at the truth of the practical information it was giving him. When he followed what the voice said, there would be an inner sense that this was right. And then beginning of May, two weeks before the breakup, it asked

Archie to do something that he thought was totally stupid. The voice began to tell him, 'You and Anne cannot continue.'"

Archie said, "At first, I asked why, but the voice just kept repeating that phrase. And then I tried to bargain with it. The voice ignored me. It was just this calm, steady, persistent thought, 'You and Anne can't continue.' After I told you to get out of the car, all the way home I was thinking, *What am I doing? This is nuts!*" With the voice, Archie lived in the duality of what he wanted and what he was told.

"When you phoned and asked me to go swimming the day after, was that a ruse?"

"No, I really wanted to go swimming. But after I hung up, the voice said, 'That's enough.' I fully intended to go meet with you the next evening. The voice said, 'Don't go.' I said, 'I'm just going to talk to her.' And it just kept repeating, 'Don't go.'"

"Why didn't you call to let me know you weren't coming?" Anne asked.

"What was I going to say? How could I possibly explain? There was nothing I could say." Jane continued to narrate Archie's words. "After he broke up with you, a full twenty-four hours passed before the voice came and said, 'You made the right decision.' The voice helped to steady him. Archie says there's no hell, but that day he created hell for himself. He wants you to know that you both picked a tough lifetime. It was an unbelievable test of your bond, and both of you demonstrated a lot of integrity. The guides were always monitoring you, helping you without making it too easy, without pushing you over the edge. Nevertheless, they let it be hard for you. The breakup was a test for Archie, asking him, 'If we guide you, will you listen?' Archie didn't, in fact, understand at all, but he did listen."

"Did the voice tell you to write the letter?"

"Archie says, 'No.' The letter was a test for both of you. Archie had felt led to write it. He was hoping you would call or get in touch with him, but in the end, as you know, the letter left both of you confused and hurt."

Archie said that after he married, during the middle of his life, he shut the voice down. In his mid-fifties, however, Archie was given the dreams of Anne. And with the dreams, the voice and its messages returned.

"Archie had no idea where you were, Anne, but the images of you were magical. At the time, he was both pleased and amazed at how connected the two of you were. He so loved what he saw you doing. The dreams were a series of vignettes of what he now knows to have been your time in Ireland with the goddess group. He says your energy was so high, it was easy for him to tap into it. The dreams kept him present and aware. It could have been a huge danger point, as you were so hugely compelling for him."

Anne was deep in thought and was thus startled by Archie's change of tack.

"Archie is so proud of you and how you're managing having a foot in both worlds. You still have a vulnerability that he doesn't have. On his side of the veil, he doesn't have an ego. He is telling me that sometimes you are very brave, but that you're also very shy. He wants you to know that this is your tough time. His advice is: First and foremost, trust him, your connection, and your conversation."

"Archie is definitely the extrovert and I'm the introvert."

Jane noted that Archie was agreeing with her. Nevertheless, Archie had felt Anne needed to hear, to know that what she was doing in her life, what she was writing about, was a testament to how truly courageous she was. Because of Anne's shyness, one could often miss or overlook her bravery, even Anne herself.

~~~~~

As Anne worked on the final chapters of their book, something was troubling her. Actually, a lot was troubling her, and not just the book. COVID-19 and the subsequent lockdown had introduced a new normal—one Anne was struggling to deal with. As introverted as she was, she was finding the isolation hard to handle. Not being able to see and hug her kids and grandkids was especially painful.
~~~~~

And she worried about Ella, her youngest granddaughter who was just two and an only child. Anne's daughter-in-law recently shared that Ella had said, "Nana no come any more. I miss Nana every day." And that broke Anne's heart. Suddenly, the writing and book seemed less pressing.

Nevertheless, with regard to her writing, whenever Anne worked on the chapters about the soul contract and 'the voice', waves of fatigue and deep sorrow would overwhelm her, so much so that she'd have to sit or lie down.

One evening while conversing with Archie, Anne decided to take the bull by the horns, metaphorically speaking, and revisit a subject she knew to be a sensitive one for Archie. It was the one part of the story she still wrestled with.

Anne: I'm still having difficulty getting around why you listened to the voice and broke up with me, all the while knowing I was the love of your life. At first, I thought this was just me. That I'm taking this too personally. Last week, however, I gave Jane a draft of our story for the purpose of getting some feedback. And with no prompting from me, Jane said this was the one part of our story she found hard to imagine—your ready compliance, Archie.

Archie: This is so hard, sweetheart, all these years later.

Anne: I just want to understand why. Why? Why did you listen to the voice, trust it over your feelings, your heart?

Archie: It was the tone, Anne. The voice felt, not like a command, but a <u>commandment.</u>

Hearing Archie's words, Anne felt their magnitude. No more needed to be said.

CHAPTER 32

A Soul Farewell

Anne regretted that she and Archie had never said goodbye to each other. The memory of their last date when they were having their most exquisite loving moment, was always juxtaposed with the awful one of Archie telling her to get out of the car. And then he had driven away without as much as a glance in her direction.

This continued to haunt Anne. In some ways, she was annoyed with their spirit guides for not allowing them a moment to speak and part on good terms. It had been one of the reasons she'd informed them that, yes, they had ensured Anne and Archie had successfully finished their contract, but at what cost?

The COVID-19 lockdown had allowed Anne time to focus on her writing. It had also provided her time and space to be alone and go within. In mid-April, as she was contemplating the end of their story, a memory from decades ago came to light. About four months after Anne had moved to Guelph, she recalled walking out of her house, standing on her front porch, and seeing a man standing by a car parked across the street. He had looked at her and, for a moment, their eyes met. And then after a minute, he got into his car and she returned into her house. Anne was puzzled. Had that been Archie?

A couple days later, Anne had a session with Jane, her first since COVID-19 where social distancing was required. She had no idea how it was going to work with Jane and Anne in two different locations, and Archie God knew where. As the appointment began,

Jane explained that Archie, as energy, was in both places. Apparently, he was gently laughing at Anne as she struggled to get onto Skype.

"He says they don't have these problems where he is."

Feeling increasingly frustrated and anxious, Anne finally said, "Let's leave it. This appointment is to help me de-stress. I think we should just use the phone."

Jane asked how she was coping. Anne acknowledged both the challenges and gifts that had come with the pandemic. Her biggest disappointment—she didn't get to a writers' workshop in Costa Rica, something she had been looking forward to. She asked if Archie had known that her trip would be cancelled.

He said no. He too had been disappointed. He felt she'd really needed the time away.

Anne silently nodded. She then disclosed her recent memory of the incident that, at the time, had seemed inconsequential. She asked Archie if he had indeed been the man parked across the street from her house.

"Archie is saying yes. He's so happy you have remembered this piece."

"Was this after you followed me to Guelph to find out where I lived and if I was okay?"

"He says yes. It was probably a month or six weeks later. After he learned where you lived, it was very tempting for him to go see you again. The voice said he couldn't do this, and Archie now knows the lesson was to stay away from you. However, it didn't rest well with him. He reasoned that he had seen you one day, and yes, you were okay that day, but what if you really weren't okay?"

Jane said, "Archie says he felt he was being led by divine wisdom. The voice had a calm, steady feel to it when it said, 'You can go one more time to say goodbye to each other.' Of course, then Archie argued with the voice about how *that* was going to work. If he knocked on your door, he worried you might be alarmed, fearing he was stalking you. And then one day, the voice said, 'Just go.' And so, he got in his car and started to drive."

"That's a long drive from Scarborough to Guelph."

Jane continued, "Archie says, honestly, he thought he would turn around before he got there. But he didn't. Once he parked his car across from your house, he had no idea what to do next. Should he go to the door and knock? And then the voice instructed him to get out of the car and just wait. 'Stay by the car. Your soul will call her soul, and she will come. She will know.' Archie says no one was around, but just in case he had concocted a story that he had a leg cramp and was walking it off.

"He didn't have to wait long. As he stood near the car, your front door opened and you walked out. You looked around and then at him, and after a minute you went back inside. It was a moment of profound awareness for Archie. He realized how deeply the two of you were connected."

Anne, sitting at her desk at home, was amazed. "That's incredible."

As she reflected back to that moment, she had no memory of why she'd gone out, only that she had. It had been early afternoon. Alex must have been napping in his crib. She had noted a man standing by a car. He was wearing a short-sleeved plaid shirt, so it must have been summer.

All these years, she thought they had never said goodbye. But now, her soul pulled that memory forth and informed her otherwise.

<center>~~~~~</center>

Later that evening, Anne and Archie shared their more personal thoughts about that momentous occasion which, until today, Anne had been oblivious to. She was so touched by what Archie had revealed to her that afternoon. His soul had called hers and she'd come.

"It's just so profound on so many levels. That you came to check on my well-being and our souls actually did say goodbye to each other. Thank you. I'm so grateful you did that. And I'm so happy to have finally retrieved the soul memory. Did you feel better after that, Archie?"

"Yes, I really did, for two reasons. First, it was such an intense awareness for me of our deep bond. My soul called yours, and you knew and responded. And for some reason, knowing that, I knew you were okay. I could let you go and move on with my life. For the next twenty years, the guides kept me very busy with family, friends, and work. I really didn't think about you till my mid-fifties."

The next day, Anne was still reeling. The memory was proving to be an enormous, almost overwhelming experience. Archie's need to check on her and say goodbye all those years ago had been so heartfelt. That Archie had done this before he moved forward with his own family made Anne's heart ache.

Some days were harder than others. She loved Archie and a part of her simply wanted him to be in-body so she could hold him again.

Archie said, "I was thrilled you remembered it. It moved me deeply when you came out—that your soul heard mine. I was blown away. The experience proved so intense that after I turned the corner, I had to pull over. I needed to stop shaking before I could drive home."

"Were you upset I didn't recognize you?"

"No. I knew your soul knew who I was. In a way, I was relieved you didn't. It was really just a beautiful moment for me, for you, at a soul level. To be honest, I don't think I could have handled you coming to talk to me. I would have found it hard to say goodbye, and it was what I had to do. You had moved on and I had started taking steps to move on with my life—preparing to get married and start a family. Saying goodbye was the last piece. After that, I was able to let you go."

For some reason, Anne felt a sense of relief. She knew their souls had come together to say goodbye, and that moment had been so full of love and tenderness. At least, that's what she felt it to be now. Anne concluded that the moment had been perfectly executed by their guides. It would have been lovely if they had included her, but she understood why they had not. That year when she and Jack moved to Guelph had been a very tough one. And thus, Anne appreciated why her guide had protected her from the encounter, just as she now felt gratitude for her ability to recall their souls' farewell to each other. Perfectly executed! *Thank you, spirit guides.*

With Anne's retrieval of one soul memory, another soon followed. It must have been one to two years later when Anne was very busy with Alex and new baby Lizzie. Perhaps she'd had a bad day. Regardless, one afternoon she remembered falling down on her knees on the kitchen floor, sobbing and saying, "I can't do this! I can't do this anymore!"

Anne was fairly certain that, at the time, she hadn't known what she'd meant by "this." But clearly, it had been her soul crying out in pain.

Shortly thereafter, Anne dreamed she was standing in a Greek temple situated high on a hill. As she stood there among the columns, Archie, clad in a toga, walked up the stairs to her, looked at her, and said "Goodbye." He then turned and walked away. Anne awoke and knew intuitively that Archie had come to her that night. The dream had been real. From that day forward, Anne let go of Archie and all memory of the two of them.

At one of their early sessions with Jane, Anne had shared her dream with Archie. Surprisingly, he knew. He said that in a past life, this particular Greek temple had been very special to them both. Anne now surmised that each of them had experienced their own personal soul farewell. After the dream, Anne enrolled full-time at university. She never really looked back after that.

A couple of months later, Anne remembered more about the day Archie had come to say goodbye—a memory she discussed with Archie in her journal.

Anne: Archie, you said that I walked out onto the porch, looked around, and then went back inside. But that's not what happened. Prior to going outside, I did see you. I was sitting in my office which was situated at the front of the house. I was on the phone when my attention was drawn to a man parked across the street—you, Archie. You were standing on the boulevard. You seemed to be walking off a leg cramp—occasionally taking your foot in your hand, bending your leg back at the knee. Nevertheless, every few seconds, you looked to my front door. It was the look on your face that drew me. You had such a yearning expression, as if you were almost willing the door to open.

Archie: I just kept thinking, "Where are you, Anne?!"

Anne: Really? It was because of your seeming distress that I went outside to see if you were okay. What you wanted. Although I had no idea it was you, Archie. As soon as I went outside, you looked at me and I at you. And then you simply nodded, got back into your car, and drove away. You said I went back into the house, but I didn't. Did you know that?

Archie: Yes. I just said that.

Anne: Why?

Archie: Don't know. I guess I was interested to learn what you remembered about that day. It was only after crossing the veil that I came to know the truth.

Anne: I didn't go back inside. I continued to stand on the porch. I waited for you to come back around the crescent—because there was only one way out and that was in front of my house again. I kept waiting but after a few minutes, your car didn't return. And I guess my mind took over. I figured you—the man—got the wrong house. I had no way of knowing that after you turned the corner, you had to pull over.

Archie: That you came out to see me reinforced our strong spiritual connection. In my entire life, I never felt anything like it. And that was why, after turning the corner, I had to stop the car. I was so shaken, I couldn't drive.

—Anne Jeffrey, *Anne & Archie's Journal,* Vol. 24
(January 14, 2021)

Or, as Anne later surmised—perhaps the voice had instructed Archie to pull over, in part, because Anne *had* remained on the porch. And Archie's guide knew this couldn't happen—Archie seeing Anne waiting for him.

CHAPTER 33

A Climax that Rocked the World

Anne: You take my breath away, Mr. M.

Archie: And who is Mr. M.?!

Anne: Very funny. Don't be smart. That was said to you with great love.

Archie: I know, and thank you. You would take my breath away, and you did often. But since at the moment, I have no lungs, I cannot say that. But your light and energy do make a big impression on me.

—Anne Jeffrey, *Anne & Archie's Journal,* Vol. 10
(August 25, 2019)

Before COVID-19 closed everything down, Anne had enrolled in a weeklong writers' retreat in Costa Rica, with the hope of getting some constructive input about her story from fellow-writers. The book was coming along well, with the exception of the climax. Anne had written various scenarios, but none of them were working. She was stumped. She had thought of possibly killing off the protagonist—herself, but Archie had vetoed that. And so, Anne had booked an appointment with Jane, in hopes that the three of them could figure out a viable option.

According to books she'd consulted, the climax in a story was the major reversal. It was the obligatory scene that must occur and bring final, irrevocable change into the life of the protagonist. It had to be surprising *and* inevitable—inevitable because it spoke to the hero's depth of character. More than once, Anne had asked Archie whether he knew what the climax was. Each time, he had answered no, but that he had every confidence she would figure it out.

When Anne arrived at the office, Jane said Archie was present, that he had been waiting for her. Anne got right to the point. "In general, I'm pleased with the story. But the climax is a problem." The book was the entwined stories of Anne's and Archie's relationship in 1975, and the second part, their present relationship. The inciting incident had been Archie's return to Anne. She felt the climax somehow had to speak to Anne's growing awareness.

Anne had given some consideration to the idea that it had yet to happen—a scary thought. If the council thought Anne was going to leave Archie, she assured them that that wasn't going to happen. They had been apart far too long, and now that they were once again together, they were going to stay together. She was committed to Archie and their relationship.

As Anne spoke, Jane was scrutinizing Archie very intently. "He knows."

"No. I've asked him multiple times. He says he doesn't."

Jane continued studying Archie. Her eyes narrowed, as if she were trying to read his very soul. "He knows."

Silence.

"What is it?!" Jane demanded.

Silence ensued as Jane kept eyeing him, and then finally said, "Your first orgasm."

Anne was stupefied. "What?"

"Your first orgasm."

"I cried after."

"He loved that you cried."

Up to this moment, Anne had never spoken about the truly intimate nature of their relationship with anyone, not even Jane. First, who would believe it? The first time she and Archie had sex together, Anne had found it incredible—and she still did, each and every time. The deep love they shared, had been sharing from almost the beginning, continued to astonish and amaze her. Nevertheless, Anne had always regarded her personal life as just that. The intimacy they shared was something very precious, just theirs and theirs alone. And now Archie was informing her that she was to write about it.

Anne glanced at Jane. She in no way seemed shocked. Rather, she was sitting quietly, waiting for Anne to speak. And so, in her mind, Anne reflected back to that day, that moment when her world, her life, forever changed.

"Believe it or not, it happened shortly after Archie returned. Christmas had come and gone, and January had settled in. I was still coming to terms with Archie's presence in my life. And one evening while sitting on the edge of my bed, I blurted out, 'I wish we'd had sex!' I wasn't even sure he heard me."

"Archie is saying, 'Oh, I heard you.' He says when you said you wished you had had sex, he wasted no time. He wasn't that dead. He had no idea how it was going to happen, but he trusted that the two of you would figure it out."

And they had. There was no going back after that.

It was early- to mid-afternoon on January 11th. Jack was at work and Anne was at her computer, working on her history book. For some reason, she remembered snow falling outside the window. From out of nowhere, she felt a stream of energy being zapped into her lower back area, near where her left ovary once resided. Instantly, she felt aroused. She arched her back, but continued typing.

Again, there were two more zaps, this time more urgent in tone, coming one on top of the other. And with that, Anne, feeling very sexually excited, calmly stopped typing, turned off the computer, and rose from her chair. She walked over to the bed and lay down.

"It wasn't like I thought about it. It just seemed the most natural thing in the world for me to do at that moment, as if Archie's soul connected with mine and I knew."

Some details of their long-overdue first sexual encounter were a bit hazy for Anne, but the feelings—that orgasm—were forever etched in her memory. What she remembered was feeling a deep penetration of love within, a merging of their energies, and that her orgasm reverberated throughout her entire body. It had been like nothing she'd ever experienced, and the orgasm took her breath away.

And then, she simply started sobbing. Forty-three years after Archie had broken her heart, they had finally consummated their relationship. As if all those years apart, they had been building up to this moment, and it felt like a huge dam of love burst open inside of her. And with that first orgasm with Archie, he later revealed, their relationship solidified. From that time forward, they were together, a couple.

Later Anne confided to Archie that when they had sex that day, she thought it would be a one-shot deal. To her delight, she realized no. Her first orgasm was simply that: the beginning of their intimate relationship. Time after time, Archie continued to take Anne's breath away, and she still was wont to cry after. She realized that beauty, his beauty, did that to her. And to this day, they continued.

About their relationship, Archie said, "We are."

As the weeks and months passed, Anne's and Archie's relationship deepened—became more profound. In some ways, they were like an old married couple, due to the great comfort they felt with each other. On the other hand, they experienced the great joy and excitement of a young couple passionately in love. Anne was in her mid-sixties and was ever astonished by their sex life. She was almost certain she'd never had this much sex in her twenties.

Before Archie's return, Anne had only ever had sex with her husband. To be fair, Jack was a considerate lover, in that he always ensured Anne had an orgasm before he came. In her mid-thirties though, Anne began to watch Dr. Sue's television show in which she talked frankly about sexual techniques that could be used to enhance the sexual pleasure of both partners. It was through this medium that Anne first learned about self-pleasuring. And, well, simply put, self-pleasuring dramatically transformed Anne's sex-life.

In private, Anne began to experiment, touching herself intimately, and she was amazed by the orgasms that she could give herself, without Jack. Her realization that she could create such pleasure on her own was very empowering. Looking back now, she realized this practice was about self-care and self-love.

When Archie's energy came to her that day in January and signalled they would engage in sex, Anne thought back to their last date when Archie had caressed her intimately, and she had moaned and arched her back. She knew that that caress had opened her desire.

As Anne went to join Archie on the bed, she felt his energetic presence gently surround her. And she began to stroke herself in the manner she used to self-pleasure herself. However, when she put her fingers deep within, she felt Archie's energy within, moving with her two fingers, indicating to her that he was present. His energy was there caressing, and slowly probing deeper, alongside her own fingers.

And then, the energy seemed to overtake Anne's control. She literally felt Archie inside her—slowly at first, but not letting up, just slowly moving with her fingers in circles within. The pleasure Anne was feeling, her awareness of him inside her, the building up of their energy together within, continuous… Anne felt slow waves start to move through her—a spiral dance of their energies. She became aware of her breath, quickening as the energy quickened within her, spiralling ever deeper, and finally the orgasm that seemed to reverberate through her entire body.

Afterward, Anne was conscious of Archie's energy within, and around her body. After succumbing to the first orgasm, Anne just started to cry, to sob. She had felt their sexual union not just physically, but emotionally and spiritually.

Because while the experience might have been initiated by her self-pleasuring, Archie had almost immediately joined her, making his energy felt deep within. And it was their energy coming together that had sent Anne completely over the edge——into ecstasy.

Until that moment of first orgasm, she had not fully appreciated the extent of their intense connection, their bond. But with that orgasm, she felt it—and she had cried, in ecstasy, in relief, and perhaps in grief——that this is what she had surrendered in her life, this great love that was Archie, her twin flame.

As Archie explained, the brevity of their relationship in 1975 spoke to the magnitude of their love and relationship. Their guides, in seeing how quickly Anne and Archie were remembering their love, knew they had to intervene. Archie had recently confided to Anne that their next date would have ended with them having sex, after which they would have stayed together, and put aside their contract. Reflecting back to her first orgasm with Archie, Anne knew this to be true.

As Anne drove home from Jane's, she started laughing. "Climax" was another word for "orgasm"—how truly appropriate! Someone on the council had a sense of humour. Or perhaps Archie had made it up. It would be like him. Anne wished she'd journaled about that first time, when it happened. At the time, however, she'd been very nervous about documenting anything that related to their early sexual encounters, lest someone discover her journals and read the entries.

Even so, she had a very clear memory of that moment of orgasm. She felt the floodgates of her heart open and an overwhelming outpouring of love, like she'd awoken from a long sleep. In her journal, she'd marked the date with a big star and the caption "A Great Day!"

Anne once asked Archie what sex felt like from his end, from his point of view.

"Take our first kiss and magnify it a million times. That's how it feels. I become filled with light. The intensity and building up culminates in a complete merging or oneness of our two spirits. I'm left with a sated feeling. One does not need a body. It's both an emotional and spiritual experience. Our light bodies and spirits become completely entwined and it's hard to disengage from each other. That's why sometimes you wake up in your body and cry." Archie explained that, unlike tantric sex that could be quite mechanical or technical, their merging was an emotional and spiritual expression of the intensity of their love. Archie said he didn't really like the term "making love." For him, the love was already made.

"People long for what we have, Anne."

When Anne asked about the sex scenes in the book, Archie had a lot to say on the subject.

He said, "The first orgasm can be the climax of the novel. The significance of your first orgasm was that it solidified our relationship, which up to that point had been tenuous, given you were still married. The first orgasm was the linchpin or connection and speaks to the continuity of our love. The separation was an illusion. The love was always there. That's the wisdom. The answer to the experiment's hypothesis is yes. The love is and will always be held and present. It's there always, waiting for us to know it, to feel it."

Later that night when Anne and Archie were in bed, she spoke of her annoyance. "May I say, you're a bit of a weasel! How many times have I asked if you knew what the climax was? And each time you played dumb. Not helpful."

Archie laughed, while still trying to be appropriately contrite. "I'm sorry, but I really needed Jane to mediate that conversation. It's interesting that climax can mean orgasm, and I thought you might think I was joking. So, how do you feel about that being the climax?"

"Well, it shocked me, for sure. And it's something I would never, in a million years, have figured out on my own. Nevertheless, it did forever change my life. It was like with that first orgasm, you loved me back to life, to love. That last year, I had felt like a dead woman walking—and then, boom, you broke me open."

Anne had been surprised to learn that Archie had been going in blind, so to speak.

"Anne, it's hard to find the words—but with you, I trusted everything. However it turned out would be okay. Your tears—well, I was so touched. Afterward, I talked to others on my side of the veil. Conversation about sex is very open here. So, our book will talk about sex, and it was your first orgasm that consolidated our across-the-veil relationship. From that moment, we were a couple, period. When I went with you to Jane's that first time, we had already established that I wouldn't be going anywhere."

"That was very early on, a month after you came back."

"Yes. After you said 'I wish we'd had sex,' I didn't waste any time. I went to our guides and said this was what we were planning. Everyone seemed fine with it."

"Well, this climax should rock a lot of worlds."

Archie was laughing. "Most definitely! I do love your insistence on writing an authentic account of our love. I applaud your bravery. But I know it's just who you are. Merlin was right. There is no one like you."

CHAPTER 34

The Last Chapter

Anne had taken the afternoon off to go to the beach. She loved the ocean, always had. She loved to hear the ocean roar, the sound of the waves rolling in and out, ebbing and flowing. Anne took off her shoes so she could wade in the water, feel the sand underfoot and the water swirling around her legs. She breathed in the ocean air. She could almost taste the salt.

In the early evening, a soft breeze came up, but it was still hot and humid. As she made her way along the beach, she closed herself off from passersby and went within, contemplating the last two and a half years. It was a good thing she was writing this book as a novel. It was the only possible medium with which to chronicle her story—their love story. There were days when even she had trouble grasping the realness of it.

She heard barking and looked up to see a dog jumping in the waves, a man tossing a ball to him and the dog catching it. She looked to the sky. The sun was slowly setting among the low-lying clouds. Perhaps she should turn around. But no, just a little further. Anne had read that there was a mermaid statue a short distance up the beach.

She picked up her pace and then felt a hand grab hers as a man fell into stride alongside her. Startled, Anne looked to her left— to see Archie, as she'd known him when they dated.

Grinning at her like no one else could, he said, "Hi," while wrapping her up in his arms. As she looked up, their eyes met. Anne felt more than saw his deep care, love, and tenderness reflected back to her—so much so that her breath caught. As Archie lowered his lips to hers, Anne watched as his eyes closed and their lips touched.

She wasn't sure how long they kissed, but when their lips parted she was reluctant to let him go, to stop looking at him, for fear he would disappear. Her arms wrapped tighter around him. It had been too long.

Archie's physical manifestation affected Anne so deeply, she wept. She leaned into his body, leaving no space between them. Feeling physically cocooned within the comfort of Archie's arms, she didn't want to let him go.

Archie nuzzled and kissed Anne's lips again and then whispered softly in her ear, "Whatever comes, Anne, we'll figure it out. When you cross, we will be going through a gate together. And while the challenges may be greater, we will be together—no more being apart. And that's everything."

Resting her head against his chest, Anne sighed. She had so missed this Archie, her Archie in-body. Being in his arms and holding him after all these years was heaven. She could finally relax, let go. She was home.

Eventually Archie took her hand in his, kissed it, and said, "Come on, let's go."

And as they walked hand in hand down the beach together, Archie pulled Anne into the waves and splashed her. And with that, they broke into laughter as they played and danced in the ocean.

~~~~~

Anne: May I ask you a question?

Archie: Always.

Anne: Were you going to physically manifest to me in Costa Rica?
~~~~~

Archie: Yes. I wasn't going to tell you. It was going to be a surprise. I had been practising, so much so that I could physically manifest for almost three hours at a time. I was even trying to figure out a way to interfere with the electrical system of the villa where you were staying, in order to free up more of your time. So we could have more time together. That time in Costa Rica would have been our time. Of course, I was reprimanded for attempting to interfere. They said I couldn't do that. But reading the last chapter of our walk on the beach, it turns out you knew what I was planning.

Anne: No, I didn't know. I guess you've forgotten, but in one of our sessions with Jane, you asked me if I would want you to physically manifest in Costa Rica. You said then that you weren't sure it was even possible, but wanted to know if it would be something I would want. Archie, you can't just say that and expect me not to imagine it! My mind kept taking me to the retreat and seeing you there. And I couldn't get that possibility out of my mind. So when the retreat was cancelled, my disappointment was almost more than I could bear. It was heartbreaking, as we were not going to get that time—our time away where we could hold each other, kiss, walk along the beach, our arms around each other. It seemed so little to ask for *after all this time. But it was what it was. And so, I decided to write our walk on the beach that never happened. It's hard to know how I would have reacted—knowing the time you would manifest would be short. I'm not sure I would have been able to take my eyes off you for an instant, or stop clinging to you lest you disappear. And so, Archie, I want you to know I had not known, but I had imagined. And when I wrote the last chapter, that walk on the beach, I wrote it as I had hoped it would be for me, for us.*

—Anne Jeffrey, *Anne & Archie's Journal,* Vol. 19
(June 11, 2020)

How had Anne and Archie coped with being apart during their lives? They kept busy, sometimes both of them running on empty. But deep within, the loneliness remained. After knowing and feeling their deep love, it wasn't something that ever completely left either of them. They loved their family and friends, and were well-loved in return. Still, when reminders of the other emerged and the love was remembered, it proved challenging. Archie suffered bouts of depression, and after his wife's death, he sank into a depression from which he never recovered.

For Anne, as she writes the book and contemplates the ending, she hesitates. Having Archie back in her life has been a gift. Truthfully, she wouldn't have stayed for the book, if not for Archie's support and presence. He had said their book was a gift for others. Even so, Anne had come to appreciate that the book had been a gift for them as well. The breakup had impacted both of their lives. Archie was very conscious of why it had happened. Anne had not been.

Ghosted, a part of herself had closed down, gone missing. Over the years, she'd struggled with anxiety and depression, never fully understanding why. And so, the writing of their book had forced Anne to go back and finally feel it (remembering the love and joy, but also feeling her grief and pain) within the safety of knowing Archie's love, their love for each other.

While loneliness could still envelop Anne, it was the deep love, joy, and peace she experienced when together with Archie that prevailed and proved compelling. After their intimate experiences, she felt echoes of him and their love throughout the remainder of her day. Ultimately, a happy ending—with Anne on Earth, while Archie was across the veil—was an oxymoron. It wasn't going to happen—that was the plain and simple truth. Yes, it would have been amazing to have Archie come back for a couple of hours, to hold and kiss each other, to feel his physical body one last time. Yet the thought of him disappearing again was almost too much for Anne to contemplate. And one night she told him so.

"I have thought of another ending. One I would love to write, one that would make me very happy."

"What's that, Anne?"

"When I took the course on twin flames, the instructor spoke of the need to be honest with yourself about how you're feeling—to use your head, heart, and soul, and honour the fullness of yourself. And if, at the end, you want to be with your twin flame, go for it.

"And so, Archie, I feel the writing of our book has been just that for me, and perhaps for you too. What I have come to know in honouring the fullness of myself is that I will ever be lonely here on Earth because the one I love most is across the veil—you, Archie. And so, as we wind up our book, I'm asking you: Would you saddle up that Howdy-Doody horse of yours and come get me? Let's ride off into the sunset together."

Archie, deeply moved, sighed. "Anne. He's already saddled up. I was just waiting for you to ask."

Epilogue

Since rules dictate that Anne has no memory of our time together on the other side of the veil (except the memories given in dreams), I offered to write the epilogue, to say a few last words. Anne is relieved and trusts that whatever I write will be exceptional. What can I say? She still sees me through those rose-coloured glasses of hers.

The soul contract of Anne and Archie has been officially and successfully completed, this book being the final piece. Our seven-year age difference was intentional. After the breakup, we would both have time to lead full lives, and after my death Anne would still be young enough to write our story. We could never have anticipated how truly tough this life apart would be for us, and so when I came back Anne did have an opportunity to exit, to come Home and be with me.

I want readers to know that Anne's decision to stay was one that took a tremendous amount of courage and love. And to be entirely truthful, I have had a hard time supporting her to stay. In this, we help each other.

When I returned Home, I was gobsmacked to learn the enormity of our contract. At the time, Anne was genuinely struggling in her own life and in her decision whether to stay or to go. I told our guides that they needed to pull her out. That it was too hard for her. They informed me that it wasn't my decision to make. It was Anne's.

I felt so helpless. The council replied, "Welcome to our world!" It turned out both of us, Anne and I, were of one mind. Each of us independently went before council, pleading our case that we needed to write the book together.

And so, the council was gracious. Our relationship that crosses the veil was a gift to us. And this book is a gift for you, the reader. Hopefully, in bearing witness to our story, you will come to appreciate and honour Anne's frank and open telling of our love, our relationship. As we have shared with you, our immense love and soul connection transcended space and time. You don't need a body to love someone, and love does not die with one's body. That was a huge awareness for Anne and me.

The end of our story? We are twin flames. It's an eternal relationship. There's no end to our love story, to our relationship. As such, we both struggled with the concept of an ending. What would it be?

After some discussion, we mutually agreed that it would be one of those simple pleasures we had not had the opportunity to share together in this lifetime—thus, the walk on the beach.

However, please know that there's no ending. And when the time comes and Anne exits this life, I will be waiting for her when she crosses the veil. And we will be together, as we are now.

We are ancient souls. It would have been easy to stay together, but we planned a spiritual journey on Earth. It was a huge learning lifetime. With this lifetime of challenge, we grew in wisdom, love, and compassion. Our soul contract that covered hundreds of lifetimes was a test of an eternal relationship—that of the twin flames Anne and Archie. In other lifetimes, we were known as:

Zulu: Kagiso and Sindisiwe
German: Clotilda and Hartmut
Welsh: Brynn and Rhys
Maori: Ahorangi and Rawiri
Tibetan: Chodrak and Thubten
Norwegian: Maiken and Gjurd

There are many more, but these will suffice.

This lifetime, the last piece of our contract, was an incredible test of our bond. It asked the question: Could we come together, remember the intensity of our love, part for the remainder of our lives, and still hold each other in love?

To set this life up, we had to build the lifetimes of experience of this immense and unconditional love. With each lifetime, we had challenges and joys. The depth of our love grew because of the shared experience of loving each other through a myriad of challenges. For without challenge, great love can't grow.

In this life as Anne and Archie, feeling the intensity of our love was essential. We had to know how much our love mattered, for the second part to have the impact it did. Trust, our trust in each other, and that we could and would do this together, is huge. Both Anne and I showed a great deal of integrity. We went on to lead full lives, independent of each other. We each had agreements to fulfil in this life and we wanted to follow through and do a good job with them.

Anne and I were extraordinary souls living ordinary lives. In telling our story and expressing the depth of our relationship with clarity, we have opened a door to unexplored possibilities. And for those interested, the answer to the question posed in the test of *this* eternal relationship—could we hold our immense unconditional love through incredible challenges, through separation and hurt, through other loves and lack of understanding—is "Yes—a resounding yes!" Ours was truly a love to behold. It still is.

—Archie McAllister (October 2020)

POSTSCRIPT: It would be remiss not to acknowledge our guides, who are the real heroes of this story. The orchestration of our contract was and is mind-boggling. While Anne and I participated in the broad strokes of its planning, our guides were the masterminds behind its successful execution and completion. We owe them a debt of gratitude; one we can never repay. And to our family and friends who loved us through this life, we are immensely grateful. Knowing we wouldn't be together, we selected an amazing cast of souls to grace our lives and to remind us of the joy and wonder of life on Earth. Thank you.

In Love and Gratitude,
Anne and Archie

Afterword

SPOILER ALERT: For those readers who read the end of a book first, please note this afterword contains a spoiler.

Dear Reader,

When the first edition (2020) appeared in print, the general reaction was deafening silence. I had put so much heart and soul into writing this love story that it was very hard for me. I was incredibly grateful when a very dear friend told me the truth— "it's a story of heartbreak, betrayal and ultimately adultery." Those words stung, but I quickly realized what the silence was about. Not to say, that in a rush to get it out, I had not exercised due diligence in getting it properly edited and securing a publisher. It was Covid and I insisted on doing it all on my own. Nevertheless, I thought the book launch had addressed all the areas that might be considered controversial, and challenging to present-day social norms and mores.

With the second edition, I knew I would have to address the sex chapter as an afterword. In writing their story, I purposely organized the book, so that it would end with Anne and Archie speaking individually about their love and relationship, their deep twin flame soul bond. With this second edition, rather than me pontificating, I have decided to let Anne and Archie take it from here, allow them to address the shock reverberations to the first edition, and have a final word.

Archie: Hello sweetheart.

Anne sighs (as long as she lived, she would never tire of hearing Archie call her 'sweetheart'): So, as you know, I sent our book to an editor who specializes in spiritual fiction. And you wouldn't believe her comments.

Archie: What did she say?

Anne: She wants more sex.

Archie: Me too. So…?

Anne: You don't have to convince me. But you remember what my friend said: our book is a story of heartbreak, betrayal and ultimately, adultery.

Archie: I know. I was there. If I'd had a body, I would have broken down and cried. Bravo for you not doing that.

Anne: What should we do? How do we deal with this situation?

Archie: Tell the truth. Be explicit. Society today is obsessed with sex. For me, sex is one part of a loving relationship—a very important part. But still just one way a couple expresses their intimacy, their love for each other. And there are all different kinds of sex. There is hot sexy sex. There is romantic sex. There is sex that comes as a result of comforting each other, soothing each other, when one is sad, upset, or grieving. There is make-up sex after one has an argument. But ultimately, sex is one aspect of a relationship, and it is only one aspect, one expression of our oneness, the deep love and relationship we share, and have shared throughout time, through the ages.

Anne: You're right Archie, as always. I am grateful for your input, because being in spirit and no longer in-body, you have a panoramic view—you can see everything from a broader soul perspective—and have a fuller appreciation of the challenge of us sharing details of our sex-life.

Archie (laughing): Our sex-life! I think that's the first time you have said it like that. I understand how hard it has been for you Anne. I loved that you have never apologized for writing that chapter.

Anne: And I never will. No matter what, I will never apologize for loving you. And yes, it is only one facet of our across-the-veil love and relationship—albeit a great one. So, if we're being honest, what are the challenges from your point of view?

Archie: Before I answer your question, I want you to know that our relationship here on the other side of the veil is equally as intimate as it is in your earthly life.

Anne: I do so wish I could know _that_ part of it.

Archie: You will, once you cross over. But if you knew it now, it would be too difficult for you to stay. And you still have soul work to do, to inspire. Actually, we both do.

Okay, the challenges? For me, there are none. I'm good. I love us and all the parts that make up what we are, what we share together. I guess the one thing that I find difficult is how emotionally challenging it has been on you Anne. I hate to see you having to deal with this. But I love that you didn't quit. After feelings of grief and disappointment, you got right back up and got an editor. She clearly gets it and I think she represents a wide readership who will be both moved and interested in all the possibilities, the magic, the majesty of having an across-the-veil relationship with loved ones who have died.

When the first edition came out, you gave me permission to host a book launch over here on my side, and they get it. Actually, there is much excitement about the second edition, that includes more details about the sex aspect of our relationship—which by the way deepened what was already a deep relationship. The sex was not an escape—it was what we did and do to experience our love, our soul oneness more deeply, more profoundly.

Anne: I'm glad to hear they are excited. To be truthful, I would have found it more heart-breaking if we had not had sex. I can't even imagine us not having sex, not having that connection. At a time when the world seems to be in such a mess—chaotic, madness abounding, and so challenging for so many—I find our love story to be a hopeful one. It opens the door and allows readers to peek through and see what is possible, by way of love, by way of connection. My growing awareness has been that death and separation are illusions—that it is possible to keep loving at all levels, and have that love transformed and transformative. Love—our love, Archie, and being together, <u>is</u> real and has profoundly transformed my life, my being. You have made it possible for me to move beyond my grief, to have courage and continue on my soul path.

Archie: Anne, I have said this before, but it bears repeating now. When I died, I was done with my earthly life. What I was not done with was our relationship. But the ball was in your court. And well, all I can say is you are amazing. It was your courage, steadfast commitment, your trust in me, our connection and conversation that *has allowed our relationship to become all that it is. So much joy! Our love is a thing of wonder and awe. And our relationship—well it is ground-breaking. You are opening a door, shining a light on what is desperately needed in the world: unconditional love and acceptance, respect of self and others, all their situations and choices, no judgement. We are all connected.*

Remember when Merlin came to your last goddess circle and said that one voice can make a difference. Trust me, Anne, when I tell you that you, in telling our story, whether you know it or not, will make a difference. You are the bridge. You are opening the doors for humanity to love more completely.

Anne: No, Archie. <u>We</u> are the bridge—our love is the bridge.

Anne and Archie, February 28, 2022

Acknowledgements

I have long desired to write a story about the immense and unconditional love of twin flames. What would that kind of love and relationship look like? How would it manifest in an ordinary life? And what would that look like if one twin flame was still alive, but one had crossed the veil?

A Love to Behold is the product of my wondering—my imagining. I poured so much of my heart into the characters of Anne and Archie that, at some point, I feel I loved them into being, much like the rabbit in *The Velveteen Rabbit.*

This book would never have been written without the love and support of my family, and the many friends and teachers who have graced my life. The following individuals, each in their own way, have held and continue to hold a meaningful presence in my life. My heart is full with gratitude.

My parents, Blake and Pauline Eatough—while they are gone, their love remains.

The Wellesley Hospital School of Nursing—even though it no longer exists, I continue to carry with me all that I learned there about the care and compassion of others.

Professors John M. Beattie, University of Toronto, and Donna T. Andrew, University of Guelph. With their wise direction, and encouragement, I successfully completed my doctoral dissertation, a feat I could never have imagined possible.

Christopher Church, associate publisher, Dagmar Muira and Teja Watson, editor, without whose insights and support, there would not be this second edition.

Ann Osborne, there are literally no words to fully express my gratitude. Her wisdom, generous support, and encouragement in these last many years as I navigated my spiritual path, my soul's journey, have been an inspiration in the writing of this novel. Her generosity of heart and spirit are without compare.

Evelyn Smith MacKay, who, along with Ann Osborne, facilitated the "On the Spiritual Path" workshops. These workshops were life-changing, affirming that angels, spirit guides, and one's High Self and their wisdom are accessible to everyone; that across-the-veil relationships are real and possible.

My wise women friends and fellow goddesses have always held a sacred space and place for me to be, to breathe. It has been one of life's greatest pleasures to have you in my life, to laugh together, to share our innermost feelings and cares, knowing you're always there when it counts. You are mirrors of my magnificence, and I'm both honoured and humbled.

To Shawna Beecroft, who designed the cover for this book. She said it was her first cover and since it was my first novel, I thought it made for a perfect match. And despite the COVID-19 pandemic, she created a masterpiece.

K. Enders, my daughter, whose creative input and cover photograph of my hands holding the wooden heart for all to see is, as I have long known, brilliant when it comes to love and matters of the heart.

To my immediate family, my children, E.J. and Katie, my daughter-in-law Kelly and son-in-law Greg, and my three granddaughters, you light my life. And whenever I drift off within myself, you ground me in the here and now and remind me how wonderfully blessed I am to have you all in my life.

To Ernie, my husband, to whom this book is dedicated. We have been together almost forty-five years and much of what I know about love comes from him, from us. He, like Jack in the novel, has little interest in the spiritual realm. Even so, he has always honoured and supported me in the pursuit of my dreams and my soul journey. Not always easy, but he has never failed me. This novel wouldn't exist without him.

References and Resources

Awiatka, Marilou, "Motheroot," in Alice Walker, *In Search of Our Mothers' Gardens: Womanist Prose.* New York: Harcourt, Brace, Jovanovich, 1983, p. 230.

Brown, Brené, *Rising Strong: How the Ability to Reset Transforms The Way We Live, Love, Parent, and Lead.* New York: Random House, 2015.

Hay, Louise L., *You Can Heal Your Life.* Carlsbad, California: Hay House, Inc., 1999.

Kai Ellis, Jackie, *The Measure of My Powers: A Memoir of Food, Misery, and Paris.* Canada: Appetite by Random House, 2017.

Kyle, Barbara, *Page-Turner: Your Path to Writing a Novel That Publishers Want and Readers Buy.* Copyright © 2016 by Barbara Kyle.

MacKay, Evelyn Smith, *Without Halos Without Wings: Connecting with Angels in the Thin Places.* Guelph, Ontario: M and T Printing Group, 2019.

Medhus, Erik, with Elisa Medhus, MD, *My Life After Death: A Memoir from Heaven.* New York: Atria Paperback, 2015.

Medhus, Elisa, MD, *My Son and the Afterlife: Conversations from the Other Side.* New York: Atria Paperback, 2013.

Oliver, Mary.
"Everything That Was Broken" by Mary Oliver,
Reprinted by the permission of The Charlotte Sheedy Literary Agency as the agent for the author.
Copyright © 2015 by Mary Oliver with permission of Bill Reichblum.

Rose, Reverend Safire, "She Let Go" (poem).

Rother, Steve, and the Group, *Re-member: A Handbook for Human Evolution.* Poway, California: Lightworker, 2000.

Schwartz, Robert, *Your Soul's Gift: The Healing Power of the Life You Planned Before You Were Born.* London: Watkins, 2015.

Schwartz, Robert, *Your Soul's Plan: Discovering the Real Meaning of the Life You Planned Before You Were Born.* Berkeley, California: Frog Books, 2009.

Wilson, Lori (and Grandmother), "Twin Flames, Soul Mates and Hard Soul Helpers"—online course, www.inneraccess101.com.